GAZE

What Reviewers Say About
Kris Bryant's Work

EF5, *Novella in* Stranded Hearts

"In *EF5* there is destruction and chaos but I adored it because I can't resist anything with a tornado in it. They fascinate me, and the way Alyssa and Emerson work together, even though Alyssa has no obligation to do so, means they have a life changing experience that only strengthens the instant attraction they shared."—*LESBIreviewed*

Home

"*Home* is a very sweet second-chance romance that will make you smile. It is an angst-less joy, perfect for a bad day."—*Hsinju's Lit Log*

Scent

"Oh. Kris Bryant. Once again you've given us a beautiful comfort read to help us escape all that 2020 has thrown at us. This series featuring the senses has been a pleasure to read. …I think what makes Bryant's books so readable is the way she builds the reader's interest in her mains before allowing them to interact. This is a sweet and happy sigh kind of read. Perfect for these chilly winter nights when you want to escape the world and step into a caramel infused world where HEAs really do come true."—*Late Night Lesbian Reads*

Lucky

"The characters—both main and secondary, including the furry ones—are wonderful (I loved coming across Piper and Shaylie from Falling), there's just the right amount of angst and the sexy scenes are really hot. It's Kris Bryant, you guys, no surprise there."
—*Jude in the Stars*

"This book has everything you need for a sweet romance. The main characters are beautiful and easy to fall in love with, even with their little quirks and flaws. The settings (Vail and Denver, Colorado) are perfect for the story, and the romance itself is satisfying, with just enough angst to make the book interesting. …This is the perfect novel to read on a warm, lazy summer day, and I recommend it to all romance lovers."—*Rainbow Reflections*

Tinsel

"This story was the perfect length for this cute romance. What made this especially endearing were the relationships Jess has with her best friend, Mo, and her mother. You cannot go wrong by purchasing this cute little nugget. A really sweet romance with a cat playing cupid."—*Bookvark*

Against All Odds—*(co-authored with Maggie Cummings and M. Ullrich)*

"*Against All Odds* by Kris Bryant, Maggie Cummings and M. Ullrich is an emotional and captivating story about being able to face a tragedy head on and move on with your life, learning to appreciate the simple things we take for granted and finding love where you least expect it."—*Lesbian Review*

"I started reading the book trying to dissect the writing and ended up forgetting all about the fact that three people were involved in writing it because the story just grabbed me by the ears and dragged me along for the ride. ...[A] really great romantic suspense that manages both parts of the equation perfectly. This is a book you won't be able to put down."—*C-Spot Reviews*

"*Against All Odds* is equal parts thriller and romance, the balance between action and love, fast and slow pace makes this novel a very entertaining read."—*Lez Review Books*

Temptation

"This book has a great first line. I was hooked from the start. There was so much to like about this story, though. The interactions. The tension. The jealousy. I liked how Cassie falls for Brooke's son before she ever falls for Brooke. I love a good forbidden love story."—*Bookvark*

"This book is an emotional roller coaster that you're going to get swept away in. Let it happen...just bring the tissues and the vino and enjoy the ride."—*Les Rêveur*

"You can always count on Bryant to write endearing and layered characters, even in stories like this one, when most of the angst comes from the not-so-simple act of falling in love."—*Jude in the Stars*

Falling

"This is a story you don't want to pass on. A fabulous read that you will have a hard time putting down. Maybe don't read it as you board your plane though. This is an easy 5 stars!"—*Romantic Reader Blog*

"Bryant delivers a story that is equal parts touching, compassionate, and uplifting."—*Lesbian Review*

Listen

"[A] sweet romance with a touch of angst and lots of music."—*C-Spot Reviews*

"If you suffer from anxiety, know someone who suffers from anxiety, or want an insight to how it may impact on someone's daily life, I urge you to pick this book up. In fact, I urge all readers who enjoy a good lesbian romance to grab a copy."—*Love Bytes Reviews*

"This book floored me. I've read it three times since the book appeared on my kindle… I just love it so much. I'm actually sitting here wondering how I'm going to convey my sheer awe factor but I will try my best. Kris Bryant won Les Rêveur book of the year 2018 and seriously this is a contender for 2019."—*Les Rêveur*

"The main character's anxiety issues were well written and the romance is sweet and leaves you with a warm feeling at the end. Highly recommended reading."—Kat Adams, Bookseller (QBD Books, Australia)

Forget Me Not

"Told in the first person, from Grace's point of view, we are privy to Grace's inner musings and her vulnerabilities. ...Bryant crafts clever wording to infuse Grace with a sharp-witted personality, which clearly covers her insecurities. ...This story is filled with loving familial interactions, caring friends, romantic interludes and tantalizing sex scenes. The dialogue, both among the characters and within Grace's head, is refreshing, original, and sometimes comical. *Forget Me Not* is a fresh perspective on a romantic theme, and an entertaining read."—*Lambda Literary Review*

"[I]t just hits the right note all the way. ...[A] very good read if you are looking for a sweet romance."—*Lez Review Books*

Shameless—*Writing as Brit Ryder*

"[Kris Bryant] has a way of giving insight into the other main protagonist by using a few clever techniques and involving the secondary characters to add back-stories and extra pieces of important information. The pace of the book was excellent, it was never rushed but I was never bored or waiting for a chapter to finish...this epilogue made my heart swell to the point I almost lunged off the sofa to do a happy dance."—*Les Rêveur*

Not Guilty—*Writing as Brit Ryder*

"Kris Bryant, aka Brit Ryder, promised this story would be hot and she didn't lie! ...I love that the author is Kris Bryant who, under that name, writes romance with a lot of emotions. As Brit Ryder, she lets chemistry take the lead and it's pretty amazing too."—*Jude in the Stars*

Whirlwind Romance

"Ms. Bryant's descriptions were written with such passion and colorful detail that you could feel the tension and the excitement along with the characters…"—*Inked Rainbow Reviews*

Taste

"*Taste* is a student/teacher romance set in a culinary school. If the premise makes you wonder whether this book will make you want to eat something tasty, the answer is: yes."—*Lesbian Review*

Jolt—*Lambda Literary Award Finalist*

"[*Jolt*] is a magnificent love story. Two women hurt by their previous lovers and each in their own way trying to make sense out of life and times. When they meet at a gay and lesbian friendly summer camp, they both feel as if lightening has struck. This is so beautifully involving, I have already reread it twice. Amazing!"
—*Rainbow Book Reviews*

Touch

"The sexual chemistry in this book is off the hook. Kris Bryant writes my favorite sex scenes in lesbian romantic fiction."
—*Les Rêveur*

Breakthrough

"Looking for a fun and funny light read with hella cute animal antics, and a smoking hot butch ranger? Look no further. ...In this well written, first-person narrative, Kris Bryant's characters are well developed, and their push/pull romance hits all the right beats, making it a delightful read just in time for beach reading."

—*Writing While Distracted*

Visit us at www.boldstrokesbooks.com

By the Author

Jolt

Whirlwind Romance

Just Say Yes

Taste

Forget-Me-Not

Shameless (writing as Brit Ryder)

Touch

Breakthrough

Against All Odds
(written with M. Ullrich and Maggie Cummings)

Listen

Falling

Tinsel

Temptation

Lucky

Home

Scent

Not Guilty (writing as Brit Ryder)

Always

Forever

EF5 (Stranded Hearts Novella Collection)

Serendipity

Catch

Cherish

Dreamer

Perfect

Gaze

GAZE

by

Kris Bryant

2025

GAZE

© 2025 BY KRIS BRYANT. ALL RIGHTS RESERVED.

ISBN 13: 978-1-63679-711-3

THIS TRADE PAPERBACK ORIGINAL IS PUBLISHED BY
BOLD STROKES BOOKS, INC.
P.O. BOX 249
VALLEY FALLS, NY 12185

FIRST EDITION: JANUARY 2025

CREDITS
EDITORS: ASHLEY TILLMAN AND CINDY CRESAP
PRODUCTION DESIGN: SUSAN RAMUNDO
COVER DESIGN BY DEB B

Acknowledgments

This is the final book in my sensory series and while I'm sad that I'm done, I love the stories that have come from this project. With book banning and groups out there trying to erase the LGBTQIA+ community, having an outlet to get queer books out into the world is of the utmost importance. Hats off to Bold Strokes Books for publishing queer books and allowing us to write our stories. I hope this will always be the case. Books make us happy. We're seen. As writers, we're proud and inspired to tell stories that fill your hearts with love, joy, hope, and validation. You are the reason we write. Because of you, this community has grown, and I hope it continues to blossom as more readers find our books.

As we all know, Ashley is the glue that holds my stories together. She's the best! Cindy is great at line edits and explaining everything to me. I don't always understand, but I know she's right. Having editors you trust elevates your story. Thank you. I owe everything to you both.

Thank you, Deb, for letting me live out my dream of becoming a writer. Writers are quirky and we have weird schedules, so thank you for giving me the space to get my manuscripts done. Massive shout out to Orange Kitty, Black Kitty, and Kiki. IYKYK. Maybe one day, I'll find another pupper soul mate, but for now, the community cats are doing a lot for my mental health. I love my friends, my patrons, and this community. I want to list everybody, but there's a book after this page that I know you want to get to so just know if you're in my circle, I love you, I need you, and you mean more to me than you know.

Dedication

To Vita
Thank you for always reading our books
and making us smile every day

Chapter One

Brianna Jameson—Lawyer at Titan and Spector Law Firm

What do you mean no? This case is money in the bank, Charlie. Just trust me." I clenched my teeth to keep them from chattering. I crossed my legs and leaned back in the chair refusing to show any signs of weakness. The chair was unbelievably uncomfortable. The leather was too slick, the scoop too deep, and it was rock-hard. I knew from his assistant that he picked the chairs because he didn't want people to stay long. All the partners in the firm had posh, buttery-soft, sink-into, comfortable-enough-to-nap-in leather chairs except Charlie. I dug my heel into the carpet and balanced myself on the chair. This whole thing was ridiculous.

"This is not a case for us. No attorney in their right mind would take this dumpster fire." He made a dramatic gesture of opening the folder and reciting key words from the police report. "Crossed the median. Crashed head-on into a Lickety Split delivery truck. Cops reported smelling alcohol on his breath."

"But not legally drunk. Just one beer at a friend's barbecue," I quickly interjected. He scowled at me for interrupting. I held my hands up in a surrendering gesture and motioned for him to continue.

"The delivery driver's medical bills are over twenty thousand. And you want to sue Lickety Split? Their driver was the one who got crashed into." He paused to find the name of the client I was pitching. "Gabriel Andrews is damn lucky he's not in jail. Or maybe he is. Either way, we're not touching it."

"We're a personal injury law firm and he has several injuries from this wreck." I started listing them. "Broken vertebrae, crushed wrist, smashed knee, and he's wearing a colostomy bag. I'm the only one listening to his story. And it's completely believable. Charlie, he swerved to miss some kids who darted into the street. I just need the resources to investigate. If we accepted it, I would keep it trim." I heard the pleading in my voice and hated that I sounded desperate. I didn't need the case. I wanted it. I was on the cusp of becoming partner and needed to show them I could turn any case around, even the ones that seemed impossible. I was damn good and they knew it. Charles Spector III, my boss, aka Charlie, told me to keep taking the easy ones so I could slide into partnership with a higher win/ loss ratio, but that's not who I was. I climbed the ladder at Titan and Spector quicker than anyone else. I wasn't afraid to get my hands dirty or take the small cases that nobody else wanted. Charlie was firm on Gabriel's case though.

"You'd be fighting a police report where every witness interviewed said it was his fault. The case is too risky. He can work it out with his insurance. The answer is no, Brianna."

I fucking hated when he called me by my full name. It reminded me too much of my father when he was stern with me, or whenever I got into trouble at school. A flash of me snatching the folder out of his hands, announcing my resignation, and storming out of the firm gave my heart a kick and made me inwardly smile. Instead of living out my fantasy, I politely plucked the folder off his desk.

"Whatever you say, boss." I forced a shrug and stood. I tapped the edge of the folder into my palm several times and chose my words carefully. The sharp jabs were a reminder to keep myself in check. "Is there anybody in town who would take the case? I'd like to give Mr. Andrews an option instead of slamming the door in his face. I mean, he called us because of our commercials where we promise to help everyone in our community. And don't say Smythe and Wessol because they're out."

He pointed at me. Pointed! "There's your answer. If an ambulance chasing team doesn't want him—and Smythe wants everyone—then walk away." His features softened a fraction. "I know you are trying to prove your worth here, and as much as I appreciate your dedication, you have to know when a case isn't going to bring in money. We can't just throw money at it because you have a feeling. Hunches work for cops, not lawyers."

"Noted," I said. I excused myself and kept my emotions in check while I marched down the hall.

Sebastian, my legal assistant, was at my heels the moment I entered my office. "Well, how'd it go?" he asked.

He waited until I slammed Gabriel's folder on my cluttered desk before handing me a mug of hot, black coffee. I cupped it and closed my eyes while I inhaled the sharp, nutty bouquet before taking a sip. Sebastian was my right hand. He knew how to read me better than anyone in the firm even though today was only his six-month anniversary and I had been with the firm for eight years. He was hungry, like me, and wasn't afraid to push the limits to get me information.

I gave Sebastian a thumbs down. "He wouldn't even listen to me." I slid my jacket off my shoulders and threw it around the back of my chair. I kicked off my heels and paced in the small space between my desk and the credenza. My elbow brushed against a two-foot-tall stack of folders that were perched precariously close to the edge. Out of the corner of my eye, I saw Sebastian wince expecting the papers to tumble. They wobbled, but I steadied them quickly with my palm and continued my trek. It wasn't as though my office was messy, but I had a lot of cases going at once. Sebastian knew not to touch anything unless I gave him permission. My organizational system was chaotic to the naked eye, but I knew where everything was. "He wouldn't even give me the name of another firm." I had a ton of lawyer acquaintances, but everybody wanted something for nothing and I didn't want to pull my favor card yet. I still had hope somebody would take it. Since Charlie wouldn't allow me to sign it, I couldn't secretly work on it pro bono because it would be affiliated with the firm. Selfishly, I couldn't take the professional hit. "Who do we know who's eager but careful?"

"We've hired them all," he said.

I sighed. He wasn't wrong. "Well, fuck." I sat down and took another sip of coffee. My day started off shitty and plummeted.

"If it helps, Edwin Williams called," he said.

I dropped my head in my hands and groaned. "Was he gloating or did he sound defeated?" I'd never had a case bounce back and forth so much. They lowballed my client and threatened to take it to trial. I challenged them. Four times. This was the fifth reach out from them. I ignored the last two and had Sebastian take the calls. It was the same bullshit.

"It sounds like Midwest Trolley wants to settle. For real this time."

I sat up straight. "Well, we can hope. Get him on the line." I quickly added, "Please. Sorry. It's been a day." I promised myself that I would never treat any interns or assistants the way my mentor, Robert Howth, did. He was an asshole to all the first-years. Correction. I could've just stopped at asshole. He was a hateful little man with bad breath but was a shark in the courtroom. He respected no one and it showed.

"Mr. Williams is on line one," Sebastian yelled from his desk.

I shot him a look that made him cower. He winced and mouthed an apology. I waved him into my office and motioned for him to shut the door. "This is Brianna Jameson. Are you ready to make all of this go away for your client?"

Our client had given us a number he'd be happy with and Midwest Trolley came in three hundred thousand higher than his bottom line. It was obvious they were done. I wanted to push, maybe even take it to trial, but I also had to do what my client wanted.

"Send over the paperwork and I'll present it to our client. Always a pleasure working with you." I high-fived Sebastian as I disconnected the call. It was a huge victory in the scheme of things, but my joy was overshadowed by the looming dread of having to tell Gabriel I couldn't help him.

"Want me to get Mr. Bradley on the phone?" he asked.

I held up my hand knowing all too well how shady the firm Midwest Trolley used was. "Let's wait until we have the settlement in hand. If we get it in time before the weekend, maybe we can take a field trip and tell our client. It's a nice day." Anything to get out of this stifling office. I didn't want to run into Charlie any more today. "Speaking of nice days, I'm going to head up to the rooftop. Let me know when we get the documents." I looked at my watch. "The courier should be here by three." I gathered my laptop and a few files and slipped them into my briefcase. "Listen. Sebastian, you did a great job with the Bradley case. Lister's deposition was a game changer. Great job chasing him down."

He puffed his chest a bit and crossed his arms. It was normally a strong stance, but the constant clicking of his pen in his right hand gave his nervousness away. "Thanks, Bri. Glad I could make a difference."

"You've made a difference to me since day one." I winked at him. "Now, don't tell anyone where I am. Just let me know when we get the papers." I brushed past him and quickly made my way to the elevator before somebody stopped me for advice or small talk. I pressed the up button twice and pretended to be engrossed on my phone to avoid all chitchat. Out of the corner of my eye, I saw my nemesis, Tyler Orlach, approach. He shoved his hands in his trouser pockets and slowed his gait. I loathed him. He was part of the good ol' boys club even though he was my age, thirty-four.

"I hear your dry spell is over," he said. He purposely drew out his words thinking he sounded sexy, but I found the nasally drawl as irritating and annoying as the start of a headache.

I turned to him as emotionlessly as I could. How did this asshole hear about the Bradley case? I just closed it five minutes ago. I knew Sebastian didn't tell this bottom-feeder. Tyler probably had a spy on my side of the office. Great.

"Weird that I didn't even know I was having a dry spell," I said. He looked at me with that cocky grin I'd seen too many times. I clamped my lips together to prevent sneering at him.

"Well, maybe dry spell is a bit over the top. I mean, your numbers aren't where they should be." He leaned back and opened his mouth like he burned me.

I took the bait knowing he didn't know that even at a reduced rate, it gave the firm close to a million dollars. I took a step closer. "Why are you so concerned with me? We're on the same team. You know that, right?" He scratched his chin and moved his wrist so I was sure to see the silver monogrammed cufflinks. I almost rolled my eyes. He worried more about fashion than I did. He'd had one good case and thought that made him superior to everyone else. It was annoying.

"Come on, Bri. Where's that fire we're used to?"

I damned my luck when he hopped into the elevator with me. I hit the fifth floor insinuating I was going to the library instead of up to the sixth floor to a workstation outside. I didn't want him to ruin that oasis for me. Mostly paralegals and vapers went up to the rooftop. I was one of the only lawyers who still frequented it on nice days. Kansas City had four seasons, so when spring came, I took advantage. Working seventy hours a week gave me little time to enjoy sunshine with my heavy schedule. I was fooling myself when I thought I'd work fewer hours if and when I became a partner. I was a woman at a law firm in one of the most patriarchal states in the country. I had to work harder, smarter, and prove my worth more so than any one of my peers. I was one of four female lawyers in the firm. Two worked at our plaza branch and the other one who worked downtown with me was such a bitch, even I stayed clear. I purposely hired a male legal assistant just to thumb my nose at the partners, but it ended up being the best decision I ever made. I wanted the world for Sebastian, but I also never wanted him to leave me.

"What are you working on?" Tyler asked.

I forgot he was standing next to me. "Just researching a few basic refresher things. What about you?"

"Here to pick up some case studies I asked for."

"I'm surprised you didn't send your assistant. This errand seems beneath you," I said. He barked a laugh at me and the moment I stepped into the library, I knew. The new librarian was a twenty-something petite blond with big boobs and a bright smile. Her hair was piled high on top of her head in a messy bun and her blue eyes were amplified by sharp, angular glasses perched on her nose. "You're such a pig," I hissed at him.

"Hello, Mr. Orlach. It's good to see you today," she said to Tyler. She looked at me and arched her brow. "Hello, I'm Hazel. And you are?"

"Brianna Jameson, one of the associates. Welcome to Titan and Spector." I shook her hand with emphasis to let her know I wasn't to be trifled with nor was she to snub me.

"Oh, well it's sure nice to meet you, Ms. Jameson," she said. Even though her voice was soft, her Oklahoman accent cut through like nails on a chalkboard and made the small hair on my arms stand at attention. I never realized how sensitive I was to voices until right now. I could tell she was sizing me up. I was not her competition. I didn't care about Tyler one bit.

"If you ever need anything, just let me know," she said.

"Thank you, Hazel. I'll do that." I already missed Emily who went on maternity leave. I wasn't sure if Hazel was a temporary or a replacement.

I excused myself and walked to the back of the library where I was far enough away but could still see them. I didn't want to head out until after Tyler left. I grabbed a book off the shelf and pretended to read, flipping the pages for full effect. It took him eight minutes to grab his paperwork and finish flirting with her. Tyler was a good-looking man who got a lot of attention because of his looks. He used them to his advantage. I didn't. I kept my professional look as clean as possible. My hair was always pulled back, my makeup light, and my conservative suits pressed. Even on Fridays when it was business casual, I still wore a suit. Tyler had a year-round tan, maintained a perfect five o'clock shadow, and always had a bad boy disheveled look about him. He wasn't a great lawyer, but he was a good one who got a lot of perks because he was a pretty boy. For everything I was fighting against, he was embracing and exploiting. It was disgusting.

"Did you find what you were looking for?" Hazel asked.

I didn't even stop. "I sure did. Thank you, Hazel." I pressed the up button and breathed a sigh of relief when the doors opened to an empty elevator. "Have a nice day." I gave her a sweet smile as the doors were closing.

When I got to the rooftop, I was happy the first workstation next to the giant outdoor chess board was available. It was private, the closest to the side of the building, and the view was spectacular. I plugged my laptop into the weatherproof monitor and adjusted the brightness. Only a few people were up here. A cluster of vapers presumably on their late lunch break were horsing around in the designated area but stopped when they saw me. Eventually, they drifted off until I was the only one taking advantage of this magical place. The late spring air smelled fresh and the welcoming breeze weaved itself into the sleeves and collar of my button-up blouse. My mood was improving even though I still didn't have a clue what to do with Gabriel. I looked at the surrounding buildings wondering if I should give up my crappy townhouse north of the river and move down here. Some of the lofts looked gorgeous. After finally paying off student loans, I was squirreling away my money for a house. A really big one with a huge kitchen I'd never use and a big backyard with an eight-foot-tall privacy fence because I was discouraged with the human race and hated the thought of making small talk with neighbors I didn't pick.

A gorgeous long-hair tuxedo cat peeked out from behind curtains in a window a few stories up in the building diagonally across from ours. "Hey, pretty kitty. How are you today?" I figured it couldn't hear me, but its ears twitched as though it could. "Are you enjoying this beautiful day, too? Are you?" I wasn't even a cat person, but something about it made me pause. It was so relaxing to watch its fluffy tail sway to and fro. "You've got the life, pretty kitty. Fresh air, free rent, probably really good food, and parents who love you." It pawed at the screen as though waving. Huh. Smart cat. I waved back before I even realized what I did. Weirdly, it looked like it was waving again. I looked around hoping somebody saw that. "Well, aren't you a smart one?"

As I looked away, the curtain parted and a woman's face peered out. She caught my attention. For about three seconds, I held my breath. I could tell she was beautiful even though her features were too far away for me to see clearly. Her strawberry shoulder-length hair was pulled over one shoulder and rested against fair skin. Was she only wearing a towel? Tiny zaps of electricity tingled my clit as I focused on the soft swell of her breasts right above the top of the light blue material. The cat was forgotten and I was blatantly staring. I should've looked away when our eyes met, but her gaze held me in place. The polite thing to do was to pretend I didn't see her at all, but we were past that option. Even from this far away, I saw her smirk—as though she knew I was looking and did nothing to cover up. I waved. It was a fast, single wave that she didn't return and I quickly looked down to focus on my laptop as though whatever was on it was the most important thing ever. I waited ten very long seconds before I looked up. She was gone, but the floofy cat was still staring at me. "You really are a lucky kitty."

CHAPTER TWO

LUCKY CHANCE—MARKETING SPECIALIST
AT WEB PIONEER

L ook at you flirting with the sexy woman on the roof. I'm so
proud of you." I scratched Tito's head before backing away
from the window feeling unnerved by the woman watching us. Not
because it was uncomfortable, but because it was kind of hot.

I sighed thinking how pathetic I was getting excited about a
stranger glancing my way. It was the most action I had since getting
dumped. What the hell was I thinking moving to Kansas City? I
had the perfect life in Boston. I landed the company their biggest
client ever, but instead of sticking around reaping the rewards
including a massive promotion, I made the stupid grand romantic
gesture of following my girlfriend, Mia, to the Midwest so she could
attend medical school. With hearts in my eyes, I transferred to Web
Pioneer's Kansas City branch. She dumped me after two months.
I was alone in a small city that was nothing like the East Coast. I
sighed again, feeling sorry for myself. I wallowed for three more
minutes while the coffee finished brewing and snapped out of my
funk when it beeped announcing it was done. I tucked the corner of
the towel tighter across my chest and padded into the kitchen for a
hot dose of caffeine that I was going to need to stay awake.

*Are you ready for Monday's presentation? I'd like to see a
mockup before we meet with the client.*

I snarled at my phone. My boss, Miranda, had zero faith in me. Kansas City was a different vibe and a lot more conservative than my East Coast clients. I needed to get a handle on this audience.

I'll have you something by Sunday. Stay tuned. I really didn't like her.

We need a touchdown from you.

Of course, she was going to make a reference to my big client back east. Landing the account for the NFL's latest expansion team, the Connecticut Cheetahs, was a career high. The stress of not having a successful client here weighed heavily.

I'm going to knock their socks off. No worries.

I had all weekend to mock up a website for a cracker company. They wanted something fresh and exciting, and for the life of me, I couldn't come up with anything. It was frustrating. How did one make a plain, round butter cracker exciting? Moonlight Crackers was looking for a boost in sales with nothing new to offer their customers. They thought an online makeover was good enough. I knew that while graphics dazzled consumers, what they really needed was a new and improved product.

What was going to make people want to order a plethora of crackers? Why did people eat crackers? These weren't even made with healthy grains. They were chock full of carbs, butter, and a bunch of ingredients that were manmade. I had a sleeve of them on my table. Even Tito wasn't interested. I grabbed some cheese from the refrigerator and tried to disguise the bland taste of the cracker with the boldness of the asiago. It gave me an idea. Maybe they could have a chart of which one of their crackers paired the best with what cheese. Maybe they should have an online store where people could buy gift baskets of crackers and cheese. I pulled up their present website and it was only informative. The *About* page was historically interesting, but the cracker rolling across the page was rudimentary. It was as if whoever designed their page in the nineties never updated it. Anything I offered would be better than what they had.

I looked up when Tito meowed. "Are you still flirting with that woman?" I crept over to the window and tried to see if she was still there. She was, only her head was down reading a stack of papers instead of looking up at us. It gave me a moment to study her. Her dark brown hair was pulled back in a bun and she was dressed impeccably. I could tell her suit was nice quality, probably high-end designer. What did she do for a living? I didn't know the businesses in that building, but she seemed very important like a CEO or owner of a firm. When our eyes met earlier, she didn't flinch or look away. She was definitely a boss or extremely sure of herself. Or both. Of course, wearing only a towel was a pretty bold move on my part.

I pulled back the curtains as though I wanted fresh air, but I really wanted to get a better look at her. A young, energetic man was beside her laughing and gave her back-to-back high-fives. I couldn't hear what they were saying, but I could tell they were really happy about something.

Tito nudged me for attention and purred as I stroked his silky fur. "I wonder why they're so happy?" He meowed his answer. "Maybe celebrating that it's a gorgeous Friday here." I hadn't left my apartment in days. Working from home was nice, but lonely. I needed to get out, but I was on a deadline and my pool of Kansas City friends I could call out of the blue was extremely shallow. I lost the good ones during the breakup. To be fair, most of them were people she met at medical school. It was time for me to find new friends and maybe even start dating again. "Should I try one of these dating apps? What happens if I run into Mia?" I groaned thinking about starting over. I groaned again when I saw that my mother was calling. I answered knowing that if I didn't, she wouldn't stop until I did.

"Hi, Mom."

"Hi, honey. I haven't heard from you all week and just wanted to make sure you're doing okay." My mother was sweet but was constantly pushing me to either find another girlfriend or move back home. Those two things came up every conversation. By trying to make me feel better, she was making me feel worse. I didn't want to think about Mia daily. At least we got past the "I told you so" speech.

"I have a presentation to give Monday so I'm going to be working all weekend," I said.

"Is this for the barbecue restaurant?"

I smacked my forehead. That was a complete failure. I hadn't found my footing here so it was a miss with every other client. Like Miranda said, I needed a touchdown. "No. I tanked so they gave it to Jared."

"The man who smells like mothballs? Why?"

My mother always remembered the weirdest things about people, but it made me smile. "He's the one. Apparently, I'm too progressive. I have a niche and it's not food." The irony of my words didn't fail me. I picked up a Moonlight cracker and bit off a corner. For inspiration, I thought.

"They don't even know how lucky they are to have you," she said. I waited for it. "And if they don't figure that out, you can come back home." There it was. I tapped my phone to my head and counted to three.

"Thanks, Mom, but I have to give this city a try. It's really cute. You should come for a visit. Well, when I'm done with this project."

"Your father and I could come out over Memorial Day weekend. Send me the names of some hotels nearby and we'll make reservations."

I wanted to invite them to stay with me, but I only had four walls. My studio was large, but there wasn't any privacy. Besides, my parents were used to a certain lifestyle and this wasn't it. Tito would lose his mind if he had to give up any of his favorite sleeping spots like the back of the toilet, the left side of the couch, or God forbid, the kitchen sink. My mother would faint at Tito curled up in the stainless steel sink hoping I'd drip some water for him. "Sounds good, Mom. What else is going on?"

"Nothing. I just missed you and wanted to check in," she said.

My mother spent the next ten minutes catching me up on the family and neighborhood gossip. I wasn't fully invested, but I dropped all the appropriate non-verbal exclamations in the right places. Eventually, she was done sharing and made me promise to call her next week after the meeting. She, too, believed Moonlight Crackers were just meh. They lacked pizzazz.

Talking about the project stirred up a lot of creative juices so I sat at the computer and started designing their site with a drop-in template. By midnight I was exhausted. Everything was boring. I came up with a few eye-catching graphics. During the initial meeting with the client, they told me they would be interested in anything that could generate more sales. In case they really meant it, I added a page where customers could pair different crackers with cheese and if the customer liked that, then they might like my out-of-left-field suggestion of printing names and events on the crackers. Is your child graduating college? High school? Have their name and graduation date printed on the cracker. Baby shower in your future? How about a cracker gender reveal party? Or print the baby's name for a baby shower or first, second, third birthday. This was well out of the scope of the project, but I had a similar account back in Boston and they loved the idea. I was proposing something that was going to change their whole product line, but I felt it was a good change for them. If it went well, then we would look good to the client. I would look good to my boss.

I rubbed my eyes and yawned so hard that I startled Tito who was sprawled out on my desk fast asleep. I scooped him up and threw him over my shoulder. "Let's go to bed, boy." I walked behind the screens that hid my bed and flopped on it without even taking off my clothes.

❖

"What do you mean you never got the pitch? I emailed the link yesterday afternoon at three." I gripped the steering wheel and hissed out my anger low enough that Miranda couldn't hear me. I waited all afternoon for changes but never received any. It was eight thirty Monday morning and I was on my way to a nine o'clock meeting with Moonlight Crackers. She was going to meet me there.

"Wait for me in the parking lot when you get there. What's your ETA?" she asked.

My shoulders slumped. I was going to get there five minutes before the meeting. "Well, there was a wreck crossing the river, so I'm only going to get there five minutes early."

"Lucky."

I waited for her to say more than just my name. She said it with such disdain that it made me wince. I knew I wasn't clicking here with the people and the clients, but something great was going to stick and when it did, Miranda was going to realize that I was a valuable asset.

"It'll be fine. I'm happy with it." I really was. I went over the top for Moonlight Crackers. My graphics were impressive, the drop-down menus were easy, and the rolling crackers only showed up on certain pages instead of every single click. I barely slept last night ensuring this was going to be a big hit. Or, as Miranda said, a touchdown.

"This is so unprofessional. I can't believe you put me in this position."

What was I supposed to say to that? I kept quiet. Pregnant pauses were the worst. I never knew what to say in tense moments. I stammered before spitting out, "I'll see you in a bit." I disconnected the call and turned on my women empowerment music playlist. I needed to focus. I needed to believe in myself. Going in there without Miranda's blessing was unnerving. I belted out the lyrics to Rachel Platten's "Fight Song" telling myself that I was strong and brave and could do this job. By the time I pulled up in the parking lot and slid next to Miranda, I was ready to go.

She motioned me over to her car. "Get in," she said.

"But we're supposed to be inside in six minutes," I said. I shaved off a minute by racing through questionable yellow lights in the Fairfax District. I shrugged and slid into her Mercedes. As nice of a car as she had, I couldn't enjoy it. I was two feet from a woman who just yelled at me. It took everything to stay in a small space with her. I was way too uncomfortable.

"I guess I owe you an apology. I found the email, but there isn't enough time for me to review it here since you're so late. Tell me what you can in three minutes."

I quickly launched into the changes I made including the ones they didn't know about. Her lips pinched into straight line and she stared at me as though I just kicked a puppy. She shook her head.

"We should reschedule for later this week. That way I have time to review it and remove all that unnecessary stuff you added. You know these are very conservative clients. It's a family-run business and we're dealing with a seventy-five-year-old CEO. They haven't updated the website in decades because he thought it worked."

I placed my hands over my heart for emphasis. "I promise that the customer will love my idea. It's the touchdown you wanted. And I reached out and specifically asked his daughter, the VP, if they would be open to suggestions and she said yes. If the climate isn't right, I won't even bring up the extra pages. Let's just see how they react to the little changes first."

She held up her finger. "If this goes sideways, I'm stopping the presentation, and we'll go back to the drawing board and offer them exactly what they want. We aren't the only ones presenting. Moonlight might not give us a second chance."

I knew that was a warning. This weekend and even when I woke up today, I had the best feeling about this design. Now, sitting next to my boss, I was doubting every decision. With more determination than I felt, I nodded. "Let's go wow them."

By the time we were in front of them in their small conference room with mismatched chairs, I was sweating. I launched into my spiel and pulled up their mocked-up website, hoping for excitement. All attention was on me, but there wasn't a single smile on any of the five faces in the room. I paged through the mocked-up website emphasizing what changes were necessary and which ones were outdated and could be replaced by other things like a testimonial page or a contact page. I looked at Miranda for encouragement, but she gave me the same pinched look the owner did. I took a deep breath and pulled up the page where customers could pair crackers with various cheese. A few people nodded as though they approved of the extra page. "And to piggy-back on that, I thought maybe Moonlight Crackers could offer personalization."

"No, no, no," the CEO interrupted me. "We don't want any of that horse crap. We want exactly what was there. I don't know why you're trying to change our business. That's not what we wanted at all." He slapped his palm on the desk. "We're done here."

Miranda finally spoke. "Mr. Fox. Lucky is new to our branch. She's still learning how we do things in the Midwest. Let me work with her and we'll have something more your style at the end of the week." He grumbled and looked around the room. The people nodded at him. Fox's daughter even shot me a quick, sympathetic smile. Her father must be awful to work with.

"Okay, but we plan on making a decision by then so get it to me sooner rather than later." He stood and walked out without shaking our hands.

I felt like a total failure. I smiled politely to the few employees who stuck around and walked us out.

When we were out of earshot, Miranda shook her head. She gripped her briefcase and squeezed her fingers deep into the leather material. It was unnerving that she was so angry. "What were you thinking? I told you a hundred times to give them exactly what they asked for. Nothing more, nothing less. And you come in with this crap? It's embarrassing. You've embarrassed Web Pioneer and yourself."

Whoa. What the hell was happening? "Miranda, I'm quite capable of pitching to a client. Maybe it wasn't the home run that you wanted, but my ideas had merit. I could tell everyone else liked my idea."

"Well, you weren't there to please everyone else, just the one who would sign the contract and give us the check."

"I checked with the VP who informed me she was excited about the proposed changes."

Her eyes were narrow slits as she sized me up. "Run all changes by me, not the client." She pointed behind her. "And definitely not to his insipid daughter who is afraid of her own father. Now get back and make the changes before we lose this client, too."

I slipped into my car and drove home feeling like a failure. Miranda wasn't providing any actual guidance and my customers weren't willing to listen to proven success stories. What was I still doing here in Kansas City?

CHAPTER THREE

BRIANNA JAMESON—LAWYER WITH THE BIG WIN

I stopped at the small coffee shop inside Downtown Square's food court on my way back to the office. It was another nice day after a gorgeous weekend. The storms that were predicted over the weekend split west of Kansas City and shot north and south of us. I spent Saturday in the office, but Sunday I sat on my deck and read a book. Not rulings or motions but a mystery novel from the New York Times best-seller list. My best friend, Avery, sent me a TikTok about it. I understood the hype. It was hard to put down.

"How are you doing today, Ms. Bri?" the barista, Bill, asked. He was the nicest guy. He always had a smile for everyone, regardless of how they ignored him because he wasn't in a suit or behind the desk in an office upstairs.

"Hey, Bill. I'm good for a Monday. How was your weekend?"

He handed me my coffee and yogurt in a flash and motioned for me to swipe when the payment terminal was ready. I loved that he was living his dream. Even though there was a long line behind me, he didn't shuffle me off. "It was wonderful. The grandkids stayed with us and helped me and Dorothy get the garden ready for flowers."

"That's precious. How are they doing?"

"Growing like weeds. Rowan is in kindergarten this year and Allison is in preschool."

"That's amazing. I swear you just showed me their baby pictures last week." I put my card back in my wallet and took a step back so he could ring up the next customer. "I'll see you later, Bill."

"Enjoy the weather," he said.

A flash of strawberry blond hair caught my eye as I left the shop. I did a double take. Was that my mystery girl? Her back was to me and as much as I wanted to stare and find out, I felt and probably looked ridiculous standing in the empty space in front of Bill's store gawking. I grabbed my phone and pretended I was on a call. I casually paced to the left of the line trying to get a glimpse of her. She was pointing to a pastry behind the glass. I couldn't tear my eyes away. Her profile was exquisite. Strong cheekbones, slightly upturned nose, and full, dusty pink lips. I was so intrigued by the color of her hair and the paleness of her skin. She wore a light gray blouse and a black skirt that hit above her knees. Her outfit was basic but everything else about her was anything but. Her black heels weren't designer, but that was me being a snob. It was definitely the same woman whose cat was chatting with me last Friday.

We made eye contact while she was standing in line to pay. I couldn't even pretend to talk on my fake phone call. I was right. She was breathtaking. Her brow furrowed for a split second as though she recognized me but didn't know from where. I gave her a soft smile that she didn't return. Oh, I was even more intrigued. When my phone buzzed against my head, startling me, I pulled it away and looked at the screen. Horrible timing, Sebastian. A slight smile perched on the young woman's lips before she looked away. I was busted.

"Bri, are you there?" Sebastian asked.

"I'm here. What's up?" I was going to tell him his timing was less than perfect, but his voice held a note of panic.

"I still can't get ahold of Aaron Bradley. I called him all weekend."

That was disturbing. "Let's not panic. He's probably off celebrating. You left him a message, right?"

"Yeah, I told him to call the office when he had a free minute because we had some good news."

I tapped my forehead trying to focus. "Call his mother. She might know something." Aaron was in a wheelchair and wasn't working because of the pain medication. Thanks to the settlement, he wouldn't have to work again unless he wanted to. He'd moved back in with his mother so she usually had an idea of his schedule. During our last conversation, he told me he was writing a memoir. He was a thirty-one-year-old extremely active engineer who not only got hit by the river market streetcar, but got run over by it and had his leg severed. His life was forever changed.

I watched the young woman tap her card and walk the opposite direction from where I stood. Sadly, we weren't destined to meet today. Maybe I'd see her later if I got up to the roof this afternoon.

"Keep me posted. I'll be there in ten." Could I just have a workday that started and ended well?

As I hung up, a text from Charlie came through. *Swing by when you get back from lunch. I have a project for you.*

I rolled my eyes. Charlie never texted unless it was important. He learned a long time ago that I never answered my phone unless I wanted to. Texting got my attention and he knew that. He also knew my schedule was full. The last thing I needed was a project. Pro bono? Favor for one of the partners? Let Tyler do it. I had a hot case going to trial and several I was trying to settle.

On my way back to the office now. I'll be there in fifteen to discuss. And turn down, I thought.

I needed to find out about Aaron Bradley first. I wasn't officially worried. He was probably out with his friends. He liked to fish and it was a gorgeous weekend. At least that's what I was telling myself until I knew for sure.

When the elevator opened, I quickly marched back to my office, avoiding eye contact. It was great that I had one of the largest offices, but it was also a million miles away from the elevators.

"Bri, do you have a moment?" one of the paralegals asked.

"No." I wanted to shoo her away, but then I remembered getting help around here was virtually impossible. I stopped. "Not now. Call

Sebastian and he'll squeeze you in today. How much time do you need?" Her smile improved my mood.

"Ten minutes tops."

I nodded. "Okay, ten minutes. Call Sebastian." I made it to my office without further interruption only to find Charlie in my office and Sebastian nervously hovering. I didn't slow down until I sat behind my desk. "Charlie, I told you'd I'd be up to see you in fifteen." I checked my watch. "That still gives me six minutes." He smiled at me but didn't budge. I sighed. "But this saves me a trip. What can I do for you?" Sebastian quickly closed my door.

"You're a young woman who knows what's hip these days," he said.

Who said hip anymore? I folded my hands in front of me. "What do you mean exactly?"

He held his palms up and shrugged. "We're looking to update our website and maybe shoot a few commercials. We'll be reaching out to several marketing firms over the next month to pitch us their ideas and since you're the future of Titan and Spector, we'd like you to sit in on those meetings."

I never fell for fake compliments. "What about Tyler? This seems like something more up his alley than mine."

Charlie nodded. "He'll be invited, too. You're more responsible than he is." He stuttered over the word responsible. "He's fresh but he's not focused. You'll be able to give us a real evaluation of what we have and where improvement is needed. I trust your judgment. I always have."

That's all I needed. More time away from billable hours. "I can't afford to give it a lot of my attention, but I'm more than happy to sit in on the meetings. I can't be responsible for decisions, though. I have too much on my plate."

"That's all I'm asking. I'll have my assistant keep you posted on when." He stood and shook my hand. "Thanks for being a team player, Bri."

I gave him a fake smile. "No problem. Anything to help the firm."

Sebastian sprang into my office the second Charlie left. "I got ahold of Mr. Bradley. He was on a fishing trip down in Branson, like you thought, and left his phone in the car. He's home if you want to take a drive."

"Did you tell him anything?" I asked. Selfishly, I wanted to give him the good news, but Sebastian deserved a lot of credit.

"Just that we wanted to meet with him. He said he's home now so we can stop by anytime."

The customer almost always came to the office to sign settlement paperwork, but since Aaron Bradley was in a wheelchair and had been through so much already, we made an exception. "What are your plans this afternoon?"

"Only the Bradley case."

"Perfect. I'll drive."

He thumbed behind him. "What did big dog want?"

I hated when he called Charlie that. "He wants me to sit in on our website design makeover. Hey, you're young and you have a pulse on the internet. Join us."

Sebastian waved me off. "No, no. I wasn't invited."

I steepled my fingers as I thought about sending Sebastian in my place. Charlie would be furious. "I'm officially inviting you. That way we can put our heads together. Not a request." His shoulders sagged. "It'll put you in good standing with the big dog." I almost puked the words out. I couldn't understand Sebastian's fascination with Charlie. "Anyway, what's on my schedule for this afternoon?"

❖

"Thank you so much for coming, Brianna." I didn't mind it when Kristen Bradley said my full name. It sounded soft and charming. She invited us in. "Can I get you anything to drink? I have iced tea, lemonade, water, and Coke. And since it's after five, I can offer something stronger."

"Well, if they're here and smiling, maybe we should crack open the beers." Aaron wheeled into the room with wet hair and a positive attitude. If what happened to him happened to me, I would still be sulking in my room avoiding people for the rest of my life. Or worse.

"Hey, Aaron. You look great today."

"Mom made me shower. After a weekend of fishing with the guys, I was ripe," he said.

"He didn't have a choice. I could smell him before he even got to the front door," Kristen said. She had a nice, large open floor plan house that helped accommodate Aaron's wheelchair.

"You smell fine now," I said.

"Have a seat, please." Kristen was nervously wringing her hands.

I felt her anxiety and touched her hand as I sat on the couch next to Sebastian. I looked at their eager faces and smiled. "Let's get started." Sebastian handed me a folder. "Midwest Trolley understands that this incident has altered the course of your life and have offered a hefty settlement." I slid the letter in front of Aaron and Kristen.

Tears gathered in the corners of Aaron's eyes and his chin quivered, but he powered through and squeezed his mother's hand. Kristen's sobs cut right through my heart and had I not braced myself emotionally, I would've crumbled.

"I know there is nothing that can compensate for the pain and suffering you've had to endure over the last six months, but we hope this is enough to keep you comfortable and afford all the rehabilitation you'll need in the future." I knew he was getting fitted for a prosthetic and that he was already suffering from phantom pain. That was the nail in the coffin that made Midwest Trolley fold.

"Thank you so much," Aaron said.

I had to stand behind our acceptance. I didn't like that it wasn't more, but I was honoring my client's wishes. I felt that going to trial would at least double the money, but that would've meant appeal after appeal and Aaron wouldn't see any money for years. He needed to put this behind him to move forward. "How are you going to celebrate?"

"Order a nice dinner and finish these drinks. We would love for you to join us. I mean, without you, none of this would be possible," Aaron said.

I had dinner plans with two friends, but quickly sent them a text message that I needed to reschedule. Claire understood. She was a lawyer or used to be. She closed one of the biggest cases in Kansas City years ago. I slipped my phone into my message bag and folded my jacket over the chair. I glanced at Sebastian who nodded. "We would love to have a celebratory dinner with you. What sounds good?"

Chapter Four

Lucky Chance—Not Living Up to the Name

Hugging Tito always made me feel better, even if he squirmed at the attention. "I know, big guy, but I'm going to need some love after that disaster." I plopped on the sofa and held him until his claws came out signaling that he'd had enough love. I couldn't believe Moonlight Crackers hated my design. Even though his team thought what I proposed was good, Mr. Fox shut me down before I could really shine. What he wanted was garbage. Miranda's harsh words when we left had made me feel broken. My morning was crap, but because I stopped in at Time for a Break for a coffee and a cinnamon roll, my afternoon felt like redemption on a different level.

"I'm pretty sure I saw your girlfriend today," I said. Tito looked at me and meowed. "Yep. That one. I even busted her staring at me." I smiled recalling how our eyes met and how she pretended to be on the phone. She was very attractive and her body language screamed power boss. Most women didn't look at me the way she did.

On a whim, I jumped up from the couch excited to find out if she was on the rooftop. The curtains were already pulled so the only thing I had to do was peek out. Why was I so nervous? I smoothed down my hair and looked. I was disappointed to find the space unoccupied. Of course, she wasn't there. I padded to the closet to change into short shorts and a tank top. I threw my hair back in a ponytail and sat at my computer to finish the changes on Moonlight Crackers. I was going to have the updated site back to Miranda by tonight.

After two hours of hunching over my laptop, I rubbed my eyes and stretched. I was stiff and needed caffeine. It was almost three and I was over halfway done with the changes. I opened the window to let fresh air in and quickly backed away when I saw her at the workstation. Did she see me? Why was I even hiding? I took a deep breath and stepped into view. Either she was scouting my window every ten seconds, or looked up right at the exact moment I looked out. A funny feeling tickled low against my ribs and made my heart quicken. I couldn't look away.

She gave a small wave and I had to stop myself from looking behind me. I gave a small wave back. She yelled something, but I couldn't hear her over the traffic below. I shrugged and pointed to my ear. Was I actually having a semi-conversation with hot boss lady? Me? Wearing a threadbare tank and shorts that left little to the imagination? I wish I hadn't pulled my hair back in a childish ponytail. It didn't complete the sexy girl in the window look. I wanted to fade away and do something magical to my hair, but also, I was glued to this spot.

"What?" I half-whispered knowing she couldn't hear me but hopefully she could read my lips.

She shook her head and pulled out a legal notepad. She wrote something and held it up. *CAT?*

Weird. Yes, he's a cat, I thought. I stroked his fur. Oh! She wanted to know his name. I held up my finger and grabbed my white board. I wrote *Tito* large enough so that she could see it.

She smiled and gave me a thumbs up. She flipped the paper over. *HE'S CUTE.* I nodded. And he knew it, too.

I thought about writing my name, but she was interrupted by a phone call and turned her attention to her work. I faded from the window determined to continue working but my body was on a high at finally having a quasi-conversation with her. It inspired me to knock out my project so that I could continue this semi-flirtatious exchange with her. My mind constantly drifted to her, but I promised myself I would get the project done so I could pay bills and eat. I was surprised she was still on the roof after three hours. What kind of work was she in that allowed her to hang out on the roof all day? I quickly let my hair down, grabbed a book, and sat in the window hoping she would glance my way. I opened the copy of *The Great Gatsby* and even though I wasn't reading a single word, I flipped the pages slowly as though I was fully engrossed in the story. I pulled the front of my tank and twisted it around my finger so it pulled the material tighter across my chest and gave a hint of a side boob. Could she see from that far away? Did I dare to look at her? I slid one knee up and rested the book in my lap. It was a casual move that looked innocent, but I knew from her angle that she could see the back of my thigh if she was looking. I looked down right as she turned her head so I wasn't sure if she was looking at me or not. She grabbed her phone as though it rang and started pacing while talking on it. When she finally looked at me, I held my breath. She was intense and that was sexy. I loved everything about a woman in a power suit. Still on her call, she walked away, her back to me, as though I was a distraction. It made me smile.

Seeing the life-size chess board near her workstation gave me an idea. Not knowing when she would look up again, I wrote *E4* on a piece of copy paper and taped it to the window. I backed away and made myself focus on work. Tito, curious about the paper, pawed at it until he eventually gave up and plopped down on the ledge for a quick nap. Miranda popped up on my instant message wanting to do a Teams meeting. It irked me to no end that she had zero faith in me. I put on a T-shirt and shared my screen with her to show her my changes. Every single one was exactly what the customer asked for.

"Now this is good work, Lucky," she said.

Was she serious? I rolled my eyes hard and bit my tongue from adding words like boring, dull, retro but not cool retro, more like left-in-the-past-for-a-reason retro. "It's what he wanted."

Her exasperated sigh made me cringe. "Look, I know it's been hard to find your footing here, but these simple websites are our bread and butter. They are easy and everyone is happy. The company is happy, the client is happy. Happy pays the bills. You might have to tone back your creativeness for a while until we find you the perfect fit. I know you're used to flying solo, but I'm going to have you work with a team on the next few projects. Darian, Noelle, and Elliot are excellent team members who are used to doing all scopes of projects including getting in front of the client."

"Okay, Miranda. Whatever you want me to do." I gritted my teeth knowing full well it was a demotion.

"That will require you to work in the office more. I know we agreed to fully remote, but maybe for the next few months, you should come in a few days a week. It can't hurt to immerse yourself in our practices. We're different from the Boston branch."

I was furious at both Miranda and the customer. They needed to immerse themselves in the twenty-first century and learn how much the world has changed. We needed to land younger, fresher clients. Maybe I needed to land a different company. Kansas City had a women's soccer team and a women's professional volleyball team. Maybe sports was my calling. I killed the Connecticut Cheetahs logo, website, and webstore. That account was a gold mine. And to think I left it all for a woman. I smacked my palm against my forehead.

"Are you okay?"

I forgot we were on Teams and my video was on. "I'm fine. I just forgot something. I'll polish up the changes on Moonlight. When do you want me to start coming into the office?"

"I'll have a conversation with Darian and Elliot and see what they're working on and I'll get back to you," she said.

"Sounds great." It pained me to say it, but I knew it would make Miranda feel good. "Thanks for your help today."

Miranda's smirk only intensified her bitchiness. "I'm always around if you need advice. I know you're trying. Your efforts are noted."

I almost snorted at her insincerity. "Thanks. I'll firm this up and send it over in the morning. That way you can get it back to the customer since we're one of three. I don't want to miss out." I wished her a good evening and closed Teams. My head was spinning. Too many changes at once. I needed a break. I stretched and decided to see if my rooftop hottie was still at the scene. I glanced out the window. She wasn't there, but she moved my pawn and made a move of her own. Game on. For the first time in hours, I smiled.

I finalized the Moonlight changes. By the time I sent them off to Miranda it was ten. I was done with Moonlight. I had my next move taped in my window for hot boss to hopefully see tomorrow. There wasn't much I could do except scroll on my phone or watch something mindless on Netflix. I felt cooped up and needed a change of scenery. There were a few bars within walking distance but nothing queer, and the last thing I wanted was to fight off advances from men who thought I was straight. Katrina's, the only queer bar along the trolley route, didn't have anything on the schedule so I decided a cold beer and laughing with drag queens sounded a lot more fun than sulking in the dark. I grabbed a light jacket, kissed Tito on the nose, and hopped on the trolley. Katrina's wasn't a place I frequented because Mia and her friends hung out on karaoke night. I walked in like I owned the place but slowed when I realized Mia wasn't there. It was a slow night. I grabbed a stool at the bar and pretended to be interested in the baseball game that had gone into extra innings.

"Are you a Royals fan?" The bartender swooped into my line of vision. "What can I get you?" I watched her eyes travel down to my shirt. She made an unpleasant face. "Oh. A Red Sox fan. Well, I guess I still have to serve you even though you just broke my heart. I'm surprised they let you in." She winked and gave me a crooked smile.

I wasn't there to flirt. I was there to drink a cold beer and wallow in my failures. "I charmed them." Or, you know, paid the cover. "Can I get a really cold beer?"

"Tap?"

"Whatever hazy is on special."

"I've got Boulevard's Unfiltered Wheat."

"Sold."

"College student?" she asked and slid a Boulevard Unfiltered Wheat in front of me. I drank a third of the glass before I answered her.

"Graduated about four years ago. I just look young." I subconsciously patted my ponytail and slowly slid the band out of my hair so it fell around my shoulders.

"Good for you. Whatever you're doing, keep it up. I could probably take a few pointers," she said.

"I'm Lucky."

"You sure are."

"No, I mean that's my name. Lucky. Well, Lucinda, but nobody my age goes by that. Just call me Lucky."

"That's adorable. Hi, Lucky, I'm Frankie. Francesca, but nobody my age goes by that. Just call me Frankie," she said.

I hated that she said adorable, but people either loved my name or thought it was a joke. My parents had a great sense of humor twenty-six years ago. Last name is Chance, better name the kid Lucky. They were a bit more uptight now. "Hi, Frankie. Thanks for the recommendation It's good." It seemed that Kansas City had a brewery every few blocks. Every month there was a beer crawl, beer festival, brewery bash, or tasting. This city wasn't short on alcohol. I liked beer as long as it was ice cold and had some flavor. It was cheap, and holding a hefty pint glass sitting at a bar all alone seemed less sad than if I were holding a martini glass.

"What brings you out tonight?"

I shrugged. "Just finished a project that kicked my ass. I'm trying to recover so I figured getting out of my apartment for an hour seemed like the celebratory thing to do."

"Hey, you're here so that means you won." Frankie slammed down two shot glasses and poured gold tequila to the rim of each glass. She slid one in front of me and held up the other. "Let's celebrate. I hate drinking alone and since we're friends now, you can't leave me hanging."

I abhorred shots. They burned my throat, my stomach, and got me drunk faster than any other alcohol. I inwardly groaned. I skipped dinner so it was going to hit me hard and fast. "Only one. I have an early start in the morning."

"You got it, Lucky girl." She slapped two lime slices on a clean napkin in front of me and clinked her glass against mine. She was ready. I was not. Tequila didn't like me. I closed off my throat so I didn't choke on it and shot it as fast as she did. She was impressed, and I fought the urge to puke it right back up. I sucked on the lime and practically jumped off the stool as the smooth liquid quickly turned into fire all the way down to my stomach. She held up the bottle and I shook my head.

"No, thank you. One is enough. Can I get a glass of water?" Anything to keep it down. The last thing I ate today was a cinnamon roll. Come to think of it, it was the only thing I ate. "And is it too late to order any food?"

"The kitchen closed at ten but let me see what I can find." Frankie disappeared after pouring me a tall glass of ice water. I reminded myself that I wasn't a drinker and to leave after I finished my beer. I was almost done with it when Frankie came back with chips and salsa.

"It's not much, but hopefully it helps."

I needed something with bread, but chips were a close second. "Thanks," I said and dug into a greasy pile of hot chips. "Hopefully, the kitchen didn't get too mad."

"No worries. Everyone is pretty laid-back. Most of us are night owls so we understand," she said. She busied herself by tidying up the bar and putting bottles back on the shelf, but always kept the conversation going. "What do you do, if you don't mind me asking?"

"I'm in marketing with emphasis on redesigning websites. I transferred here last winter from Boston." I decided not to go into why I moved because she probably heard enough sob stories in her life, and we had a nice vibe going. I liked to keep my failures to myself.

"That sounds rewarding. Any clients I might know?" she asked.

My only Kansas City success story was a private healthcare system. Orion Healthcare loved everything I created from a new logo to a new easy-to-use website with patient portals that were so easy to use, my grandmother could use it. Truthfully, I had her run through the program after our IT department designed it to see if she could. She passed with flying colors and my grandmother barely knew how to use a smartphone. I had a few other smaller hits, but nothing as impressive as Orion. "Orion Healthcare." Frankie blinked at me. "Yeah, nothing exciting here." I needed to brag. "But back home, I did the Connecticut Cheetahs website and logo."

That got her attention. "That's amazing. I mean, working with the NFL must have been an incredible opportunity. Did you meet any of the players? What about the female coach? Did you get to work with her?" she said.

I hated to burst her bubble. I worked with their marketing team. I visited their campus once and that was only to get a feel for it. "I didn't get to work with her, but I remember it being a very big deal."

"The first female offensive coordinator? Hell, yeah. Since she became a coach, there are now over two dozen females coaches including a defensive coordinator. She's done so much for women in the NFL."

"Now we just need a few female players," I said. Honestly, I didn't care about football. I wasn't really into sports, but Mia was a massive Red Sox fan so that had made me a fan by proxy.

"We probably won't see that for a few years. Maybe a kicker or punter, but I can't imagine a female quarterback or wide receiver. The defenses would crush her just to be dicks. That coach, Sutton McCoy, had a biography written about her life and she said that playing quarterback in high school was hard for that very reason," Frankie said.

"I can't imagine. I'm not very sporty," I said.

"So, I shouldn't invite you to join our softball league?"

"Not if you want to win." I grabbed my biceps. "Look at these limp noodles. They are not for swinging bats or hitting balls."

"We can always use cute cheerleaders, too." She reached under the bar and handed me a flyer. "It's a fun way to meet new people. Just take it home and put it on your refrigerator. You never know."

I scanned the flyer. Katrina's Kittens played just across the river on Sunday afternoons and Wednesday nights. The season started in a few weeks. The name was a bit much, but I wasn't going to play so my opinion didn't matter. "Thanks." I carefully folded the paper and slid it into my back pocket. "I should probably get going. How much do I owe you?"

"I got this one, Lucky girl. Thanks for keeping me company on a slow night."

It felt good to talk to somebody about simple things. I needed to figure out if I was going to stay here or move back to Connecticut. If I was going to stay, then I needed to try harder. I might not be looking for love, but I needed friends, and Frankie was a great start. "Thanks, Frankie. Maybe I'll be a cheerleader after all." I dropped a ten on the bar as a tip and waved to her on my way out. For the first time all week, I felt hopeful. Maybe everything was going to be okay after all.

CHAPTER FIVE

BRIANNA JAMESON—LAWYER LIVING THE GOOD LIFE

I know we said we weren't going to be bougie when we hit it big, but I really like this lifestyle better than when we first met." I accepted the glass of Santa Margharita Pinot Grigio and waited until Claire's and Emery's glasses were poured.

"It's easy to get used to and we deserve it," Claire said.

I loved how direct and honest she was. "Cheers to that, my friends." I tilted my glass at both of them and smiled. It was so wonderful to see Claire happy. When we first met, she was all business. She was the first one in the office and last one out every day. I didn't work directly with her, but always admired her from afar. It wasn't until she became a judge that I started really connecting with her. We both had season tickets to the Kansas City Symphony and were on the board for the Kansas City Inclusion and Diversity Club. Being her friend was easy; finding time together was hard. We were both extremely busy because we both had something to prove. Her advice was invaluable.

"How's work? I'm starting to see a lot of Titan and Spector lawyers in my courtroom."

I shrugged. I trusted Claire, but she still kept in contact with some of the partners. "I want to sign a case, but Charlie firmly put his foot down."

"He's pretty good at sniffing out money. If he doesn't think it'll pad his pockets then he'll give it a wide berth," Claire said.

"He's playing it too safe. I think he's lost his edge," I said.

"He's comfortable," she said.

"He's very comfortable."

"Why don't you just open your own practice?" Emery asked. "You have the clients and then you could accept any cases you wanted. You'd be your own boss."

The thought of opening up my own practice had crossed my mind more and more. "It's not a bad idea. I'm just so close to becoming partner now that I'd hate to give it up after putting in so much work."

"But then all the fees would be one hundred percent yours. You wouldn't have to share. Isn't that every lawyer's dream? Owning their own practice," Emery said.

Claire put her hand on Emery's forearm. "Except your wife who wanted to be a judge."

"Touché, love." They were my favorite power couple. Emery was so supportive of Claire and vice versa. They attended benefit dinners, fundraising luncheons, and special events around town. How they found the time amazed me.

"Yeah, but Titan settles so many cases. I couldn't handle that many cases on my own," I said.

"You just settled a huge case, right?" Emery asked. I nodded. "How much did the firm make?"

I smiled. "Just under a million."

Emery pointed at me while holding her wine glass. "That would be all yours. Well, your practice. Land a few of those cases and you're set. You could hire people who would do exactly what you are doing and offer profit-sharing. There are some great up-and-coming lawyers who would love to get in on a ground-floor practice with the numbers to back it."

I blew out a deep breath. "It sounds overwhelming."

"It is, but I've known you for a few years and you're hungry. And you like challenges," Emery said.

"Don't push her, babe." Claire quietly stepped in.

Emery held out her hands. "Okay, okay. I'm sorry. Just know that we support you in whatever you do," Emery said.

"Speaking of supporting you, any luck with Kelsey? Is she somebody you'd be interested in?" Claire had introduced me to Kelsey Hawk at the last Diversity Club meeting. Kelsey was their director of communications, and while she was pretty and nice, she was also extremely quiet. I had to keep the conversation going and life was too short to spend it drawing words out of somebody.

"I don't think she's right for me. Super sweet person, but our personalities were too far apart, I think," I said.

"At some point you're going to have to slow down and enjoy life," Claire said.

"Funny coming from you," I said.

"Hey, I don't work wild hours anymore. Emery gives me a reason to race home every night," Claire said.

I wanted to tease them for being sappy and emotional, but honestly, it was lovely to see. "I think your relationship is incredible. Inspiring."

"You should try it," Emery said.

"Well, now that you mention it, I haven't been seeing somebody, but there's been some playful flirting from a distance." I was going to keep mystery girl a secret because nothing was really happening, but our interaction made my heart lighter. And seeing her in person sent little, fun shockwaves throughout my body.

"Do tell," Claire said.

"It's truly nothing. One day I was working up on the rooftop and I saw a cat sitting in a window in the building across the street. I was trying to get his attention because hello, it's a cat. Well, then I see his owner and she is beautiful. And this is going to sound weird, but we're in the middle of a chess game and the only thing I know about her is that she's really good at the game. Oh, wait. Her cat's name is Tito."

Emery snorted. "Hold up. What?"

"I know. It's hard to explain. Claire, you know that giant chessboard on the roof, right?" At her nod, I continued. "This woman and I aren't close enough to talk, so we write large notes. She gave me the first move in chess, and now we're halfway through the game. It's juvenile, but fun." I didn't tell them how her skin was alabaster white and how her strawberry-blond hair looked incredibly soft or how her vivid blue eyes bored into me when she caught me staring at her at the coffee shop. I certainly wasn't going to tell them how I was too chicken to go talk to her. Me. Afraid of nothing and nobody. I couldn't remember the last time I was literally stunned by a woman.

"This could be the start of something pretty fun," Emery said.

I drained my glass of wine feeling lightheaded but not because of the alcohol. Claire and Emery were the first people who knew about my mystery woman. She was no longer my secret. Crashing and burning when nobody knew was a lot easier to swallow than when your friends inquired about your love life every time you got together and then tried to console you when things didn't work out. I stopped sharing for a reason. Mostly it was because I was embarrassed. I could do anything except keep a relationship. Claire and Emery's relationship gave me hope though, and spending time with them didn't make me jealous. It made me realize that I could have what they have.

"Enough about me. What are you doing for your anniversary?" I asked.

"We're keeping it low-key this year. A quick trip up to Niagara Falls for a long weekend," Claire said. "I have a big trial on the docket, but we know how much lawyers like to try to settle while the court races around trying to get ready for a showdown."

"Oh, that sounds romantic," I said. I wasn't even jealous. Emery loved waterfalls and even though it was kind of a touristy place, I could appreciate its beauty. Being landlocked in Missouri made you appreciate waterfalls and oceans and sandy beaches more so than the people who were around it all the time.

"It's something different to kick off our summer. What about you? What are you doing over the long weekend?" Claire asked.

I blew out a deep breath.

"Uh-oh. That doesn't sound good," Emery said.

I shook my head. "It's fine. My parents are having a barbecue. It sounds like they invited the entire neighborhood." I took a bite of my chicken spiedini. I missed the days when I met my parents out for dinner and our conversations were just about us. Dealing with their neighbors was a bit too much. They always wanted free legal advice about the weirdest things. Who was responsible for tree limb trimming? What happened if somebody's dog destroyed your property? Was it okay to discharge a firearm if wildlife was in your backyard? All I wanted was a hot dog, maybe a cheeseburger, a cold beer, and to sit in a lawn chair while soaking up the first warm rays of the start of summer. I didn't want to work on my long weekend.

"Sometimes we have to do things we don't want to," Claire said.

"Personal experience?" I asked. I casually looked at Emery who held her hands up.

"My family is normal. Sometimes a bit much, but they never push Claire," Emery said.

Claire nodded. "They're great. I like weekends where we can spend the day in bed watching bad television, but sometimes we have to go to T-ball or soccer games."

Emery kissed her on the cheek. "I'm sorry. We're the favorite aunts so it's hard to not want to do everything to keep the title." She turned to me. "I have a large family and we're only getting bigger."

That raised my eyebrows. "Wait. What? You two?" I moved my finger between the two of them.

"Oh, no. Not us. Just everyone else in my family who's married," Emery said. She found her silverware very interesting and smoothed the napkin in her lap avoiding any eye contact. Must have been a recent conversation that didn't go well. I always assumed Claire didn't want kids and given that Emery had so many nieces and nephews, my guess was that she was the one prodding. Gently, of course. Claire wasn't one who could be coerced into anything she didn't want.

"I'm too career-driven to start a family now," I said.

"All the more reason to start your own practice now. Get it going before you get serious with chess girl or anyone else," Emery said.

I mentioned a small flirtation and they were laser-focused on it. That was the problem with having married friends. They couldn't believe you were okay being single. "I'll give it some thought." And I would, but I worked so hard to be in the running, it was hard to just walk away from all the effort I put into impressing the partners.

"How's your job, Em?" I asked.

"Thankfully, pretty chill. I get home at a decent hour most days now that I'm the boss and we were able to hire another investigator for evening shifts," she said.

"Not too many day fires?" I asked.

"Most of them are tame and not suspicious. Mulch plants, barbecues, and the occasional house fire. Open and shut cases," she said.

"Sounds pretty boring," I said.

"I like to use the term predictable. It gives me more time to work on the house," Emery said.

They were building a giant house in a new gated community up north. Emery was very hands-on in the process. It helped that it was her brother's contracting company. The photos of their house were gorgeous. I felt a little tinge of jealousy as I compared their new house to my townhouse. If I plugged my nest egg into a new practice, the dream house would have to wait. I wasn't getting any younger either. "When is it move in ready?"

"If it was up to Emery, never. But I can't imagine it not being done by the end of summer. We'll throw a party," Claire said.

"Sounds great. Really. I'm happy for you both." I was. I loved them both and wanted nothing but good things for them.

"Are you ready for Pride?" Emery asked.

"I'm so excited! Backstage passes to see Annie Foster perform? Hell, yeah. And we'll probably meet Bristol Baines, too," I said.

Pride in Kansas City was a three-day affair. It was loud and proud, and Titan and Spector were gold sponsors of the event. Our name was everywhere. We even had a large booth for free legal advice. I was going, but as a spectator, not a lawyer. And I wasn't planning on going until Sunday night when they had the big concert. Only a handful of people knew Annie was going to perform because it was supposed to be a surprise. There were whispers and rumors, but nobody knew for sure. I couldn't wait to see their faces when they found out. Annie still performed regularly, but Bristol had stepped away from the limelight and never looked back. The world missed her music, but she was doing a lot for up-and-coming artists.

"What time should I meet you?" I asked.

"We're probably going to be there by six. Music all day, but Annie's closing, so anytime before eight," Claire said. She never struck me as a concert goer. She seemed too refined for jumping around and singing at the top of her lungs. Sitting in plush seats backstage while drinking wine and listening to the music was how I pictured Claire enjoying any concert.

I never pushed for favors from Claire, but it took every ounce of willpower not to ask to be her guest the two times she saw Taylor Swift perform in Kansas City. From backstage. "Great. I'll text you when I get there. Thanks again for inviting me."

I left the restaurant on a high. I had supportive friends who still made time for me. What Emery said started creeping into the forefront of my mind. What if I ditched all my hard work to start my own practice? How did one even go about starting their own practice? I had a few acquaintances who had done it, but I didn't trust them to not make a quick phone call to somebody at Titan and Spector. That was too stressful. I needed to figure things out before I put anything in motion. The idea of going on my own was gaining momentum and Brianna Jameson Law Firm sounded pretty sweet rolling off my tongue.

Chapter Six

Lucky Chance—Turning Her Luck Around

"Hi, Frankie."

I shoved my hands in the pockets of my jeans trying to look like a normal person, but I was terrified to be around so many people I didn't know. I wanted to experience KC Pride, but I didn't have anybody I wanted to tether myself to, so I went by myself. I remembered Frankie told me that the women's softball league was going to have a booth and all the teams would be there to recruit new players.

"Lucky! You made it! I'm so happy to see you. Welcome to Kansas City Women's Softball," Frankie said. She handed me a clipboard. "There are seven other teams to check out, but if you sign up, it can only be with our team," she said.

A woman wearing a backwards hat that covered up most of her short, gray hair playfully pushed her aside. Her green-and-yellow John Queer T-shirt made me smile. "Don't listen to her. You can sign up for any team here." She sized me up and the way her voice got higher didn't give me confidence. "Do you play ball, sweetie?"

When was the last time I played a team sport? I was all about yoga and spinning, but how was my hand-eye coordination? "I don't, but I consider myself a quick study."

"There's not much to hitting a ball."

An attractive woman around my age glued to her phone didn't even look up. "Caitlyn, be nice. Not everyone eats and drinks softball." Her blond shaggy hair framed her smooth, tanned face. Her full lips were puckered as though posing for a selfie, but her finger was scrolling across her phone. Maybe that was her concentration look. I wasn't impressed or pretended not to be. "Some people have a life. Like this sweet person." She finally looked up from her scrolling. "I'm Mary and this is Caitlyn. We're on team Game of Throws."

That was my cue. "Hi, I'm Lucky."

Caitlyn snorted. "Lucky, huh?" She did everything but roll her beautifully bright green eyes. What did I ever do to her? I only showed up ten seconds ago.

"Be nice," Mary said. Caitlyn shrugged, grabbed a clipboard, and mumbled something about recruiting real players.

Mary waved her off. "Don't mind her. She was born grumpy. So, Lucky, are you new to Kansas City?"

"I moved here in December so I haven't really met a lot of queer people."

"She showed up late one night and the lure of women's softball was too much." Frankie pointed at the clipboard and nodded. She waved a Katrina's Kittens sticker under my nose as though that would help me decide to sign up. I grabbed a schedule instead.

"I promise to show up at the first game."

Frankie leaned her hip against the table. "Okay, but if you sign up, you're going to play on our team."

I pointed at the booth. "You have tons of people here. You don't want me." I held up my finger. "Correction. You don't need me."

"Ah, but we do want you," Frankie said.

I blushed. She was great at casual flirting. That's what made her a great bartender. "We'll see. If nothing else, I'll be the cheerleader as promised."

"I'll take that. Plus, summer is hard because a lot of people go on vacations, and we need bodies. Here, let me introduce you to some of the girls. If I remember correctly, you need more friends." Ouch. That stung. I frowned. Frankie touched my arm. "I didn't mean anything by it." She put her hand on her heart to emphasize the sincerity of her words. "Come on. Let's introduce you around."

Frankie commanded attention. She was very comfortable in her own skin and people smiled when she approached. She introduced me to the starting line-up for the KC Sunflowers, their biggest rivals, pointing each one out as we weaved through the cluster of people gathered in front of the giant tent. For the first time since I stepped foot in this park, I relaxed. Maybe I could give softball a try. I knew there were batting cages across the river. I could practice until I felt comfortable swinging a bat.

"Lucky? Is that you?" A warm hand touched my elbow. It took a split second to realize it was Mia and all the confidence that swirled inside my heart just a few moments ago, flatlined in my chest.

I gasped and stopped myself from jerking away. I could only stare. I knew there was the possibility of running into her, but I was so excited about meeting new people that I forgot to be on alert. "Uh, hi, Mia." I hated that she looked beautiful and happy. Two other women were with her. I recognized one. The other woman with long dark hair and hazel eyes had her pinky finger loosely linked with Mia's. The chicken sandwich I made myself eat before heading here threatened to make an untimely appearance. I felt somebody approach from behind me and before I could turn, I felt an arm casually drape across my shoulder and somebody twirl a strand of my hair. I stiffened at a stranger in my personal space.

"Hey, doll. Mary's looking for you. She found the forms you were looking for."

Caitlyn—snarky, rude, dismissive Caitlyn—knew exactly what was happening and jumped in to save me from having a meltdown in front of my ex. It looked natural but felt anything but.

I smiled and clamped my lips together to keep my teeth from chattering. "Thanks for letting me know."

Caitlyn made a show of tapping my chin and letting her gaze linger on my lips for a few seconds, letting everyone around us think that we were a couple. I quickly slipped into character by forcing a smile and telling myself to relax under Caitlyn's embrace. I ate up the surprised look on Mia's face.

"Good to see you, Mia. Have a great Pride," I said. Caitlyn steered me over to the table where she continued to stand close until Mia left. I grabbed her arm. "Thank you so much for saving me. That whole situation is icky." Since when did I talk like that?

"Bad breakup?" she asked.

I put my hands on my hips and blew out a deep breath. She was probably only being nice so I gave her a short version. "Sad story of following a girl here. Gave up my cool job, my friends and family, and moved to the Midwest."

She shook her head and clucked her tongue. "That's the saddest thing I've ever heard. Most people are trying to leave here."

"The thought of moving back home crossed my mind, but I need to give it a year."

"When's the year up?" she asked.

"Christmas." Technically, it was two days after, but that didn't pack the same punch as saying a massive holiday.

"Ouch."

I crossed my fingers. "Only six more months." I watched her run her fingers through her hair, ruffling it up even more as she processed my news. Somehow the chaos looked good on her. Everything about her screamed "I don't give a fuck," and that made her my new friend even though we didn't start off on the right foot.

"Oof. Well, if you play softball, that'll kill two months. You're guaranteed to be around a lot of people and you won't run into her." She nodded behind us. "I don't think she signed up. What's her last name? I can check the sign-up forms."

"It's Alban but I doubt she signed up. She's in med school and doesn't have a lot of free time."

She pointed at the clipboard. "Then now is the time to jump in and make great friends. Mary's right. You'll click with several people right away."

I was hesitant. "I've never played."

"Honestly, it doesn't matter. They'll put you in right field. Sometimes they just need a body. It's more about just hanging out."

"Let me guess, you're the best on the team."

Her confidence was unmistakable. I swear her chest puffed a bit. She shrugged. "I'm not the worst," she said.

I laughed for the first time. "Something tells me you're pretty good."

"Come show me your skills and we'll see if you're as bad as you say you are." Caitlyn grabbed a foam softball from the table. She took a few steps back and threw it to me.

I almost dropped the ball but managed to hold on to it at the last second. When I threw it back to her, Caitlyn shook her head and laughed. "See, I told you no one would want me," I said.

"Lucky! Maybe you should stick to cheerleading," Frankie yelled from the other side of the booth.

Frankie winked and gave me a thumbs up. Suddenly, Pride wasn't scary. I felt comfortable around these women. Everyone seemed to be having a good time and the vibe felt good. I grabbed a rainbow bracelet.

"Do you want to walk around together?" Caitlyn asked. "I'm supposed to meet my girlfriend at the entrance in twenty minutes. This way you get to see everything without feeling that gut punch of seeing your ex if we run into her again."

"That would be great. Thank you. I wanted to hang around until the concert tonight. I've always loved live music," I said.

Caitlyn grabbed a small tube of sunscreen with a Game of Throws sticker covering the manufacturing label and handed it to me. "You look like you're going to need this. I know the sun is almost setting, but I don't want you to burn."

I had sunscreen in my tiny backpack, but it was such a nice gesture, that I graciously accepted it and smeared it on my arms, face, and neck. I never went out in the sun. When I was eight, I got sunburned so badly that I had to go to the hospital. After that horrible incident, my mother made sure I always wore a hat and rash guards when we went to the beach or any event where we were outside for more than twenty minutes. "Thanks. I can't believe Pride is three days here. Back east, Pride is only one day."

"It makes for a long weekend when you're working the booth," Caitlyn said. She readjusted her ball cap and led me through the center of the booths so that I could see what vendors were there displaying their crafts, products, or services. She lit up when her phone buzzed twenty minutes later. "Are you good if I take off?" She looked around for Mia. "The coast is clear. I don't see her anywhere."

"Thanks. Go meet your girlfriend. I'm fine."

"I'll see you later. Nice to meet you, Lucky," she said. She gave me a sheepish grin. "Sorry I was such a dick earlier."

I pointed at her. "You're forgiven. Thanks for saving my ass back there." She gave me a thumbs up and disappeared into the crowd. I checked the time. Lizard Bath, an all-queer local band, was taking the stage in ten minutes. I liked them okay, but I knew they were one of Mia's favorite bands so I steered clear. She wasn't going to stop me later tonight when Annie Foster took the stage. Even though it was a surprise guest, everyone knew it was Annie. Knowing that Mia was at the concert, I felt a sense of freedom to move about the festival without running into her. I bought a couple of queer books, a few bracelets, and my first Kansas City T-shirt. By the time I made my way back to the softball tent after eating and grabbing a beer, it was almost time for Annie to take the stage.

"Anyone going to see Annie?" I asked.

"Everyone. I told them to go. I'm staying behind and watching things here," Mary said.

Frankie linked her arm with mine. "Let's go. Are you a big Annie fan, too?"

"She's great. I was a Bristol fan first," I said.

"I wish she'd release something new. It's been a couple of years now."

My anxiety was ramping up the closer we got to the concert. I didn't want to run into Mia, but having Frankie at my side gave me the strength to push through the crowd and move closer to the stage.

"I'm so excited!" She shouted so I could hear her. Everyone around us was talking and the energy was ramping up even though the stage was empty. Frankie squeezed my arm. "It's almost time."

Faces flashed in the moments the curtains flapped open and closed as roadies scurried about the stage to place equipment on black tape marks. I froze when I thought I saw hot boss lady in the flicker of the light as the curtains briefly parted. "Whoa."

"What? Who or what did you see?" Frankie leaned her head into my line of vision and strained to see what I saw. "Was it Bristol?"

"No. Just somebody I kind of know."

"Backstage? And you could've been there? What are you doing here?" she asked.

I couldn't stop looking. Not that there was anything I could do, but I was genuinely curious. "I'm not for sure that's her." I looked at Frankie. "I barely know her."

"Is she cute?"

Cute wasn't a word I would use to describe her. Sophisticated, elegant, confident, and beautiful. Not cute. The curtain rippled again. In the quick blur of the fluttering material, our eyes met. A bubble of excitement rushed through my veins as our eyes held until the curtain fell back into place. It was definitely her.

CHAPTER SEVEN

BRIANNA JAMESON—GROUPIE EXTRAORDINAIRE

That's her." I pulled the curtains back, and rather than awkwardly point, I told Claire exactly where to look. "Third row. Strawberry-blond hair holding a beer."

"She's pretty. And young," Claire said.

Emery squeezed between us to get a peek. "Yes, to both. You should go down there and talk to her."

"Annie's about to take the stage. I'll find her afterward," I said. I was already pumped because I was backstage and had already met Annie. That was the highlight of my weekend. So far. Regret hit me like a punch to the stomach when I noticed my mystery woman was with somebody. Why would I actually believe she was alone?

"Come on. They are ushering us to the VIP seats." Emery grabbed Claire's hand and Claire grabbed my shirt to pull me along. Our seats were in a roped off section to the left of the stage, but still above the crowd. We had plush seats and an open bar. There were fifteen people in our section, and I only knew Claire and Emery. There was a quick introduction before we all sat and Annie took the stage.

"Happy Pride, Kansas City!" Annie yelled into the microphone. She strummed her guitar for emphasis and the crowd went wild.

"We love you, Annie!" several people yelled.

She fixed the capo on her guitar while engaging them. "Aww. And I love you, too. It's great to be back. Also, surprise. I'm the headliner. Well, only part of it." She strummed again and even I screamed a little when Bristol Baines walked on stage with her. Emery gave me a weird look. I shrugged and continued clapping and whooping. More people flocked to the stage and for a moment, I was worried for my mystery woman's safety. She was close to the front and people were starting to push forward.

"What? They're both great," I said unapologetically.

Emery laughed and Claire squeezed my hand. "Inside I'm screaming, too," Claire said.

"Well, at least you know I appreciate the ticket," I said. I turned my attention back to the stage as they dueted a fan favorite. I snapped a few photos nonchalantly as though it wasn't a big deal that they were thirty feet away, then slipped my phone in my pocket so that I could enjoy the concert. The ninety-minute set was mostly Annie, but Bristol joined her for the first song, the last song, and a few in the middle. I couldn't remember when I had so much fun. When Annie announced her last song, I motioned to Claire and Emery that I was going into the crowd. I didn't have to tell them why. I'd been watching my mystery woman and I was pretty sure the person with her was only a friend. I waited off to the side until Annie and Bristol sang the last note and left the stage before approaching her.

"Hello, Tito's mom." Her mouth parted slightly and her brow arched in surprise.

"Hi." The woman standing next to her reached out and introduced herself. "Since my friend Lucky isn't going to introduce us, I'm Frankie."

I shook her hand and glanced at her briefly during the introduction, but my attention was on my mysterious woman who now had a name: Lucky. "Hi, Frankie. I'm Bri." I wasn't sure if she was quiet because I rudely interrupted them, or because she was scared of me for whatever reason. "Did you enjoy the concert?"

"It was amazing. I'm still on a high from seeing Bristol," Frankie said.

It was at that moment that I realized my backstage pass would allow me to hang out with Annie and Bristol, but right now, life had more important ideas like finally knowing my chess opponent's name. "They were both great."

"Were you backstage earlier?" Frankie asked.

"Yes." Both Lucky and I answered at the same time.

Frankie looked at both of us and quickly picked up on our vibe. "Okay, so listen, I'm going to go back to the booth to wrap things up. If you're not back up in twenty minutes, I'll just grab your stuff and you can just swing by the bar anytime to collect it." She shook my hand again. "Nice to meet you, Bri. Hope to see you again soon."

"She seems nice," I said. I was running out of ideas on how to draw Lucky into conversation. "So. Lucky, huh? I think that's a fascinating name."

"It's a blessing and a curse."

Her voice was soft, but not meek. I strained to hear her words in the crowd that was dispersing in our direction. I pointed to a picnic table out of the way. "Do you want to sit down for a little bit so we can actually hear one another?"

She nodded and followed my path through the throng of hot, sweaty bodies as though they'd been dancing at a rave instead of a borderline folk-rock concert. I sat across from her and smiled. Her gaze didn't waver. She was quiet. I had a flashback to my date with the silent Kelsey, but something about Lucky made me think she was stunned rather than silent. I didn't even know how to start the conversation. My energy level was off the charts.

"What's it like living downtown? I've always wanted to live in a loft."

Her blue eyes were so bright under the festival lights. She pulled her hair over one shoulder and fanned herself with a flyer. Tiny beads of perspiration dotted her temples, but other than that, she looked cool and calm. She wore a sleeveless button-down shirt, jeans, and sandals. I wanted to ask her everything and learn as much as I could about her, but I didn't want to come off as creepy or pushy. A fleeting image of Tyler from work flashed in my brain and I told myself to relax and dial my flirting down to a one or two.

"It's okay. The days are loud, but the nights are pretty quiet."

"Do you work from home?"

She nodded. "I'm in marketing. I work when the inspiration hits. What about you? Corporate boss?"

Sometimes being a lawyer was impressive, but something about Lucky made me doubt that she would be impressed. I toned my résumé down and simply said, "I'm a lawyer."

"What kind of law?" she asked.

"Injury, but I'm not an ambulance chaser." Although if I started my own business, I would be exactly that. "Not that there's anything wrong with that, but most of our clients call us."

She nodded slowly as though processing the information carefully. "Dream job?"

I pressed my lips together and thought about the question. Helping people was always a dream. Unjustified situations pissed me off. Fighting for the underdog was always my goal, but was it my dream job? "It's close. What about you?"

"I'm good at what I do, but I'm still trying to find my footing here in Kansas City. It's a different market, for sure."

"Where are you from?" For sure I would've noticed her sooner. She was hard to miss.

"Originally, I'm from Connecticut, but I went to school and worked in Boston for the last six years," she said.

Now wasn't the time to bring up how young she looked. Besides, it was rude. "And you willingly packed up and moved to this fine city of ours? Welcome."

"Hm." She looked away for the first time. That's when I knew that the move wasn't an easy thing.

I treaded lightly again. "Kansas City is small, but large enough where we get amazing musicians like Annie Foster and Bristol Baines. The Nelson-Atkins Museum houses several traveling art exhibits. Our sports teams are incredible, and you can get anywhere in and around the city in less than an hour. Those are all perks." I avoided listing all the downfalls. I was trying to lift her spirits, not make her move back home.

"I've been here less than a year and I haven't done a lot. This is the first festival I've attended," Lucky said.

"It's a good one. The largest Pride in the Midwest," I said.

"Hm."

Okay, so she wasn't a big talker. Strike one. I didn't know if she was available or even interested in me, and here I was pushing her into a conversation she didn't seem excited to be a part of. Even though her attention was on me, I felt like she was one boring sentence away from bolting from the table. I decided to surrender on my terms.

"Listen, you should probably get your things from Frankie. I need to find my friends because they're my ride. It was nice to meet you, Lucky. You're a formidable chess player and I'm looking forward to seeing who wins the game."

She stood when I did. "Loser buys drinks," she said.

So, she was interested. I repeated her sentence with gusto. "Loser buys drinks." I stopped and turned. "Scratch Tito under the chin from me."

I walked in the direction of the stage smiling so hard my cheeks hurt. Tonight turned out to be a great night. I flashed my pass to the security guards and slipped backstage to find Claire and Emery. I spotted them at a table talking to another couple so I grabbed a gin and tonic and slid beside them.

"How'd it go?" Claire asked after she introduced me to the couple, two women who were big fans of Annie Foster and worked for one of Annie's nonprofit organizations.

"It went well. We were able to talk for about ten minutes. She's new to Kansas City, worked in Boston and transferred here, and we decided that the loser of our ongoing chess game buys drinks."

"Why do I get the feeling that you're going to button up the game quickly?" Claire asked.

"Because I am. I've got her in six moves." My confidence level was high. Had I asked for her number, I would've been unstoppable, but I didn't want to push.

"What if she wins? Can she win?" Claire asked.

I closed my eyes and played out every scenario. "There's only one way she can beat me, but I don't know if she sees it. It's so deep." My confidence faltered. What if she was playing me?

"Never underestimate anyone," Claire said.

I tapped my clear, plastic glass against hers. "You're right. Either way, I still win because I get to see her again." I looked around at the twenty or so people milling about. "Did I miss Bristol? Is she even doing the meet-and-greet?"

"We're still waiting. If the weather wasn't as nice as it is, I would've bailed a long time ago. You know how much I hate crowds and heat," Emery said.

I pointed at her. "But you work with fire."

She pointed back. "Exactly. Give me snow any day."

"This is as far north as I go," Claire said.

Emery kissed her cheek. "I wouldn't dream of tearing you away from this city and our family."

I was blatantly staring. "You all are so cute. Now stop it." I smiled at them letting them know I was kidding.

"Okay, okay. Let's focus on you. Did you get her name at least?" Claire asked.

"You'll love this. And I'll learn more later when we have drinks, but her name is Lucky."

"Probably short for something like Lucille or Lucinda. I like it," Claire said.

I thought it was a cute name, but she looked more elegant. Maybe Lucky was a nickname. My attention was diverted when Bristol and Annie arrived. I was here to meet them, but my mind was on Lucky. Both women were gracious and polite. We took photos, talked about music, and after a half an hour visiting with us, they left.

"How nice were they?" I asked.

"Very. Thanks for getting us the tickets, babe," Emery said.

"Yes. I can't thank you enough for including me." So much happened tonight. I couldn't wait to unpack everything. I probably should've visited the Titan and Spector booth once or twice, but I passed the torch years ago after getting them involved in the first place. We always got business from having a booth at Pride. That was another reason my stock grew with the company. I was always trying to come up with ways to find clients. It was hard to stop networking wherever I went because work was always on my mind.

It was after midnight by the time I got home. I immediately jumped into the shower to wash off the stickiness of bug spray, sunscreen, and sweat. I slipped into pajamas and curled into bed excited to look at my photos and photos other people posted from the event. My concert pics were great. I found Kansas City Diversity and Inclusion Club on Instagram and scrolled through until I found a photo of the Kansas City Women's Softball League and zoomed in when I saw Lucky in the background. Did she play? Or did they con her into signing up? I knew firsthand how persuasive they could be. I kept scrolling until my eyes couldn't focus on the screen. I rolled over and thought about Lucky and how much fun we'd been having over our chess game. Maybe this would never go anywhere but I felt really good about the start of us.

CHAPTER EIGHT

LUCKY CHANCE—CUBICLE GRUNT

In-person meetings sucked. I sulked all the way back to my gray cubicle with blank walls and a wobbly chair that somebody switched out because theirs was broken. I rolled it out into the aisle for it to become someone else's problem and called our office manager for a new one.

"Oh, we thought you were one hundred percent remote," she said. There was a pregnant pause as I waited for her to continue.

"I'll be in the office three days a week for the summer. If you could get me a working chair as soon as possible, that would be great. I'm on the third floor in cubicle twenty-eight. Thanks." I hung up before she could confirm or reject my request. I snarled when my phone rang. "Hello, Miranda."

"Lucky. It's so good to see you in the office. I wanted to have a quick meeting with you, Darian, Elliot, and Noelle. Can you meet us in the small conference room in five minutes?" she asked.

It sounded like an ambush. I'd met with most of the Web Pioneer employees I'd be working with my first week at the company. Darian and Elliot were nice enough. Also, Elliot was gay which made us fast friends in a straight office. Noelle was a whole different ballgame. She set off every homophobic dog whistle without actually saying anything inappropriate.

I rubbed my forehead when I was stressed or tired. Right now, I was both. Working in an office was a nightmare. People were spaced too close together. My concentration was constantly being interrupted by people opening and closing drawers, doors, cabinets, and talking loudly over my cubicle to people behind me. It was annoying. How was I supposed to be creative when I was overstimulated by the environment? I sent myself a message to bring my noise cancelling headset to work and hit Nordstrom's or Macy's on the way home. My wardrobe lacked business attire. I had casual outfits and clubbing clothes and only a few things appropriate for the office. "Sure, Miranda. Let me just wrap up what I'm doing. I'll be there in five." I hung up and meditated on the hard, gray carpet of my small cubicle for four minutes. The conference room was around the corner. I could get there in twenty seconds.

"Come on in, Lucky. Have a seat." Miranda motioned at the line of vacant chairs across from my colleagues. Instead of sitting where she dictated, I rounded the table and sat next to Elliot. Everyone seemed shocked. Miranda's lips disappeared as she squeezed them in a tight line and moved her things from the front of the table to sit in a chair opposite all of us. I pretended that what I did was okay and I was alert and ready for whatever she was going to say.

"Before we get started, I wanted to inform you that Moonlight Crackers went with another company."

I almost slapped my palm on the mahogany table. My anger came up so fast and furious at her, at them, at all my hard work. I tilted my head and nodded. "Well, that's unfortunate since we did everything they asked. Did they give you a reason?"

"They just said another company presented them with everything they wanted and no extras."

I could keep my emotions in check, but I couldn't stop the flush from creeping up my neck to rest heatedly against my cheeks. I was light-headed. My stomach felt like a boulder rolled around and landed dead center of my body. I swallowed hard, trying to keep my lunch down. "I'm sorry I didn't do a better job."

"Maybe next time you'll listen to me and to the customer." She said it so hatefully that I instantly was embarrassed in front of the employees in the room. "It was such a simple request, Lucky." She held her hand up. "From now on, you'll run everything by me and your team. Do you understand?"

Did she really just treat me like a child? I froze. I'd never been talked to like that in my professional life. Nobody moved a muscle. I swallowed hard and gave her a quick nod.

"Okay, let's get down to business. We have the opportunity to help a local law firm expand their business by updating their website and creating commercials. I think the four of you working together will really create an incredible portfolio for them."

"What's the firm's name?" Darian asked.

"Titan and Spector. They have two locations—one on the plaza and one downtown. We'll be working with the office on the plaza near Fifty-first. They've scheduled a meeting next week so I want you all to study their website now and start coming up with ideas on what they can do to modernize it."

"Did they give specifics on the scope? You know, so that we don't do more than necessary?" To anyone else, that question sounded benign, but Miranda's quick intake made me inwardly smile as the strike made a mark. She smirked and gave me a look that my mother used to give me when I was a child and was acting out in public. It was a wait-until-we-get-home look. I backed down. I still needed this job.

"They are open to anything, but I want us to focus on a realistic proposal and not something farfetched like aliens in space holding a sign that reads Titan and Spector will help anyone and anywhere."

"So, they want to go from boring law firm, to young and exciting?" Darian pulled up their website and clicked through each page. It wasn't horrible, but it was dated. Like Moonlight Crackers. It was as if everyone in this city had one firm create their website thirty years ago and whatever firm it was used the same template for every client.

"Look at these head shots. They need vibrancy and less…" Darian swirled her hand at the photos of the partners. "And less old, white men. Do any minorities work here?"

"That's something we'll find out when we meet them," Miranda said.

As Darian clicked on the about us page, I noticed a rainbow in the lower right corner. "Oh, right there. Diversity. But it's so small.

How would anyone know that?" I quickly googled their name. "They are a gold sponsor at Pride. That's big. That rainbow should be out and proud instead of hiding on the page."

"We don't have to push it. I mean, they obviously aren't," Noelle said.

"Well, the copyright mark is from over fifteen years ago. Maybe things have changed and they want to emphasize it more now." Did I remember seeing their booth at Pride? This wasn't the first time I'd heard their name. "Let's add that to the list of questions to ask during the meeting."

"I just don't think it's important," Noelle said. Why was she fighting so hard about this? Well, I knew exactly why. I just thought she would keep her homophobia a little more under wraps in a meeting with colleagues and our boss.

"Okay, well I do. So I'm going to ask. Just because you might have a problem with it, doesn't mean they do. Being a gold sponsor at Pride is expensive. Queer people need lawyers, too." I could be quiet about a lot of things, but not this.

"Ladies," Miranda said. The word was laced with warning.

"I didn't mean anything by that," Noelle said. Her voice was pouty. I rolled my eyes hard. I didn't know a lot about her other than she wore a cross necklace and had several framed photos in her office of mission trips to South America. She would've been perfect for Moonlight Crackers. Before I had a chance to clap back, Miranda interrupted.

"Focus, people. Why don't the four of you do a quick brainstorming session right now? It'll be good for you to spend time together." Miranda scooped up her notes and her cup of coffee and nodded before leaving us. I wasn't about to step up. I was told that I was in a support role so I sat back and waited for somebody else to start.

"Okay, why don't we talk about things we think can be improved?" Darian asked.

"I don't know what kind of law they practice," Elliot said. He pointed to the landing page. "That information isn't found until you get to the About page."

"Testimonials are nice, but they don't need to scroll on the top of the page," I said.

"That could be a separate page," Darian said.

Noelle kept quiet during the whole meeting. I was sure to point out and emphasize diversity. After an hour of brainstorming, I decided maybe being part of a team wasn't all bad. This was a big project and I couldn't afford to take another solo loss.

"Let's circle back at the end of the week. I'll set up a Teams meeting," Darian said. At least we knew who was willing to be in charge.

"Sounds good." I gathered my notes and headed back to my cubicle. The broken chair was gone and a new one was tucked under my desk with a sticky note that said *Hope this one works*. After I adjusted the settings, I pulled up Titan and Spector's website again. It wasn't horrible, but definitely dated. I pulled up videos Web Pioneer had created in the past and started sketching out possible commercial ideas. I was able to tune everybody out and have a few things mapped out by the end of the day.

I grabbed my bag and walked a couple of blocks to Nordstrom Rack. I was looking for cheap. Wearing last season's clothes didn't bother me at all. It was almost seven when I got home and I knew Tito was going to be upset. He was waiting for me. It was hard for both of us now that I had to go into the office.

"It was a terrible morning, but the afternoon was better. How was your day, my floofy-floof?" I tossed him over my shoulder and walked with him over to the closet so I could change. I placed him on the duvet and changed into joggers and a T-shirt. "Are you hungry? Do we have anything in this house to eat?" I knew he did, but did I?

He jumped on the windowsill, and for the first time since this morning, I thought about Bri. I wondered if she had a chance to play. I looked at the board and to my dismay, somebody had moved all the pieces back to their original spots. They erased our game! My heart sank. Well, that sucked. I grabbed a sheet of paper, wrote "boooooo" on it, and taped it to my window. The crappy part was that I wasn't going to be working from home tomorrow so I wouldn't be able to communicate with Bri until Wednesday.

❖

Usually when I worked from home, I wore sweats and a T-shirt. If there was a Teams meeting or Zoom, I threw on a sweater or nice top, but the sweats stayed. This morning, I fixed my hair, put on makeup, and wore jeans and one of my new tops. Tito thought I was leaving again. I confused him when I sat at my desk by the window and started working. I checked the rooftop from time to time hoping she'd be there, but the only person I saw was a gardener pruning the flower boxes.

By lunchtime, my neck was hurting from sitting at an angle hoping she would show up. I got up, stretched, and grabbed an apple. I turned on some music and walked around my loft to loosen up. I had a bad habit of hunching over my computer and forgetting about time. I cracked my neck, popped my back, and glanced out the window before I sat. Bri was sitting at the workstation, but her eyes were on my window. I threw up my hands and mouthed "what happened" knowing she couldn't hear me. She shrugged and held out her hands like mine. I grabbed my iPad and held it against the glass. *I WAS WINNING*. She strained to read and laughed when the words became clear. She shook her head and smiled. I shooed Tito off the windowsill and took his place anxious to see what she was writing. I hated that I was smiling so hard, but I was enjoying getting to know somebody in such a unique way.

Bri held up another piece of paper. *DREAM ON* she wrote in big, block letters. I smirked and shook my head. She grabbed another piece of paper. *DRINKS ANYWAY?*

The hair on my arms stood up and I shook off the shiver. I typed on my iPad. *KATRINA'S?*

She nodded and held up an infinity sign. I cocked my head trying to figure out what she was saying. She pulled the paper back and laughed and turned it ninety degrees. Eight. She was giving me a meeting time. I gave her a thumbs up. Bri returned my thumbs up and a gave a soft wave before packing up and heading inside. I walked away from the window and did a little happy dance. Tito looked at me in alarm. I patted him on the top of his head.

"Guess who's got a date with your girlfriend?" I pointed at myself and continued dancing. "That's right. Me. I do." I tried to include him in my hip-shaking, finger-snapping dance, but he bolted. I cupped my hands over my mouth so he could hear me over the music. "Your loss, big boy." I danced over to the couch and flopped on it exhilarated.

What was I going to wear? Katrina's was a step above a dive bar so I couldn't overdress. Bri was a lawyer so she probably had a full wardrobe of expensive clothes and accessories that I would love. I decided on a pair of dark jeans, a taupe-colored sleeveless top, and a pair of slingback sandals with a small heel. It was nice, but casual. I still had seven hours so I had to pull my head down from the clouds and try to focus on the project.

Darian was pinging me asking me a lot of questions for somebody who jumped at the chance to be team lead. I kept my answers tight. The last thing I needed was for her to blame me for something. This was going to be clean. I didn't trust Noelle and the jury was out on Darian and Elliot. They were very cliquish. One of the perils of working from home was that you missed a lot of office drama and gossip.

I shut down at five and made a quick sandwich. Today was taking forever. I ordered my Lyft for seven thirty, took a long, hot shower, and watched the clock. Tito jumped on the couch and stretched out for belly rubs. I smiled when I saw my mom's name pop up on my screen.

"Hi, Mom."

"Just checking in. How was going back into the office?"

I stroked Tito's fur and smiled when his purrs were louder than my mother's voice. "It was as I expected. Degrading and not enough productive hours. I'm on a team now for this upcoming client meeting. I have to work with three people I don't know and it's just going to take some time." I didn't have the heart to tell her I lost the Moonlight Crackers account. "In other news, Tito and I are hanging out just waiting until my date."

"Oh, you have a date? Why didn't you lead with that? Who is she? Is it somebody you work with?" she asked.

Not that my mother would know anyone. We didn't run into a lot of people when she and my father visited a few weekends ago. "It just happened earlier today."

"I'm going to need more, Lucky. What's she like?" she asked.

"I'm still getting to know her, but her name is Bri and she's a lawyer."

"Oh, a lawyer. How exciting. She must be very smart and successful," she said.

Now wasn't the time to lecture my mother about being presumptuous. "I'll get all the details later. She's tall, very pretty, and has good energy." I didn't have a lot of specifics to share yet.

"How did you meet her? At Pride?" she asked.

"Yes and no." It was going to be hard to explain to my mom how we started communicating. "I'd seen her before. She works in the building across the street. I'll just have to call you tomorrow and tell you how it went. I should probably go. I don't want to be late. Wish me luck."

"Good luck. Be safe and responsible," she said.

"Got it. Drive fast and take chances. I love you." I disconnected the call and ran a quick lint roller over my clothes. I was too wired to sit. I triple-checked my reflection and practiced ways to say hello. The longer I practiced, the more critical I was. Why was I flattening my lips? What was I doing with my hands? Why was my hair flat on one side? I growled in frustration and gave up. Obsessing wasn't a good look.

CHAPTER NINE

BRIANNA JAMESON—SUCCESSFUL LAWYER WITH A HOT DATE

I couldn't remember the last time I was at Katrina's. Five years ago? Six? Other bars had queer nights on the weekend, but Katrina's had weathered political storms, religious boycotts, and even a grease fire to be the only lesbian bar left standing in Kansas City. There wasn't anything special about it other than what it represented. A safe space for lesbians and queers to have a drink, sing karaoke on Tuesday nights, and find connections. I pushed through the simple black door and waited for my eyes to adjust to the low light. It was darker than I remembered and slightly shabbier. Or maybe my memories were fuzzy and my expectations higher. The nostalgia hit me in the heart and I smiled remembering all the fun I had at Katrina's after concerts, queer events, and most Friday nights during the summers when I was in law school. They got rid of the pool tables and made room for dining tables, but the dance floor with the giant disco ball was still here. I remember standing against the wall with my friends secretly pointing out who we thought was attractive and wondering if we should approach them. I was a different person back then.

"Welcome to Katrina's. Oh, hey. Nice to see you again. Bri, right? Can I get you anything to drink?" Frankie waved me over to a seat at the bar. I looked around the room before taking a seat just in case Lucky was already here. I put my purse on the bar in front of me and slid onto the swivel stool.

Staring at the vast beer taps that separated me and Frankie, I wondered if they had something a little more sophisticated. "Do you have any pinot back there somewhere?" I put my elbows on the polished bar top and peeked at the bottles on the bottom shelf behind Frankie. She pointed to a 2021 unopened bottle.

"This is a decent one. Drinking alone or should I pour another?" she asked.

"I'm meeting Lucky here and I don't know what she drinks."

Frankie nodded. "Will you be snacking on anything? We have a lot of deliciously greasy after dinner appetizers half-price right now."

I'd never heard of after dinner appetizers before and realized they were probably just trying to sell what they had. My stomach growled as my brain pulled up images of cheesy mozzarella sticks. I had a quick dinner a few hours ago so it didn't make sense that I was still hungry. "Let's see what she's in the mood for."

"Did you have fun at Pride?" Frankie asked.

"It was great. I try not to miss it."

I knew when Lucky arrived because Frankie's already smiling face lit up even more. I didn't turn around.

"You're late," Frankie said.

"What do you mean? I'm early," Lucky said.

I turned and held up my hands. "I didn't say a word about anything. And you're early, but then again, so am I." I pointed to the chair next to me and moved my purse so it wasn't in her way. "Hi." Her soft perfume made me want to lean closer to her. Everything about her made me feel light.

"Hi. How are you?" she asked.

The intensity of her blue eyes was unnerving. She was classically attractive with smooth, fair skin and rose-colored lips. The shape of her mouth was perfect. The soft arch of her cupid's bow softened the look of her full mouth. I was going to have fun kissing her later. "I'm doing well. It's good to see you again. What would you like to drink?"

"What are you having?" she asked.

"A glass of pinot. It's not bad," I said. When Frankie was out of earshot, I added, "But it's not great either. I'd recommend whatever you normally drink." Stop talking, I scolded myself. You sound like a snob. "But you can't go wrong with a local IPA. We might not have the best local wineries, but we have great beer."

"That's what everyone tells me. The Boulevard Wheat is good, and an ice-cold beer sounds delicious. Summer here comes a lot faster than summer in Boston," she said.

Frankie slid a perfectly poured pint in front of Lucky and quickly disappeared into the small kitchen in the back. I turned my attention back to Lucky. "That's right. You're from the East Coast and you recently moved here for reasons unknown to me." A soft sigh escaped her lips. Either she was tired of telling her story, or she was embarrassed by it. I doubled down and told myself it was because of a woman. "Now you have to tell me."

"I followed my now ex-girlfriend here. She attends UMKC med school."

Ding ding. Point to me. I looked for any telltale signs of distress or heartbreak. Her brow furrowed in anger for a moment, so I knew there was a story there, but I didn't press. "Her loss." I took another sip of wine. "Tell me about Tito. He's beautiful." I knew the girlfriend story would come out eventually, but that's not what I was interested in. My entire focus was on the woman sitting two feet in front of me with delicate hands and short, polished nails holding a pint of beer she barely sipped from. Her smile got me. I couldn't help but smile with her. Her whole demeanor changed when I mentioned Tito. He was her safe topic. Her shoulders relaxed and she loosened her grip on the glass.

"He's the nicest cat and never met a person he didn't instantly fall in love with. He's three years old and his two favorite pastimes are eating and sleeping. I got him from a shelter in Boston when he was a kitten."

"He seems like he's a real talker. Sometimes when it's quiet, I can hear him meow," I said. I loved the change in her. She wasn't nervous talking about him.

"Wait until you hear his purr. It's so loud. I never need an alarm for anything. Smoke alarm, wake-up alarm, burglar alarm." She held up a finger after every alarm she listed. "He lets me know."

"Ahh, he's your protector. You saved him and now he's saving you. That's sweet."

"He's my pride and joy."

"Why Tito? That's a distinctive name," I said.

"When I first got him, I couldn't get him to stop sniffing vodka martini glasses. He really liked Tito's Vodka. What about you. Do you have any pets?"

"I always say I'm going to wait until I get a house for a pet, but truthfully, I work long hours in the office so I don't think I'm the right candidate for a pet. I love cats and dogs, but they need to be with somebody who is home more."

"How many hours a week do you work?" she asked.

I was embarrassed because I didn't want to give her the impression that work came first, which it did, but I would slash my hours in a heartbeat if it meant I could spend time with the right person. I wasn't looking so I put all my energies into casework. "It depends. Sometimes I work more when I have cases going to trial and sometimes I sit on the rooftop and pretend to work."

She shook her finger at me. "Somehow, I think you're lying. You don't strike me as a woman who sits around and waits for action. You make it happen." A delightful blush brushed her cheeks when she realized her double entendre.

I smiled at her. I wondered what made her think I was exactly like that. I held up my glass. "Touché. I don't have a lot going on other than work at the moment."

"I've been pretty busy at work, too, but I decided I want to spend a lot of time this summer getting to know Kansas City," she said.

"I just happen to know a wonderful tour guide." I pointed at myself. "So if you need somebody to show you around, I'm available."

"Thank you. I just might take you up on your offer," she said.

It was the way she looked at me that ignited a spark low in my abdomen. Nobody had looked at me like that in a long time. Or if they had, I didn't care. There was something different about Lucky. She was young, but that didn't deter me. I almost always dated older women. Maybe that's why my relationships never lasted. We were all set in our ways. One of my biggest flaws was the inability to bend because I never left my job at the office. This time, things would be different. This relationship started so organically that the romantic in me ignored the practical side. This was a fresh start. "I'm free most weekends." And I vowed to be available if our relationship took off like I was hoping.

"Well, this coming week is Restaurant Week and the weekend is PorchFest KC so I'm going to recommend we do both. Grab a nice dinner somewhere and listen to bands play on porches in Midtown. Obviously, we both like live music and I'd love to introduce you to several nice restaurants here in the city."

She nodded. "That sounds great. Speaking of live music, did you get to meet Annie and Bristol since you had the VIP pass?"

I wanted to tell her and everyone how awesome it was, so to minimize the jealousy, I downplayed the meet-and-greet anytime somebody asked me. "It was nice. They are very sweet and so in love. We took photos, had a drink, and left."

"Show me your photos."

Her voice was light and I could tell she was excited. Lucky didn't strike me as the jealous type. At least not about this. She seemed genuinely happy for me that I had the experience. I pulled up photos of the concert and handed her my phone. The grip she had on my phone was loose as though she was holding something precious.

"These are great pictures. Especially the one of you and Bristol. You look like sisters," she said. She held up my phone and showed me my favorite photo of the night. She wasn't wrong. We had our hair styled similarly and had the same dark eyes and complexion.

"Thanks. I'm just going to tell people I'm her older sister."

She scrolled out of photos and started typing on my phone. My natural instinct was to yank it out of her hands, but I realized she wasn't a threat and I didn't have anything on my phone that was controversial. After twenty seconds of nearly sweating, she handed it back to me.

"Now you have my number so we can talk on anything other than large letters for the world to see."

I searched my contacts and found her. Lucky Chance. I looked up in surprise. "Your last name is Chance? Really?" At her nod, I laughed. "I love that. You have the coolest name."

"My parents were going through a phase when I was born." She rolled her eyes as though she was annoyed but I knew that was far from it.

"Well, Woodstock was 1969. You're definitely not over fifty, but I'm pretty sure there was one in the nineties and you could be mid-twenties," I said. Her eyes widened when I mentioned Woodstock. "And I'm totally guessing on the Woodstock thing."

"That's totally true. My parents went to Woodstock '99 and here I am. That's amazing. Nobody has ever put that together before," she said.

I wanted to be a tool and say "that's what makes me a great lawyer" but Tyler's face popped up and silenced my ego. I was going to have to thank him for being the part of my conscience that shut down stupid remarks that I almost said to women. "Lucky guess." I gave her an exaggerated wink.

Her laugh was delightful. "Yes, I'm twenty-six."

"I'm thirty-four." I waited for her to process the difference.

"Eight years. That's not terrible."

"Well, that's encouraging," I said.

Her warm hands covered mine for a few moments. "No. I was just doing the math out loud. Eight years is nothing." She shrugged like it wasn't a big deal. Eight years to me was a big deal. I hadn't dated anyone younger than myself since college but I wasn't going to let it deter me. "Or is it?" she asked.

I made direct eye contact and held it before answering very clearly. "It's not a problem at all for me. As a matter of fact, I find you refreshing." I also found her quiet confidence very exciting. I was a take-charge kind of woman, but a part of me knew that

Lucky wasn't a pushover. She would challenge me and wouldn't back down. I was ready for this kind of relationship. When the DJ started playing loud music at nine thirty, I suggested we head down the street to a wine bar that I knew only played swing music and very softly. I wasn't ready to say good night. We had a nice rapport going. "Let me settle with Frankie."

"So, you admit that you lost?" she asked.

I froze mid-stand so I was leaning over the table. I leaned closer and looked down at her lips. Her eyes widened. "I'll admit to nothing. Not until we have a proper game."

"So, what I'm hearing is that you're a sore loser."

I smiled and stood. The Tyler in me came out. I couldn't help it. "I never lose. Anything. Ever." I practically glided over to pay the tab.

"Are you headed out?" Frankie yelled over the music.

I nodded and handed her my credit card. After leaving a fat tip, I told her good night and pointed at the door so Lucky could meet me there. Talking was almost impossible with the heavy bass thumping in my head.

"Good call on getting out of there when you did." Lucky opened and closed her mouth trying to pop her ears. "That was the loudest I've ever heard the music in there."

"I haven't been inside Katrina's in years. It was always a fun place to go before I threw myself into work." I liked that sometimes our hands brushed while we walked two blocks to the Blue Hare.

"Are there more places for queer people to hang out? I've only ever known about Katrina's and Hamburger Mary's."

"Not really so when there's an event like Pride or a concert with LGBTQ artists, all the queers come running," I said. I remember years ago there was a bar called Tootsie's that was in direct competition with Katrina's but it, too, faded away. My friends sneaked me in with a fake ID. When it closed, we had nowhere to go. "They also have meet-up groups where you can find other queer people who like to play board games, or go on hikes, or play Dungeons and Dragons."

"It's been hard meeting people. Either for friendship or dating," she said.

"Unfortunately, it's probably not as easy as it is in a larger city like Boston."

She nodded. "It's hard. When was your last long-term relationship?"

I didn't even mind the questions. "It's been a while. Maybe a year ago." Before she had a chance to ask more, I volunteered the answer. "I was working a case that took all my time and she didn't like to be put second. It was completely my fault."

"Don't say that. You have a right to your career and your partner should respect your ambitions. Sometimes you get thrust into situations where you have to put in the long hours. You should have your partner supporting you, not making you feel bad about working late."

I sensed that was more for herself than for me, but I went with it. "Agreed. I want to help people and sometimes that's not an eight-to-five job. My ex wanted to go out to all the plays and concerts and dinners, and I missed a lot because I was doing casework."

"Okay, well then that's on you." She bumped her shoulder against mine and smiled to let me know she was kidding. "I mean, don't buy tickets if you aren't going to go to something."

"I have season passes so she got to go to everything. Eventually it got to the point where she just took them whether I could go or not."

"Ouch. That's harsh," Lucky said.

"Yeah, we didn't last long. But she was my last steady relationship," I said. I had a friend who I sometimes hooked up with when we were both too busy to date, but that hadn't happened in months. My vast supply of dildos and vibrators kept me sated between visits. Lucky didn't need to know that. It was time to shift the focus. I opened the door for her to Blue Hare and found us a small table in the corner. After ordering martinis, I shifted the focus to her. "Tell me about the girl you followed to Kansas City."

She grimaced. "There's not much to tell. We were together for four years and the thought of not being with her was so strong that

I packed up and followed her here." She sounded like she was still bitter about it, rightfully so.

"I'm sorry that happened to you. It's always hard when life doesn't go the way we'd hope."

"It just opens the door to new possibilities."

I held up my martini glass. "Here's to new possibilities and for the old ones to fuck off."

"I will definitely cheers that."

CHAPTER TEN

LUCKY CHANCE—GETTING HER GROOVE BACK

L et's talk about the bravest thing you did this week." Darian made eye contact with everyone on the team to emphasize how important she thought it was.

"About work or life or what?" Elliot asked.

"Anything you want to talk about. Anything at all," she said.

I was trying to be positive. I liked Darian and Elliot, but this was the stupidest thing I'd ever done at work. I felt like I was in an episode of *The Office* and half expected cameras to suddenly focus in on my perplexed look. How was that relevant to our focus? These people didn't care one bit about my life. They barely spoke to me outside of these required meetings, but I had promised to try with them.

"I added my contact information to a woman's phone last night without her asking. I thought that was pretty brave." I said it because it was brave, but also to annoy Noelle who acted exactly how I expected. I knew Darian was an ally because she and Elliot were tight, and Elliot was gay. Why they were friendly with Noelle was beyond me. Being a team player was one thing, but to deal with her asshole behavior was something else. She rubbed me wrong.

"Good for you. That's progress and probably something you don't do every day," Darian said.

I overemphasized my smile. "I sure don't, but she's incredible and I'm excited to see where this goes."

"I think Darian means work, not personal conquests," Noelle said with disdain. "I signed another client yesterday. That gives me five for the month."

"Are we bragging? How is that brave? Are they a tough customer?" I was being a bitch because I found my confidence. Maybe not at work, but my personal life was improving and it stored hope in my chest like a squirrel stashing nuts for the winter. Last night when I walked Bri back to her car, she gave me a soft kiss on the cheek and a hug that lasted one or two seconds longer than most hugs in my life. There was something assertive about her that made my blood race. Our relationship was progressing and I was on a high. Not even hateful Noelle could bring me down.

Noelle huffed a breath. "Closing isn't always easy. I don't like pushing the customers, but I convinced them to go with me—I mean Web Pioneer—and they signed. It was very satisfying."

"Good for you," I said. Everything I was saying came out condescending, so I pulled back. "I've learned firsthand that you're not going to please every customer every time so good for you." I erased the bite from my words so I sounded more believable and less like a jerk.

Elliot mentioned something about doing a stand-up routine on open mic night which surprised the entire room.

"I didn't know you were a comedian," Darian said.

Apparently, they weren't as close as I thought. "That's really cool," I said.

"You should totally do a routine here for us." Darian's excitement and pride were unmistakable. "We'll give you a full critique, won't we?" We nodded enthusiastically because it was hard not to now that Darian had sounded so positive. Anything to stall. We were far from agreeing on the design because Elliot's ideas were stodgy, Noelle's were bland, and mine were underappreciated. It was break time.

"I'm not used to doing it around a group of friends. I'm rusty," he said sheepishly but stood and strolled over to the front of the conference room table.

As much as I wanted to tell everyone to focus on work, I wasn't the team lead, and I wanted to see if Elliot was funny. I'd never seen him in front of clients so I was curious if he was as aloof with a crowd as he was every day around us. It also gave me time to think about my evening with Bri. She kissed me. I touched my cheek remembering how it tingled after she slowly pulled away. Bri was out of my league. What did she see in me? She was a successful lawyer, drove a really nice car, wore designer clothes, and was super smart. What did I have to offer her? What did she see in me?

"What did you think, Lucky?" Darian asked.

Well, so much for bonding with my team. I zoned out and missed Elliot's thirty-second routine. Darian was beaming. Noelle was hard to read, but Elliot's flaming cheeks sporting a cheesy grin let me know that he thought he nailed it. "That was great. Good for you. I couldn't imagine getting up in front of strangers. Now that's brave." I ignored Noelle's scowl.

"Thanks, Lucky," Elliot said. He was adorable. I was really starting to warm up to him and Darian.

"Back to it, team. Today's meeting is to let you all know we have a meeting scheduled with Titan and Spector this Friday. I think we have a good idea of what they have so let's create a soft outline of talking points," Darian said.

I swear I was stuck in a time loop. We had the same meeting every time we reserved the conference room. Maybe it was Darian's way of pumping up the team, but I was over it. I wondered if Miranda knew how much time was wasted for no reason. "Do you think we need to review? I think we're in pretty good shape." I was trying to be confident, but it came across as dismissive and they all scowled at me. I shrugged.

"Team player much?" Noelle asked.

"Rude," I said. At this point, I had nothing to lose except my job. I already knew moving home was a solid option and even if this branch didn't want me, I could probably transfer back to the Boston branch. "What I meant was we have solid bones going into our initial meeting. I think we're set and we're confident."

Darian stood so abruptly, her chair scooted back several feet. "Well, I guess we're done here. Lucky thinks we've got this in the bag."

"Darian, please don't be like that. We've been discussing the same thing over and over. We can't sit here and waste valuable time trying to guess what the customer is going to say about this or that. Let's have the meeting with them first and go from there." I looked at my watch for the effect. "Besides, I have a project that I need to button up before the end of the day."

"She's probably right. I have a few things to get ready for as well. I mean, if that's okay, Darian?" Elliot asked.

Her shoulders sagged. "I guess so. We should be fine for the initial meeting. But I expect all our heads together Friday afternoon, so clear all schedules."

She looked directly at me. I smiled to let her know I didn't mean to be such a bitch about another meeting. Truthfully, I liked how my newfound boldness made people think twice about me. "We could always grab a beer after work on Thursday. Maybe coming at this in a different environment is what we need."

Darian's smile lit up the room. She high-fived me. "I like that idea a lot," she said.

Feeling empowered and like I was finally a part of a team, I gathered my iPad and headed back to the cubicle farm. While having people around me was somewhat nice, I didn't feel a connection with them like I wanted. They didn't feel my vibe and we came from totally different schools of thought. Baby steps, I thought. And lots of patience.

On the way back to my cubicle, my phone rang. I glanced at the screen hoping for Bri but was excited to see Frankie's name instead. "Hey, Frankie."

"You've been very difficult to reach the last several weeks. What's going on?"

I turned down the volume on my phone as Frankie's voice boomed in my ear. "Work's been busy. We have a big client visit that we're getting ready for. How are you? How's work? Oh, my God, are you finally recruiting me for softball?"

"No way. I saw you play catch with Caitlyn. I was just checking in. I saw you on your date, but we haven't talked in a couple weeks so I got worried," Frankie said.

I smiled because that was a genuine friend thing to say. "I'm sorry. My boss put me on a team and now I have to go into the office for a bit while we work on landing this account. I'm not used to going into an office so by the time I get home, I'm wiped."

"I get it. Changes are hard. Are things improving at your job?" she asked.

I didn't want to talk about it within earshot of anyone. I glanced around. "It's an adjustment trying to make everyone happy, but I'm trying." I was. Sort of.

"Well, don't be a stranger. Softball's coming up and Mondays and Wednesdays are slow at Katrina's. Pop on in. Bring Bri. She seems cool," Frankie said.

Just hearing Bri's name made my pulse throb. "I'll do that. Thanks for checking on me, Frankie." I disconnected the call and smiled. Kansas City was slowly growing on me.

I scrolled through my emails, finished up my project, and pulled up Titan and Spector's website. I already knew it forward and backward. There was no way I was going to tank this one. If I went down, three other employees were going with me.

I spent the next hour updating the design for a daycare website. Thankfully, the changes didn't take long. I switched out photos, changed contact information, and sent the mock-up to the coding team. Easy work.

I jumped when I felt a tap on my shoulder. I turned to find Miranda standing in my cubicle chewing on the temple tip of her glasses. I pulled out my earbud. "What's going on?"

"I'd like to have a chat with you. Do you have a moment?" she asked.

I nodded and followed her to the nearest conference room. She pointed for me to take a seat and sat opposite me.

"How do you think you are fitting in with your team?"

I knew she didn't want the truth. "I think we're working out some wrinkles, but I think we're all excited for the upcoming meeting with Titan and Spector."

She waved her glasses at me. "That account is everything to us. That's why I put you on this team. I want you do to everything you can to make this a successful venture for your team and the client."

"That's what I'm doing." It dawned on me that somebody complained. I gripped the table. "Wait. Did somebody complain? Is that what this is about?" Darian and I just high-fived and Elliot sided with me about not having another meeting. It had to be Noelle.

She leaned back as though attacked. "I just want my employees to get along."

"I thought we were."

"I know the meeting you had earlier didn't go smoothly."

"I thought the meeting went well. I'm here to work. Truly. I came into the office because you told me to and I agreed, but I'm used to working on projects, not team-building exercises. I'd rather spend the time working and billing customers." I leaned back and folded my arms across my chest. "If you don't think I'm the right fit here, let me know now."

She slowly tapped her red nails on the conference room table. The repetitive sound echoed in the silence between us. "I know you think I'm focusing on you and maybe even pushing you more than anyone. That's because I know what you are capable of. I just want you to try harder with your coworkers. That's all. I know you think team building is a waste of time, but positive working relationships make for a better end product. This isn't an attack. It's not a reprimand. It's just a reminder that working in an office requires more work on your part to bridge gaps."

I hated being on edge in a work environment. That's why I insisted on working remotely. It was less productive when you were worried about other people. Darian and Elliot were fine, but I had no interest in connecting with Noelle. And she obviously wasn't interested either. "I feel like you're punishing me by making me come into the office. And now I have to worry about people running back to you every time I don't say or do the right thing? We both know Noelle doesn't like me for personal reasons that have nothing to do with work."

"I very much doubt that. This is what I'm talking about. You're looking for an attack where there isn't one."

"Come on, Miranda. Even you know office politics suck when you're the outsider," I said.

"Then don't be the outsider. Work with your team and knock it out of the park. If this goes well, then you can go back to one hundred percent remote," she said. The stupid sports metaphors were irritating.

I'd never been in this position before. I was always the one people leaned on. Deep down I knew I was being somewhat difficult because I'd never had to work so hard to fit in. "I will try harder. As a matter of fact, I recommended grabbing a drink after work Thursday to prep for Friday's meeting."

Miranda tapped her forefinger on the table before standing. "That's good, Lucky. I just want us all to get along."

I smiled and waited until she left to figure out my next move. A part of me knew confronting Noelle would be a mistake, but I couldn't let her know that she was getting under my skin. I meditated for several minutes before exiting the room. I made it back to my cubicle without issue. I knew somebody was watching me, so I smiled and hummed a few bars of a popular song just to let them know I was unfazed by my meeting, but truthfully, it stung.

"Hey, Darian, can I talk to you for a minute?"

Darian looked at me and practically jumped up from her desk. "Of course. Here? Or where?"

"Maybe one of the conference rooms?" I looked around. Noelle's cube was three down and I didn't trust her to not crawl on her hands and knees just to eavesdrop, so going somewhere away from the cube farm seemed like the logical thing. We walked back to the same conference room I just vacated and sat next to each other. "Look, I want to apologize for my standoffish behavior. I haven't worked with a team before and it's taking a bit of time for me to acclimate." I briefly touched her hand. "I'm really sorry for being difficult. You're a great team lead and I stand to learn a lot from you."

The look of pure joy in her eyes made me almost regret laying it on so thick. She put both hands on her chest. "Thank you so much for saying that. I'm sorry it's an adjustment for you, and honestly, we haven't done the best job getting to know you." She frantically waved her hand at Elliot who happened to be walking by and motioned for him to enter the conference room. "I think it's important for Elliot to be included. He's been a fan of yours since day one."

Elliot sat across from us and nodded. "What's going on?"

I couldn't believe she dragged him in here. "Should we get Noelle, too?" I was only halfway being snarky, but they both shut me down fast.

"Come on, you know she's super homophobic," Elliot said.

Darian looked around before lowering her voice to answer me. "Besides, anything you say to her goes straight to Miranda. They're best friends."

I sat back in shock. "Really?" They both solemnly nodded.

"So be careful of what you say or do around either one," Elliot said.

"Good to know. They seem like an unlikely pair." I reviewed the conversation I'd just had with Miranda. I didn't think I'd said anything too bad about Noelle.

"Not really. Both love drama, both love getting people into trouble. Noelle has a privacy issue and Miranda has anger issues. It's just better to watch what you say around Noelle," Darian said.

I gasped. I knew Miranda was a bitchy boss. "Anger issues? Like what do you mean?"

Darian looked visibly nervous and with Elliot's encouraging nod, she explained. "Miranda's been attending anger management classes after two very significant bullying incidents at the office. She belittled and degraded one of our sales reps during a meeting with a client. Honestly, I was surprised she wasn't fired after that. And that was her second offense."

"She must have something over somebody to only get a slap on the wrist," Elliot said.

"What happened?" Gossip wasn't my thing, but I was totally invested.

He lowered his voice, too. "Just treated him like trash. She was stopped when she started attacking him personally. It was ugly." He shuddered after recalling the event.

"I'm surprised it lasted that long. In Boston, Web Pioneer's human resources department would've shut that down immediately," I said. I wasn't bragging. I was letting them know that elsewhere, Miranda's behavior wouldn't be tolerated. That was one thing I liked about the Boston branch. There was a respect that came with employee and employer relationships. This felt toxic.

"I'm sure it's because Miranda has tenure and has been with the company for years. Still doesn't make it right." Darian clucked like a disapproving mother. "But don't worry about either of them. We're going to do great things with this law firm."

"Hey, thanks for sharing. I appreciate the heads up. Now, let's get out of here before Noelle sees us or worse, Miranda does." All three of us bolted from the conference room and scattered in different directions. For the first time, being a part of a team felt right. They had my back and I was going to try harder to be a team player.

Riding the high, I picked up my phone with the intention of asking Bri if she wanted to grab a drink but chickened out. I needed a friend to deal with the petty crap today, but I didn't want to seem like a complete jerk for not being able to get along with people. That wasn't going to impress her. I pushed my phone away only to have it vibrate letting me know that I had received a text message from Bri.

Thinking about going to watch a softball game tonight. Feel like joining me?

I didn't believe for one minute she was going to the softball game just to hang out. It was an excuse to see me. *I could use some gay fun and cold beer. I didn't realize the season started already.* Keep your cool, Lucky, I told myself.

It's a fundraiser. For the Parkville Animal Shelter. Regular season starts next week. Want to meet at ballfield ten at seven? Bri texted.

It was already in the nineties. Seven sounded hot and dusty. Spring didn't last long in Kansas City. *A week? Guess I wasn't drafted. That's fine. I don't even know how to hit a ball.*

You dodged a bullet. When you're in, it's almost impossible to get out. She threw in a sad face.

You got out. I remember Bri saying she played a long time ago. *It took a lot of persuading. And tears. Big crocodile tears. And maybe even bribing. I can't remember. It happened such a long time ago.*

I was smiling so hard for so long it hurt my mouth. I looked around in case somebody saw me. *Okay. I'll see you at seven.* I pushed my phone away and tried to focus on a small fabrication shop, but my mind kept drifting. I left the office a few minutes after five and headed straight home.

I scooped up Tito and loved on him while I reviewed my wardrobe. I decided on longer shorts and a white T-shirt from a 5K run last summer in Hartford. I looked like I was going to play ball, not watch it with somebody I was there to impress. I found a simple sleeveless shirt that looked good, but still felt casual. I carefully styled my hair in a French twist and grabbed sandals. I knew it would be dusty, but wearing practical shoes was out of the question. I wanted to look my best. I ate a quick salad and brushed my teeth before heading out the door. Tito meowed and it made me stop in my tracks.

"I'm sorry, buddy. I won't be too late. And you'll get all the love from me this weekend, I promise." I grabbed a few treats and sprinkled catnip on his cardboard scratcher before heading out the door.

CHAPTER ELEVEN

BRIANNA JAMESON—PUTTING HERSELF OUT THERE

For as big as my wardrobe was, I had nothing to wear tonight. I had nice casual outfits, but nothing for ninety-degree heat with a lot of humidity. I found a pair of linen shorts and a vee-neck tank that still looked good and wouldn't show a lot of sweat. Trying to impress a girl at the ballfields while not looking wilted was hard to do. I pulled my hair back and slipped on a pair of Tory Burch sandals.

I looked at my watch. Shit. I was going to be late. Parking was a nightmare, especially when all the lesbians in the area were raising money for animals. It was an amazing time, but it was a lot. I figured Lucky could use a few new friends based on our conversation from the other night. Being in a new city was a struggle. Plus, I liked spending time with her.

I jumped in my car and drove the ten minutes to the ballfields. As expected, the traffic was bumper-to-bumper. I waved to a few women I knew and let them turn in front of me. At this point, I was going to pull into the first parking lot even if it cost me fifty dollars to park. I didn't want to keep Lucky waiting. I charmed the attendant to park up front and was only five minutes late to field ten.

I scoured the stands, and everything stopped when I saw her leaning against a tree near the field. I slowed my gait and enjoyed the view as I walked toward her. She was the kind of woman who was really attractive and didn't know it. Or maybe she did, but she never acted like it. That was refreshing. I gave her one last long look before I walked to her.

"Hi. You made it." I didn't like that she was wearing sunglasses because her eyes were amazing. I slid mine up on the top of my head. I smiled when she did the same.

"This is amazing. There are so many people here. I was only expecting a handful," she said.

"Nothing can stop lesbians and their support of animal shelters. Honestly, I'm surprised at the crowd, too. I knew it was going to be crowded, but this is quite the turnout," I said. I liked the way her eyes darted down my body and how she didn't even hide the fact that she was checking me out. She slid her sunglasses back on her nose. I could only imagine what she was looking at. "Let's find a cold drink and a place to sit." Crowds were thickening up around the concession stand, but Cathie, a good friend I'd known for years, was running it. I got her attention and held up two fingers. She gave me the solid lesbian nod and had her son run out two summer shandies. I slipped him a fifty. "Add the rest to the donation jar." I motioned for us to move to the side and find a seat. "I know it's not a beer, but hopefully it's okay."

"It's cold and refreshing. It's perfect," she said. She licked her bottom lip and made a slight smacking noise. She put her hand up to her mouth in shock. "I'm so sorry."

"Please try to be more adorable," I said. Her blush was delightful.

"Brianna! Over here." My friend Avery pointed to empty seats beside her and her girlfriend.

Lucky lifted her eyebrow. "Brianna. It suits you."

Getting to Avery was tricky. Out of instinct, I held out my hand for Lucky to hold as I weaved through the crowd. I yelled over my shoulder. "Why are we always in crowds?" I tried to pretend that her warm, soft hand in mine wasn't a big deal, but my chest felt lighter with her so close. I was acting like somebody with a crush. I barely knew her, but I was already adjusting my schedule to spend time with her. Granted a softball game wasn't a proper date, but it was time with her and it seemed innocent enough. Except when she linked her fingers with mine. That was a little bit more personal than just holding hands. Avery's eyes widened for a fraction and I knew she wanted the tea. I dropped her hand and put my hand on the small of Lucky's back as I directed us into the row. Avery bumped me softly as I stepped past her to sit. She leaned over me when we sat.

"Hi. I'm Avery. You must be Lucky. Very cool name," she said. She shook Lucky's hand and turned her attention to me. "It's nice to see you again, my friend. How long have you been hiding her?"

"Ha ha. We met a few weeks ago," I said. I smiled at Lucky who could hear everything Avery said.

"Do you play softball, Lucky?" Avery asked.

She shook her head. "We all decided I'd make a better cheerleader than player. Womp womp."

"Count your blessings. It's a lot of fun, but they are die-hard players here," Avery said.

"So, I've heard. I'm excited to watch them play."

I leaned back so that Avery and Lucky could talk about softball and their love for the clever names the teams chose. Katrina's Kittens wasn't a great name because Katrina's sponsored the team, but the others in the league made us laugh like Pitch Please, Bat to the Bone, and Base Invaders were their favorites. Tonight's game was the best of each team. The Kansas City Gay and Lesbian Choir sang the national anthem and one of the gay television meteorologists threw the first pitch.

"I can't believe how popular this is," Lucky said. She looked around. "Boston has a lot of queer people, but this turnout is impressive. Also, they obviously don't need me. Look at the crowd. I was stressed for nothing."

"I think just showing up and supporting them is good enough. Hey, there's a woman walking around selling hotdogs and peanuts. Are you hungry?" I asked. I was starving. Lunch was a peach. While heavily processed foods weren't healthy, sometimes it was okay to indulge.

"Maybe we can get a late dinner? There's that cute diner in North Kansas City that's open all night," Lucky said.

I looked at my watch. It was seven thirty. This game would drag on until ten. And getting out would be impossible. Plus, I had a meeting tomorrow morning that I was dreading. I wanted to be fresh and alert for it, but also, I already told myself that I was going to try harder with Lucky.

I held up my finger. "Or, hear me out, I can whip us up something at my townhouse. I'm about a ten-minute drive. Where did you park?"

"I took the streetcar down here. It's not that far. I was thinking of walking home."

"Then my solution is perfect. I can fix something light and drive you back to your place," I said.

"Perfect," she said.

"Let me know when you're hungry. I'm not the greatest cook so don't expect anything incredible," I said. I was a good cook, but I couldn't brag this early. Plus, the meals I liked to cook took longer than twenty minutes to prepare.

We sat through the first few innings cheering both teams. Lucky was mostly quiet but cheered when Frankie and a few people she met at Pride were at bat. Even though I was having a good time, I was more than ready to leave. I wanted alone time with Lucky.

"Are you hungry yet?" I asked.

We had both taken our sunglasses off as the sun set behind us. Her eyes twinkled when she looked at me. I felt a stirring when her gaze dropped down to my mouth and I froze when she concentrated on my lips. I resisted the urge to wet them with my tongue. Not in a sexual way, but in a way that hid my nervousness. I was Brianna Jameson, a successful lawyer who stood in courtrooms and battled for underdogs everywhere, and I was nervous as hell.

"Yes. What did you have in mind?" she asked. She was definitely flirting with me.

"I can make flatbread pizzas." I shrugged as though it was no big deal. "Wanna get out of here?" The second she nodded, I stood and turned to Avery. "Listen, we're going to go but I'll call you tomorrow." I read the message behind Avery's bright smile.

"It was so nice to meet you, Lucky. Have a great night," she said.

"It was nice to meet you, too," Lucky said.

She didn't hesitate when I reached for her hand. "My car is just around the corner." I pulled her closer to avoid a group of very loud and very drunk people on their way to the game. I almost moaned when her bare arm pressed against mine. She didn't seem to mind the closeness. I walked over to my Mercedes and touched the handle to unlock it.

"Nice car," Lucky said.

"Thank you. She's a few years old and completely worthless in bad weather, but I love her." I slipped in beside her thankful that the sedan's noise-free cab reduced the rest of the world into a slight murmur. I heard Lucky's soft breathing and the sound of the leather beneath her legs adjusting to her movements as she slipped on her seat belt. I eased out of the parking lot and squeezed into traffic. People were still piling into the parking lots trying to find spots. We made it to my townhouse in under ten minutes. I unlocked the door and invited her in.

"Nice car, nice place," she said.

"I'm saving up for a house somewhere. Probably in Overland Park. This is a nice transition place."

"Why Overland Park if you work downtown?"

"They have the nicest neighborhoods," I said.

"I like your neighborhood. And Briarcliff looks like it has some nice gated communities," she said.

"Do you come here a lot?" I asked. Briarcliff was a cute but posh neighborhood north of downtown. The view of the city and the river was incredible, but it was a newer community. Most of my friends and co-workers lived in Kansas. It was always my goal to move there.

"It's close for me to get upscale treats for Tito and splurge on really expensive coffee," Lucky said.

"I'm surprised we haven't run into each other then," I said. Then I remembered I worked too many hours so most of the shops were closed by the time I got home. "Have a seat anywhere. Make yourself comfortable." She followed me into the kitchen and sat at the bar. It was nice that she wanted to be close. "Would you like a glass of wine?" I pulled out a bottle and handed it to her. Her eyes lit up at the label.

"This looks delicious. If you hand me the corkscrew, I'll open it for us," she said.

"Great. I'll get started on the food." I handed her the tool and pulled out possible ingredients. "I can make a yummy feta cheese and pear, or a more traditional marinara, mozzarella, and black olive."

"They both sound incredible," she said. She looked at the wine label. "Maybe with the white, we should have the feta cheese and pear."

I thanked her when she handed me a glass and took a sip of the chilled, fruity wine. "Good call on the pairing."

It took a total of six minutes to make two flatbreads. I topped them both with a drizzle of balsamic vinegar and popped them into the oven. Since they would be ready in less than ten minutes, I decided to stay on this side of the kitchen. I was afraid I'd get handsy if I sat on the high barstool next to her. I rested my hip on the counter and gave her my complete attention.

"What's your favorite restaurant in Kansas City? I know you're somewhat new, but is there a favorite or a favorite type of food?" I asked.

The tip of her tongue briefly swiped at her bottom lip after taking a sip. I could stare at her mouth all day. I wondered how long it would take before I gave in to temptation and kissed her. Normally, I liked the buildup, but something about Lucky just made me want to dive in and take everything she would give me. She was like nobody I'd dated before. Most of the women before her were super flirty, confident, and let me know exactly what they wanted, when they wanted it, and how I was supposed to give it to them. Lucky was different. I sensed her attraction, but she was hesitant and that made me pause. Was I so used to one-night stands and friends with benefits, that I'd forgotten how to date?

She was also younger and just got out of a heartbreaking long-term relationship. Was she even ready for somebody like me? I scolded myself for overthinking and tried to just enjoy the moment. It was nine fifteen on a Thursday night and I was home enjoying a bottle of wine with a sexy woman. If I didn't have this planned, I would just be getting home from working a fourteen-hour day at the office.

"I haven't been a lot of places. Mostly restaurants in the Crossroads. Simple bar food. I work weird hours so a lot of times I just pop something in the air fryer," Lucky said.

"Same. I have a couple of friends who make me go to nice restaurants probably just to make sure I'm eating."

"You still haven't told me how many hours a week you work," Lucky said.

I had to be careful. I didn't want to say a high number that was going to scare her away, even if it was true. "I have a lot of cases that are in the process of closing now so I put in about sixty to seventy hours a week." Lucky gave a low whistle when she heard the amount and I felt a drop in my chest. I knew I was a workaholic.

"I average about sixty hours so I get it, but most of the time I work from home. Except now I'm on some kind of probation where I have to work with a group in the office for a few presentations." She shrugged but I could tell that it stung.

I treaded lightly. "Working well with others isn't my forte. You do something for so long and you know what works and what doesn't. And office politics suck so I'm considering opening my own firm."

I was sure I looked as surprised as she did.

"Really? That's great. Good for you. What made you consider it?"

Her approval widened my grin. Not that I needed it, but it was nice to have support from the beginning. "I feel like I could do more on my own. Like right now, I know somebody who could really use my help, but my company won't touch the case. And I know a lot of people in Kansas City who would send business my way. I want to help people and not just do it for the money. Don't get me wrong, I want bank, but I want my work to mean something."

"That's very brave. And noble," she said.

I waved her off. "I think we start our careers wanting to make some sort of legacy for ourselves and be successful."

"I'm pretty sure you're well on your way to a very successful career. I'm sure it's hard being a woman in a male-dominated field."

"Thankfully, we're closing the gap."

"Would your boss freak out if you quit?" she asked.

"Charles would probably tell me to leave on the spot. I've been with the firm since I passed the bar. I think it would hurt his feelings, but he would never admit it." The timer shrilled to let us know our very late dinner was ready and that maybe it was time to change the subject. Lucky was so easy to talk to.

"Those smell delicious and I didn't realize how hungry I was until just now," she said.

We didn't even move from our spots. I slid a plate in front of her and cut the flatbreads into manageable sizes. We talked about Boston, countries we'd visited, and childhood pets. Before we knew it, it was eleven thirty and I had to get her home.

"I can Lyft home," she said.

"Absolutely not. I made a promise and I always keep my promises," I said.

It took less than ten minutes to get to her loft. As much as I wanted to walk her up to her place, I knew we both had busy days. I pulled up directly in front of her building. The city was quiet. I could hear the clicking of the traffic signals directing empty streets, the soft hum of the car engine, and the blood rushing in my ears as the thought of kissing Lucky swirled around in my head. I parked and got out. She closed the car door and leaned against it.

"Thank you for a really nice night," she said.

"Wait until I really try," I said. I held my hand up. "No, wait. I didn't mean that. It was a very fun night and I enjoyed our time together." I sounded like a complete tool. I touched her cheek and ran the pad of my thumb across her chin, barely grazing her bottom lip. My meaning was clear, but I still asked. "Can I kiss you?"

"I've been waiting for you to."

I moved closer so my body was almost flush against hers. I could feel her body heat and her warm breath against my mouth. I was tired of waiting. I pressed my lips softly against hers expecting a nice, end of the evening kiss, but was blown away with how powerful it was. It made my knees weak and my stomach flutter. Her mouth was softer than I imagined. I braced my hand on the car when I felt her tongue run along my bottom lip. When she sucked my lip into her mouth, I pressed my whole body into her. We both moaned at the contact. A burst of heat raced inside my body and it took so much effort to peel myself off her.

"I should go even though I don't want to." I kissed her swiftly again. "Stop looking so sexy. We both have to work in the morning and as much as I want you to invite me up, this will definitely keep."

She steadied herself when I gently pulled her away from the car. "Okay, wow. So, good night," she said.

My legs felt wobbly like a newborn calf so I stood in place until she entered her building. I gave her a small wave before the door closed. I couldn't stop smiling. What was happening to me? My energy level was off the chart. I felt like going for a run, but it was late and I knew tomorrow was going to be challenging with all the meetings I had scheduled. My phone dinged when I pulled into my garage.

Did you make it home safely?

I smiled harder. *Just got home. Thanks again for a great night. Thank YOU. Sleep well.*

You, too. Only I knew I wasn't going to sleep. My body was humming with excitement. There were too many new things. Everything felt right. Life just clicked.

CHAPTER TWELVE

LUCKY CHANCE—A NEW OUTLOOK

The twenty minutes I spent with Elliot and Darian at Boulevard Brewing Company before Noelle showed up was the most fun I'd had with my team ever. We sobered up when Noelle slid into the chair beside Elliot. She looked at her watch. "Am I late? What'd I miss?"

"No. We just got here early," I said. Totally planned, but we needed a few minutes to chat without our conversation getting back to Miranda.

It occurred to me that Noelle reminded me of Selma Blair's character at the beginning of *Legally Blonde* and I suppressed a giggle with a snort. I didn't think the beer I had affected me already, but here we were, laughing in Noelle's presence with no explanation. She snatched the menu off the table and flagged over our waitress. I cringed when she rudely ordered and dismissed our server with a flip of her hair. Time to get down to business.

"How does everyone feel about tomorrow's meeting?" I asked.

Elliot nodded. "I feel great. I have the list of questions that we came up with. Do we want to divide up the questions, or just wing it?"

Noelle huffed. "Winging it isn't professional. We definitely need to divide them up. Who's taking the lead?"

Darian was best suited to drive the initial interview and I would do the final presentation. "I assumed Darian would take the lead since that's literally her title." I couldn't keep the snark from my voice. Another huff from across the table. "Am I wrong about that?" I was starting to doubt what the team lead did.

"No, Darian is fine," she said. Her tone indicated that it was chewing-on-glass level not fine.

Then what the actual fuck was her problem? Noelle confused me. I bit my tongue and sat back in my chair knowing that whatever was said here would get back to Miranda. I was damn sure going to look like I did a one-eighty on my team. Honestly, I had, just not with her. Thankfully, Darian pulled the focus off me and listed all the talking points we planned on covering in tomorrow's meeting. After two pints each and an hour of reviewing questions, we were set. Elliot had to go home to take care of his dog, and Darian had an online game that started at eight. I sure as hell wasn't going to spend any unnecessary free time with Noelle so I bolted, too.

The next day, I thought everything was great until it wasn't. We met an hour before the meeting with the client to review everything. Unfortunately, Noelle and Darian got into an argument that got personal quickly and everyone stormed out of the conference room to head to the client's office. The tension in Titan and Spector's waiting room was explosive. I was afraid to move for fear of causing a spark that ignited my team. I was the only one in a good mood. I wasn't worried about the presentation because Darian came across as professional and I trusted that Elliot would rise to the occasion, too. Noelle was the wild card, but I hoped she would be on good behavior in front of a client. We sat in silence. Elliot fidgeted with his tie so much that Darian leaned over and placed a hand on his knee.

I couldn't stand it any longer. "Does anyone want anything to drink? Water?" This waiting room was posh from the comfortable plush chairs to the small refrigerator that offered clients water, soda, and healthy snacks. I grabbed four bottles and returned to my team. I lowered my voice. "Let's get it together. We're about to pitch a client who could drop a ton of money. I would like it if everyone shook off the bad vibes and put on a smile. We know what we're doing. Let's leave the political bullshit back at the office and start acting like the professionals we are." I handed everyone a small bottle. Noelle turned her nose up and looked the other way.

"Lucky's right. Let's do this," Darian said.

I sat and tried hard to stay focused on the presentation we were going to give in less than ten minutes. My job was to review all questions we came up with and ensure they were asked. That meant I had to pay attention but not say anything unless necessary. Darian shook out her arms and rolled her neck.

"I'm ready. Thanks for the swift kick," she said. She drank her water and recycled the bottle. I nodded and did the same.

"They're ready for you now." The receptionist was stunning. Her hair was pulled back in a bun accentuating her sharp features. Her makeup was impeccable, and her suit fit her perfectly.

I felt underdressed and plain compared to her and I was wearing a new outfit. We followed her into a large conference room where eight people sat around an oval walnut table. It wasn't until I pulled out the chair and looked at faces opposite me that I saw her. I froze. Everyone else sat, but I just stood there in disbelief. How did I not know Bri worked at Titan and Spector? Did she ever mention the name? Did they have several offices around town? A knowing smile perched on Bri's fantastic mouth with lips that I tasted last night. I finally sat when Darian cleared her throat. My eyes never left Bri. She looked lovely. Her brown hair was loose around her shoulders and her eyes sparkled mischievously.

"Thank you for giving us the opportunity to discuss new marketing ideas for your law firm. I'm Darian, team lead for Web Pioneer. With me are my colleagues Elliot, Noelle, and Lucky." All eyes were on me when Darian said my name. I lifted my chin a fraction and nodded to them.

Darian and Elliot launched into their spiel and I tried hard to focus on the questions and answers, but my God, I couldn't stop staring at Bri. She looked powerful and beautiful and every time she looked at me, I felt a jolt. Hours ago, her hands were on my face and around my waist and her lips on mine. Heat spread throughout my body and rested uncomfortably between my legs. I uncrossed them to alleviate the throb. We were in the middle of a very important meeting and I wasn't paying attention. Instead, I was remembering Bri's warm lips pressed against mine and wondering what would've happened if she hadn't stopped us when she did.

Bri adjusted her collar drawing my attention to her neck and purposely ran her fingertips down her neck and brushed the soft skin right above the second button of her blouse. She was teasing me! Anybody else wouldn't have noticed, but I knew exactly what she was doing. I twitched my eyebrow to let her know I was on to her. She smiled and for the first time, broke eye contact. I smiled victoriously and tried hard to focus on Elliot's words. I marked off several questions on the list as my mind raced to recall everything we'd talked about. After an hour of back and forth, Darian looked to me for final input in case she missed something.

"We noticed you have a rainbow on your website and that you're a gold sponsor at KC Pride. How visible do you want that to be?" I knew it was a sensitive subject, especially in the Midwest. It blew my mind how conservative it was here, so I always treaded lightly.

Several people looked at Bri. She didn't hesitate. "I think it's important and needs to be more prominent than it is," she said. She looked at her colleagues who nodded emphatically. I just recognized the young man sitting next to her. It was the same guy who was always on the roof when she was there. He was important to her. "I can get you more information. Maybe after the meeting here."

"Sounds good. Thank you." I was screaming inside. I scribbled words on my iPad that didn't make sense like rainbow, diversity, hot, blouse, softball, dinner again? And other clips of phrases that I would be embarrassed by if anybody saw my notes.

"Thank you for coming in. How much time do you think you'll need before you submit a formal proposal?" one of the attendees asked. He looked important and I wondered if he was Bri's boss. I was pretty sure his photo was with the partners on the current website.

We looked to Noelle who stumbled over her answer. We had good bones, but it would take us at least a week to put everything together. This was a larger project than we anticipated.

"We should be able to get it done by Monday or Tuesday," Noelle said.

I felt Darian and Elliot immediately tense. I quickly spoke up. "Let's go with a week. We'll have our proposal to you next Friday," I said. That seemed to appease them. I expected fireworks back at the office upon our return. We spent a few minutes shaking hands and exchanging business cards. Good thing I grabbed some. I learned early that a lot of people still liked the textured rectangular cards to hold and throw in a drawer only to dispose of them years from now. We were in a digital age, but people around here liked traditions.

"Lucky, is it?" Bri slowly walked over to me and shook my hand.

I nodded. "Yes. Ms. Jameson?"

"Please, call me Bri." She briefly squeezed my hand. The private look she gave me was scorching. Every part of me felt like it was on fire. She handed me a business card. "My office is on tenth street. If you have some free time, please stop by and I can give you more information about our LGBTQ+ representation and how we want that presented."

"I live downtown so I can stop in later this afternoon if you're available," I said. I couldn't look away. She was amazing. Powerful, in control, and fucking sexy. She turned to the guy I recognized from the rooftop. "This is Sebastian. He's my assistant. Do I have any openings this afternoon?"

He pulled up his phone and quickly scrolled. "Today's tight," he said. She put her hand on her hip and shifted her weight to lean against the table. I felt the power radiating from her. Apparently, so did Sebastian. "But we can juggle a few things so that we can give Lucky fifteen minutes at four." She didn't move. "Oh, I mean thirty minutes."

Bri dropped her hand and turned to me. "Does that work for you?" she asked. I was mesmerized. I stared at her completely enthralled. She repeated herself. "Does that work, Lucky?"

I nodded and cleared my throat. "That sounds perfect. I'll see you later. At four. At your office. Thank you."

She nodded to my team and left. I blatantly watched her leave. What were the odds?

"I don't know who she is, but are you going to be okay meeting her by yourself?" Darian asked under her breath.

I grabbed my messenger bag and kept the smile off my face. Be professional, Lucky. Be professional. "Oh, I'll be fine. And plus, it looks like she's in the building across from where I live." I waved her business card at my colleagues. "I'll get as much information as I can from her." I'll get as much anything as I can from her, I silently added.

"Sounds good. Let's break for lunch and meet back at the office in an hour," Darian said.

I didn't even care that it was going to be stressful. Nothing could bring me down from this high. Not Noelle, not another screaming match between my teammates, not even Miranda. Bring it, I thought.

"See you later," I said. I wasn't hungry, but I needed to get away and expel this energy. I needed to process that Bri was the potential client. A weed of doubt popped up. What was the rule about dating clients? We were seeing one another before either of us knew we might be working together. Then I remembered they weren't our client yet. We technically weren't in a professional relationship. I hopped into my car and drove to one of the many parks around the plaza and parked under a tree.

Well, that was a wonderful surprise.

My heart leapt in my chest at Bri's text. *You were flirting with me, Ms. Jameson.* She baited me by touching her throat and playing with the buttons on her cleavage and drawing my attention to her chest. I almost moaned in the meeting recalling her body pressed against mine last night.

I know how much you like to watch me. She followed it with a winking emoji.

I had so much to say, but I wanted to play it cool. Bri was definitely way out of my league and it wasn't until today that I realized how much. Seeing her in her element was magnificent. How was she single? *Mm-hmm. Huge flirt.* I decided to push a little. *It's a good thing there was a table between us.* I hit send before I changed my mind and instantly regretted it. That was too much.

Well, there won't be a table between us later. Just my desk…

Fuck. I felt my clit twitch demanding attention. I blew out a deep breath. How was I supposed to respond to that? I knew I pushed, but I didn't think she would come back with words that dripped with promise. *Don't make promises if you're not going to follow through.* What was I getting myself into? I turned the air conditioner on full blast, but it didn't help at all.

You'd be surprised what I can do in 30 minutes.

This exchange had me so worked up that I seriously thought about touching myself. I looked at the clock and groaned. I had only a few minutes to get back to the office so no release for me until I got home. This afternoon with Bri was going to be very interesting. I just had to get through the follow-up meeting first, but how was I going to be able to concentrate? My panties were soaked and my thoughts were on Bri and her mouth and different ways she was going to seduce me. I splashed cold water on my face before heading to the conference room for a meeting recap. Darian didn't disappoint.

"Why would you even say Monday? That would give us zero time to finalize numbers. We would have to work over the weekend, and we rely on different departments who don't work on the weekends. We went over this a million times. One week is always the minimum." Darian was still upset at Noelle. I sat back and quietly listened.

"We have a lot of the work already done. I thought we'd be able to pull numbers together and use an existing proposal. I can do that quickly. Let me remind you that we're not the only ones in and we need this account," she said.

"We can't afford to mess up the numbers. A weekend isn't enough time. If it wasn't for Lucky stepping in and pushing the deadline out immediately, we would have been up shit's creek without a paddle," she said. Noelle shot me a nasty look. I smiled politely in return. She was getting pretty good at scowling when I was around. "Look, let's just move on. Elliot, please get with the AV team and find out their schedule for the first part of August. Titan seemed excited about the commercial ideas. I can't imagine they don't want to use their own employees. Everyone there was beautiful. But get headshots of professional actors just in case they back out. Lucky, you're meeting with Brianna Jameson today. I know they want to go bigger with the rainbow, but find out from her what that really means. What time is your appointment?"

Minutes felt like hours. The afternoon was dragging. "Four. I'll head out about three thirty." That was in two hours. I knew I was going to get nothing done between now and then. I tuned out Darian while she doled out the rest of the responsibilities. Ultimately, I would be the one to tie everything together once the client signed on the dotted line. Right now, my only obligation was Bri and I couldn't be happier.

I stopped by my place to quickly freshen up. My meeting was in twenty minutes and I didn't want to get there too soon. On a whim, I glanced out the window and stopped when I saw Bri on the roof talking on her phone. Her eyes were on my place. Tito was sprawled out on the sofa so she wasn't looking at him. She was looking for me. I smirked. She raised her eyebrow and cocked her head. I looked down and realized my shirt was only halfway buttoned and my lacy, cream-colored bra was very visible. I should've gasped and clutched my shirt together and stepped back from the window, but I didn't. Instead, I very slowly and deliberately buttoned my shirt and adjusted my collar. I held my hands out as though I was waiting for her approval. She fanned herself with her fingers and smiled. Her approval was hot. I watched the sway of her hips as she turned on her heel and disappeared into the building.

Titan and Spector had several floors in the building. Brianna's office was on the third. My heart was pounding with excitement. I had no idea what was going to happen, but I had high hopes it would involve her hands on my body. That was more fantasy, but it was one

GAZE

that was on repeat in my mind. "I have a four o'clock appointment with Brianna Jameson. Lucky Chance." The receptionist gave me a blank stare. I repeated my name. "I'm Lucky Chance. That's my name."

"Oh. Okay." She looked at her computer. "Please have a seat, Lucky. Sebastian will be here shortly to collect you."

"Thank you." I was too excited to sit so I walked around the room and looked at the artwork on the walls. They were all local artists according to the information plaques by each one. I pretended to study them even though my mind was one hundred percent on Bri.

"You're early," Bri said.

Chills popped up and I resisted the urge to shiver. I turned slowly.

"Can you blame me?" I asked.

Her smirk was ridiculously sexy. I slowly looked her up and down and bit my bottom lip to hold back a moan of appreciation. When I finally met her gaze, she crossed her arms and arched her brow. "Perhaps we should take this to my office." Her voice was low and commanding.

I walked toward her thinking she would turn and walk to her office, but she didn't move. I was inches from her. She looked hungrily at my mouth before turning on her heel. I took the time to look at her toned legs, how her ass looked in her tight skirt, and how the jacket accentuated her small waist. She looked over her shoulder and caught me staring. I shrugged. She smiled.

When we got closer, I saw Sebastian hang up the phone and stand. "We're not to be disturbed."

"I'll hold all calls," he said. He focused on me. "Can I get you anything to drink? Coffee? Water?"

I waved him off. "Thank you, no. It's nice to see you again."

"Let me know if you need anything," he said. He sat and continued working on his computer. Bri ushered me in and closed the door. When I heard the click of the lock, I smiled. This wasn't going to be all work.

I turned and smiled. "Did you just kidnap me?"

"Legally, kidnapping means I'm taking you somewhere," she said.

"You just locked me in. I think kidnapping is holding someone against their will. I've watched enough *Dateline* and *20/20* episodes." I moved closer to her.

"Am I? Are you here against your will?" She unbuttoned her suit jacket and placed it on the back of her chair before walking over to me. "Maybe I'm keeping you safe from the world outside."

"Or maybe you just want me all to yourself." Where was my confidence coming from? I closed the gap until I was in her personal space.

"Today was hard."

God, if she only knew how hard I was today. "Agreed." Just her voice was making my sensitive spots throb.

"Should we get work stuff out of the way first?" she asked.

That meant she felt it, too. "No," I said.

CHAPTER THIRTEEN

BRIANNA JAMESON—STEPPING UP HER GAME

Seducing Lucky in my own office during business hours didn't cross my mind until she walked into Titan and Spector's conference room. A flutter of excitement tickled every part of me. What were the chances?

Now, instead of working, we were making out like teenagers. I was trying not to wrinkle her, but I needed her close to me. Our mouths found a perfect rhythm and it was hard not to moan at how good she felt in my arms. I pushed my nameplate and other items back from the front of my desk and made room for Lucky to sit.

Lucky pulled her skirt up past her knees to accommodate me. I put my hands on both thighs and softly caressed them. She tilted her hips slightly as if wanting my hands to move up.

"Lucky. What are you doing?" The correct question should've been what are *we* doing, but I knew exactly what was happening.

"Just making myself comfortable in your office. That's okay, right?" she asked. Her fair skin was flushed and her blue eyes sharp. At some point in the last two minutes, she'd unbuttoned two buttons so her lacy bra peeked out from her shirt. Of course I looked. She wanted me to.

"What's going on here?" I ran my fingertip down her neck and between the soft swell of her breasts. She gave a soft moan. I looked at the clock on the wall opposite my desk. I had to take my next appointment. I'd pushed the client back an hour to accommodate Lucky's visit. There was a very good chance she was already waiting for me. Even though I had chairs outside my office for clients to wait, I gave Sebastian specific instructions to keep the rest of today's clients in the formal waiting room. I didn't care if Sebastian heard anything suspicious; I just didn't want clients to hear.

"I was getting hot. I unbuttoned my blouse so I could enjoy the cool air," she said.

I kissed her hard knowing that she was offering herself to me and even though I would've preferred touching and tasting her for the first time in the privacy of my home, my office had an element of taboo. I moved forward so that she had to spread her legs more. I stroked her thighs and smiled when she moaned.

"Is this really the place?" I asked. I wasn't playing fair by pushing myself against her. My intent was clear. So was hers.

"What time is your next appointment?" she asked.

"Fifteen minutes, but she's probably already here."

She dropped her gaze to my mouth and quickly licked her lips. "I've been turned on since I saw you sitting in that conference room earlier." Her hair was slightly disheveled, and her clothes askew. She was incredibly beautiful and willing.

I was torn between wanting to fuck her on my desk, or being the sweet, romantic woman and waiting for a more appropriate time for us to further our relationship. Last night was sweet and wonderful and everything I wanted. Today's surprise was hot and unexpected. This side of Lucky was a massive turn-on. I expected our first time to be in a bed, under the sheets, with the lights off—not on my desk in the middle of the day. That amplified everything tenfold.

The look of longing she gave me almost made me sink to my knees. I wanted to do the right thing, but her parted lips and slight panting pushed me over the edge. I slid my hands under her skirt until I reached her panties. Her mouth dropped open and her eyes pleaded with me. I slipped my fingers under her lacy underwear and scrunched them into my fists. I felt them tear but didn't let go. I wanted her to give me permission. She lifted her hips and that was all I needed. I pulled them down and barely gave her time to kick them off. I kissed her hard and slipped my hand back under skirt. She was smooth, wet, and velvety soft. We both moaned when I pushed apart her lips to find her swollen clit.

"Shh. We have to be quiet," I said. I stroked her softly even though I felt her hips push hard against my hand. Her back arched and her eyes closed when I entered her. She bit her lip to keep from crying out and her body shook with excitement. I'd never been with anyone so responsive before. She leaned back on her elbows and opened her eyes. The intensity of her hard stare made me weak. Lucky knew what she wanted.

"Deeper."

My hand was already drenched. I added a second finger and pressed as far as I could. She threw her head back and softly hissed. I put my hand on the desk next to her for leverage and fucked her hard and fast. I watched my fingers slide in and out of her pussy and when I added my thumb to rub across her clit, she clamped down and stifled a shout. She was still louder than I wanted, but watching her entire body quiver as an orgasm hit was incredible. Her legs shook for at least thirty seconds and her hips jerked and rolled as she rode it out for as long as she could. I kissed her softly.

"I wish I had time for more." The only thing preventing me from dropping to my knees and making her come again was my schedule.

"Tonight," she said.

I nodded and helped her off my desk. We were both shaking. Her with release and me with need. I took a deep breath. "You're beautiful when you come." She smiled and looked down as if suddenly shy. I didn't want her to feel embarrassed by what happened. I lifted her chin. "Ask me what I'd do if we had more time."

She licked her lips and buttoned up her blouse. "Tell me."

"I'd bend you over my desk and taste you." I liked the way her eyes lit up and how she looked at my lips longingly.

"I'd like that. A lot."

I stepped away so she could straighten her skirt. "I have a washroom if you'd like to fix your hair. While I very much like the tousled look, I'm afraid you might not like the stares." I walked to the door that most people assumed was a closet. It had a sink, a small shower, and a toilet. I quickly washed my hands before giving her the room.

I had five minutes to get my office organized before Sandra Prince, victim of medical malpractice, arrived to review her offer. As much as I wanted to reschedule, I couldn't. Sandra simply didn't have time to wait. I straightened out my desk and picked up pens that fell to the floor in our haste. Lucky's panties were under one of the guest chairs. I picked them up and noticed where I had ripped them. They were mine now. I unlocked my desk drawer and gently put them inside.

"I guess we'll have to talk about queer company things some other time," Lucky said. She was completely put together and looked as fresh as she did when she walked in. Her skirt was slightly wrinkled, but it wasn't enough to draw anyone's attention. I still felt frazzled and needed a few minutes myself.

"Thank you for an amazing surprise. Everything about you is incredible and I can't wait to see you again. I'll call you later." I gave her a quick kiss and walked her to the door. "Are you ready?" She nodded. I opened the door. "Sebastian, please escort Lucky to the elevators. Lucky, I'll be in touch soon."

"Thank you very much, Ms. Jameson."

"Bri, please." I leaned against the doorframe and watched them leave. Today was the best day and the night was even more promising. Remembering Sandra, I quickly spritzed an air freshener so my office didn't smell like sex and left my door open to push the subtle sandalwood and cedar scent out. I checked my reflection in the mirror. Everything outwardly appeared fine. Inside, my pussy was swollen, my heart was beating at a faster pace, and my mind was replaying the visual of Lucky on the edge of my desk—her legs spread wide and my fingers deep inside her. It threatened to knock the wind out of me every time I thought of her moans. As much as I loved being a lawyer, I wish I could've blown off this afternoon and spent it with Lucky, but I had clients who needed me.

"Brianna. How are you?" Sandra walked into my office and shook my hand. I respected her. She was forty years old, a hard worker, and a single mother of three. We accepted an offer sooner than I would've liked, but Sandra wanted to spend whatever time she had left with her children and not fighting in court. She wanted to take them to Disneyland, the Grand Canyon, and several amusement parks across the country.

"Can I get you anything to drink, Ms. Prince?" Sebastian asked.

"A glass of water would be great. Thank you, Sebastian."

I hated when bad things happened to good people. "I know this has been a horrible and draining journey for you." I had to look down at my paperwork to keep my emotions in check. I flipped a few pages before I tamped down my sadness and shared the news with her. I knew it was what she wanted, but I wanted to fight for more. Settling quickly was the best option for her. Her doctor had missed both lung and liver cancer. The gap in time meant she was stage three for both by the time they realized it. At least this settlement would allow her to enjoy her last few years with her kids and leave them with some college money.

"Thank you so much," she said. She turned to Sebastian who walked in with her water. "And thank you, Sebastian. You both have been so nice and honest with me. I appreciate this so much. What do you need from me?"

I slid the contract over to her. "We just need you to sign everywhere you see a tab." I excused myself and Sebastian swooped in to guide her. Sandra's case was probably the hardest I fought in my entire professional career. It was people like her who got me started on this path.

"If there's anything we can do for you, please reach out. You have my number," I said. Sandra put her check in her purse and her settlement papers in her bag. She tired easily and I felt bad for having her come in. Sebastian and I should've gone to her house, but she insisted she would meet us at the office. When she hugged me, I was careful not to press too hard. This time I didn't tear up. Neither did she. "And I want you to send me photos of your trips."

She laughed. "I'll do that. Thank you so much."

It was almost six by the time we were done with today's work. Sebastian scurried off because he had a hot date. I didn't tell him I did too because he probably knew. I wanted to shower and freshen up before I saw Lucky. I shot her a quick text. *Finally wrapping up here. Do you want to have dinner?* I packed up my briefcase while I waited for her response.

I can DoorDash something easy, she texted.

Would you like me to bring anything? Besides my libido, I thought but didn't type.

A bottle of your favorite wine. Apartment 808.

❖

It was almost seven thirty when I showed up at Lucky's. I had a bottle of wine and a cat toy I picked up at QuikTrip on a whim. I thought since Tito was the reason we met, I should bring him a gift. I knocked softly. Why was I so nervous? She answered the door wearing a light blue cold-shoulder top and white leggings. Her hair was pulled back in a messy bun and she was barefoot. She looked amazing.

"Hi. Come in," she said.

I walked into her arms and gave her a soft kiss. We were interrupted by a very vocal Tito who meowed his introduction. I squatted. "Hello, big boy. It's nice to finally meet you. I'm Brianna, and I brought you a present." I dangled the catnip mouse in front of him. He pawed it but was more interested in rubbing on me. Just like his mama, I thought but wisely kept that thought to myself. I stood and reached for her again. "And hello. You look incredible."

"Thank you. I wanted to look nice for you," she said. Her voice trailed off. The "for you" slipped out but it was more of a whisper.

"You succeeded." I peeled my eyes off her to look around her loft. "Your place is great. I love the high ceilings and the exposed brick." She moved ahead of me, fluffed a pillow on the couch, and invited me to sit. I knew we couldn't just jump right back to where we left off, so I told myself to relax and enjoy the evening. We had plenty of time.

"Thank you. It's enough space for me and Tito. And there's just something cool about living downtown," she said. She seemed nervous. I linked my fingers with hers.

"How are your neighbors?"

"Decent. A retired school teacher lives next door and a twenty-something computer programmer and his girlfriend live across the hall. They're quiet, but I've talked to them the most. It's a pretty diverse building and that's why I like it."

"You picked a great spot," I said.

"For so many reasons," she said.

Her body language changed with every minute that passed. Her shoulders relaxed. The pillow she fluffed and clutched to her chest was on her lap. Tito jumped up and put himself in the space between us. It gave us more time to adjust. I pulled up my DoorDash app. "What sounds good for dinner?" I asked.

"I didn't eat much today. Too nervous so I'm hungry now," she said.

Eat first, play later, I thought. "How about a few bowls from Chipotle?"

"That sounds good," she said.

I placed the order and put my phone on the coffee table. This conversation was too polite. I wanted the heat. I craved the passion from her. The blood circling my body thumped against my skin every time my heart beat. It was getting faster and I was getting antsier. "When do you want to talk about work?" I asked. She seemed surprised.

"Definitely not now. It's Friday night," she said.

"We didn't get to say much earlier and I know you have a deadline," I said. Did I really want to talk about work? Absolutely not. Did I want her to think about earlier? Absolutely yes. "It's a safe conversation until the food gets here."

"Safe?" she asked. She shooed Tito off the couch and scooted closer. She looked at my mouth.

"Safe only if we talk," I said.

"Then let's not talk."

CHAPTER FOURTEEN

LUCKY CHANCE—GETTING LUCKIER BY THE MINUTE

Nervous didn't begin to explain how I was feeling. I couldn't stop thinking about this afternoon. For the last three hours I replayed Bri fucking me on her desk over and over. I wanted to be loud and pull at her clothes and do the exact same thing to her, but I knew we didn't have a lot of time and I selfishly wanted her to fuck me. I was greedy for her touch. Now that I knew what she was capable of, how was I ever going to be okay with us just sitting around chatting about the weather? I was desperate for her, but I didn't know how to let her know that. Work? She wanted to talk about work? I was trying to figure out a way to get her interested in me so we could pick up where we left off or do it all over again. With Mia, I always took control. Most of our friends thought I was a pillow princess. I never corrected them. It was none of their business. With Bri, I wanted her to take control—at least tonight. She was a powerful woman and how she handled me so effortlessly today was hot and exciting.

"If we were still in my office, what would you do to me?" Bri asked. The huskiness in her voice gave me shivers.

I kissed her passionately and moaned when she wrapped her arms around me. Her warm, wet mouth was demanding and hungry. I gave her everything I could. Her hands slid under my shirt and when her fingernails grazed my back, I moaned and leaned up to look at her.

"What are you doing to me?" I asked.

"Everything we couldn't do in my office." She grabbed my hips and flipped me so that I was underneath her.

"You left me so turned on today. It's hard to work when all I've been thinking about is your warm, wet mouth and sexy body," she said.

"What do you want me to do about it?" I asked.

"I want you to touch and taste me everywhere," Bri said.

"Like this?" I shifted so I could crawl up her body and rest my hips between her legs lightly pressing against her core.

"Just like that." She blew out a quivering breath. "But more." Her mouth opened and she gasped when I rolled my hips again. I kissed her softly several times until we found the perfect rhythm with our lips. I ran my tongue over her bottom lip until she opened her mouth. I slipped my tongue inside and moaned when hers touched mine. Bri had the softest tongue and I couldn't wait to feel it all over my body. I pressed my hips into hers and elicited another delicious moan. This time she rolled her hips against mine. She wanted friction.

I slipped my hand between our hips and pressed against her warm pussy. Her nails scratched the back of my neck and her mouth demanded more. The desperation in her touch was too much. I sat up and unbuttoned her expensive linen pants.

Bri lifted her hips so I could tug them off. I stopped when I saw she was wearing a white lacy thong. I ran my fingertips along the edge marveling at how soft her skin was and how warm she felt. "I'm all yours," she said.

I unbuttoned her shirt and kissed her warm skin under each button. When I pushed the fabric aside, I leaned back on my heels to look at her. She wore a matching bra that held beautiful breasts. I ran my fingers over her erect nipples and slightly pinched them. Bri was the most beautiful person I'd ever touched. I ran my hand down her firm, flat stomach and slipped my fingertips under the lacy waistband of the wisp of underwear she was wearing. I pulled the tiny strip of lace to the side, bent down, and licked her pussy hard and fast. She grabbed the back of the couch and spread her legs further apart. Just as I was about to pull the thong off, my doorbell rang. Shit. The food.

I pointed. "Don't move. I'll be right back." I stumbled to the front door to buzz the delivery person up. As I waited, I could see her moving on the couch and felt weak when I saw her drop her thong on the floor. "Fuck," I whispered.

"Yes," she said.

I was torn between abandoning my post of waiting for the delivery or going back to my new favorite place in the world—the spot between her legs. I was so busy watching her, that the knock startled me and I yelped. I pulled the door open a fraction. I didn't want him to see her.

"Thank you." I grabbed the bag. I shut the door and dropped the food on the counter on my way back to her. Food was going to have to wait. I didn't think either of us minded.

I knelt on the couch and ran my fingers up and down her thighs. She squirmed and lifted her hips every time my fingers got close to her core. It felt like teasing, but I was trying to take my time. I still tasted her on my lips. She was swollen and I knew she wanted release. Still on my knees, I watched Bri's face when I slid a finger inside. Her back arched slightly and she nodded. We kept eye contact. I slipped another finger inside. This time she closed her eyes for a few moments and when she opened them, they were darker with passion. She felt really tight, but the more I slid in and out, the easier it was. I tried a third finger. She cried out softly and clutched the armrest. Her hips became more demanding and met my thrusts.

My hand was starting to cramp, but I didn't want her to come yet. I wanted to bring her to the brink without falling into a hard orgasm. The faster I went, the more Bri moaned. This wasn't what I wanted. I wanted my mouth on her pussy when she came. I wanted to feel her body stiffen and jerk and taste her release. I pulled out slowly. Bri groaned her disappointment. I knew I would make it up to her. I moved from the floor up to slide my body next to hers on the couch. I ran my fingertips over the smooth swell of her breasts admiring how soft she was. She looked stunning in lace, but I wanted her completely naked.

"Do you want me to take this off?" she asked, as though reading my mind.

I nodded and helped her unlatch the hook. "You are so beautiful." I repeated myself and ran my hand over her breasts, over her hardened nipples, down her flat stomach and back to the juncture of her thighs.

"I need you inside me," she said.

I loved that she was okay telling me what she wanted. I watched her expression when I slipped two fingers inside. Her back arched slightly and she blew out a breath.

"More," she demanded.

I obliged. I was beyond excited when her pussy accepted a third and seconds later, a fourth finger. She was so tight that I was afraid I was going to hurt her or somehow split her in half. I moaned with her and watched her pussy clench my fingers. This was the closest I'd ever been to fisting someone. I didn't care that my hand was bent at an angle that was uncomfortable. I only cared about giving Bri what she wanted. I didn't care that she was loud and probably scaring my neighbors with her deep moans and guttural cries. "Is this okay?" My voice sounded hoarse and I wasn't sure she heard me, but she managed to answer.

"It's perfect, but I want your mouth on me when I come," Bri said.

Her words sent lightning through my body. Every part of me was on fire. Her voice was husky and I could tell she was ready. I gently pulled out so I could move down between her spread legs and taste her. I could feel her legs tremble. She put one leg on the back of the couch to give me more room. We both deserved the release. I spread her apart with my hands and ran my tongue up and down her slit. When I sucked her clit into my mouth, I felt her hands in my hair. She softly held my head in place and moved her hips against my mouth, bruising it, but I didn't care. I knew she was going to come fast. I slid two fingers inside and continued to lick and suck until I felt her walls quiver. Her body felt tense and she sped up her hip thrusts.

"Just like that, just like that," she repeated over and over.

I didn't stop. My jaw hurt and my hand was cramping again, but I wasn't going to stop. When Bri cried out and loosened her grip on me, I fucked her harder until she came again. My couch was drenched from her and I didn't care. I wanted her to come a third time, but she stopped me.

"That's enough." She couldn't finish her sentence because she was panting so hard, but I stopped immediately and watched as her hips slowed and her legs stopped twitching. When her body grew limp, I moved up the couch and slipped in the small space behind her. I pulled her in my arms and held her until her breathing returned to normal. "You're good at following instructions," she said.

I laughed and kissed her cheek. "You're very good at giving directions." I leaned up on one elbow so she could reposition herself.

Bri touched my face. "That was incredible."

I kissed her fingertips when they got close to my lips. "Everything about today was incredible," I said.

"You surprise me," Bri said.

I looked at her swollen lips, flushed cheeks, and bright eyes. I traced the slight tan line she had around her neck and moved my hand to cup her breast. It filled my palm nicely. I wasn't done getting to know her better, but I needed to stay in the moment. "I surprised you? The woman who bent me over her desk and fucked me during business hours was surprised by me?" I feigned shock.

"But you knew exactly what I needed when I came here," she said.

"I was just following your lead."

Bri snorted. "Yeah, but I wasn't expecting that. My body is still humming. And it hasn't hummed this hard in a long time."

It was hard not to feel a burst of pride for being able to pleasure her so completely our first time. "I'm going to enjoy getting to know you better."

"I am, too," she said.

"Are you hungry? I can reheat the food." I wasn't sure if five minutes had passed or two hours.

"That sounds good. I'll just excuse myself."

I pointed her in the direction of the bathroom and dug through the bag. She ordered us a lot of food. I removed the aluminum cover from two bowls and put them in the microwave for two minutes.

Bri sneaked up behind me and put her arms around my waist. "I probably went overboard," she said.

I nodded. "There's enough food to keep us going for a long time." I smiled when her hands drifted down my hips, over my ass, and start rubbing between my legs. Dinner could wait. I couldn't. "Fuck."

"Yes?" she asked.

I nodded. "Yes. Oh, yes." My clit was rock hard and the pressure of her fingers was going to make me come in less than thirty seconds. She peeled down my leggings and panties leaving the material low on my thighs. It was binding and hot as fuck. I stopped prepping the food and held onto the counter for stability. Bri put one hand on my shoulder and slipped the other one between my legs. I couldn't spread my thighs apart so she gently pushed me forward, bending me at the waist for better access. I clutched the corner when she started fucking me.

"Oh, God, yes," I said. I remembered those magical fingers inside me hours ago. The hand on my shoulder moved to my waist and held me there while the other hand was in the sweet spot between my legs.

Her teeth grazed my shoulder and she nipped a path down my back until I felt them press into the tender flesh of my ass. The sharpness rivaled the pleasure building in my pussy and I erupted into an orgasm. It was completely unexpected and I didn't have enough time to try to be quiet. I clutched the sink as though holding on for dear life fearful that my knees would buckle. Standing was hard and I couldn't move because my pants were restricting me. I had to wait until the aftershocks were done before I could stand without help from the counter or her. I pulled up my pants and faced her.

"I wasn't expecting that." I kissed her hard and wrapped my arms around her neck.

She smiled victoriously. "That's when it's best. When it's least expected," she said. She kissed me swiftly and washed her hands. "I'll take over here."

On shaky legs, I grabbed a pair of fresh panties and new leggings and cleaned up in the bathroom. My hair was messy, my cheeks were rosy, and I was sporting a grin that only Bri could have put on my face. Is this what dating was like now? Sign me up.

She didn't leave until after two in the morning. We ate, we talked, we even discussed the rainbow representation on the website, and we had sex in the bed. It was just as exciting as it was in her office or on my couch. I was exhausted by the time she left, but I had enough information on how Titan and Spector wanted to show LGBTQIA+ representation and a sore body from sex all over my apartment. Bri was insatiable and I loved it.

CHAPTER FIFTEEN

BRIANNA JAMESON—READY FOR THE NEXT STEP

Even though I was having a record month, things felt off. I should've been celebrating every case closure, but I was stressed instead. The vibe in the office was different. I felt like I'd stepped in a cobweb and was fighting an unknown nuisance. Somebody was going to be named partner any day now.

"Are you hearing any chatter?" I asked Sebastian. We had this ability to find one another in the office when we needed each other without much difficulty. He fell into step with me on the way back to my office as though we planned to meet at the copy room.

"Nothing. Nobody's talking. Maybe they don't want to be the leak."

"I swear if Tyler gets it, I'm going to be pissed." I clenched my teeth in anger just thinking about that unjust decision.

"Don't get worked up yet. Nothing's happened. And if you go, I go," he said.

We grew silent walking past a cluster of interns. They were the worst gossipers and knew everything. Sadly, neither Sebastian nor I were close to any of them. I had a feeling we were going to have to wait it out with everyone else. "Don't even Jerry Maguire me. You take care of yourself." It was the right thing to say even if I didn't mean a word of it. I wanted Sebastian in my professional life until I retired.

"I'm sure we'll know soon. There's too much tension for a decision not to be on the table," he said.

That movie was starting to hit me in the feels when I thought of leaving Titan and Spector. And they most definitely would escort me out if I announced it Jerry Maguire style. No, if I left, it would be on my terms. I would tell Charlie after work or on a weekend and never return to the office. Walking out with a box of personal effects and two security guards was unsettling and embarrassing. I pushed the thought from my head and focused on the here and now. What a bananas week this had been. It was already Thursday and I hadn't seen Lucky since Monday night. She was working on the proposal for us, and I didn't want to get in her way. I was working on two new cases and had one coming up for trial. I had a feeling we would settle in the eleventh hour, but I still prepared like I was going to war. "Well, I don't like all this secrecy."

"Only because you're the subject of it," he said.

"You're not wrong." I continued walking into my office and Sebastian stopped at his desk outside.

Dinner tonight? I know you're busy but tacos sound great and you need nourishment.

I smiled at Lucky's text. I wanted to see her, too. *How about Manny's at seven?*

Perfect. I'll see you there, she texted.

I liked how she respected my time. Most women were clingy, but not Lucky. She was trying to get back to her promising career, and I didn't want to interfere with that. She also respected my career and that spoke volumes. Even though we were brand new, she didn't press for time with me. I decided I would just leave from work instead of trying to get home in time to come back into the city. *Why don't you meet me downstairs at seven and I'll drive us?*

Late night?

Just getting ready for trial that probably won't happen but it's good if I review the case. See you in a bit. Only I couldn't concentrate on work anymore. I missed Lucky. I picked up my phone. "How's the proposal? Are you going to be ready tomorrow?"

"Hi. I'm glad you called. I think I'm ready. We should have something concrete. If you can tell me, how many companies are you considering?" she asked.

"You are one of three, but one completely tanked so one of two. But you didn't hear that from me." I trusted Lucky to keep that information private.

"Thanks. So, were you calling to find out about the project or is something on your mind?" she asked.

"I decided that seven was late and maybe we could have dinner earlier? If you're up for it," I said. I heard her smile.

"That sounds great. When do you want me to be ready?" she asked.

"How about one hour? I'll still pick you up out front," I said.

"I'd love that. I'll be ready."

"See you soon," she said.

I answered five emails and signed off ten minutes before I was going to meet Lucky downstairs. I scowled when I saw Tyler waiting for the elevator, but I decided to be cordial. "Hello, Tyler. I'm surprised to see you here."

"It's only a little after five. I usually stay until six," he said.

"Interesting. I never see you past five. And I work late. Almost every night," I said. I was being bitchy, but something about him just made my skin crawl. His sleeves were already rolled up to his elbows and his hair tousled. His tie was in his back pocket. "Going somewhere casual?"

"Meeting a client for drinks. Big client. The kind that's going to bring millions to Titan and Spector." He clapped his hands once with glee. "I see your numbers are back up."

"Soon to go even higher. It's so much fun being in the top spot this month." Why was the elevator taking so long? There were only two floors below us. It finally arrived and I followed him in. He hit the first-floor button. I hit the garage. He shook his finger at me. "Never count me out. I always have something up my sleeve." When the doors finally reached the lobby, he sprang out. "Have a great night, Bri. I know I will." He wagged his eyebrows at me and jogged out of the building. He was so secretive.

I clicked the down button repeatedly as though that would speed things up knowing full well the action was worthless, but it made me feel a fraction better. What game was Tyler playing? Did he have a ringer? Was he getting ready to sign a big customer? I hadn't heard anything about it. Either Sebastian's spies were very bad, or Tyler's underlings were very good at keeping quiet. Well, I had a date so I squelched the need to figure out what he was up to. By the time I left the garage, my heart felt lighter and the dark cloud of doubt was pushed aside by sunshiny thoughts of Lucky. Catching her at the entrance to my garage caught me by surprise. I lowered the window. "Hi. Get in." I watched her slip into my car and adjust herself quickly knowing there was a car behind us waiting patiently to leave.

"It's nice to see you earlier than I expected," I said. Rather than kiss her like I wanted to, I pulled into traffic and drove the seven blocks to Manny's. "I love that color on you."

She wore a dark gold top and wide-legged pants. On anyone else, it would've looked chic. But Lucky accessorized differently and she looked more bohemian and carefree. Her hair was down and wavy and I wondered if it was always this way and she straightened it daily or if she styled it differently. There was so much I needed to learn about her still. As much as I enjoyed sex with her, we were doing things backwards. Our courtship, if that's what we were calling it, had included sex but not dinner in a restaurant.

"Thank you. I'm glad you agreed to dinner," she said.

"I haven't been to Manny's in forever. Great idea."

I parked outside the restaurant and put my hand on the small of her back when we walked in. We were seated immediately because it was so early and placed our orders with the waiter. Tacos. Enough said.

"Are you going back to work after this?" She wasn't asking me because she wanted me to come over. She was asking because she knew I was busy and leaving the office before six wasn't something I did.

I shrugged but then nodded. "Yes. If this trial sticks, I need to make sure I'm ready for it." I could feel my heart pick up thinking about the fight ahead of me.

Lucky must've sensed my tension because she changed the subject. "Enough about work. Tell me about your family. What was it like growing up here in the Midwest?"

"Exactly how you would imagine. Conservative," I said. It wasn't bad. It just wasn't good. "I'm sure the East Coast is twenty years ahead."

"I had a pretty easy time of it. At least in regards to my queerness. Most people didn't care. I had my first girlfriend in the eighth grade."

"Oh, so you were out at an early age? That's great. Did you have a lot of support?" I asked. My parents struggled for a bit, but once I got through law school and became a bona fide lawyer, my sexuality was forgotten. They didn't care. Being a lawyer outweighed being gay in their eyes. They had bragging rights. Their only child was a successful lawyer.

"My parents always knew and always supported me. I went to school with a large queer alliance," she said.

"What do your parents do for a living?" I asked.

"My mom is a pharmacist and my father is co-owner of a sports equipment company. I grew up never needing anything. Not that we're rich or anything, but I had a very comfortable upbringing," she said.

"Your father owns a sports equipment company and you've never played softball?" I threw up my hands in disbelief.

"Look at me. I'm not sporty at all. I was a nerd in high school. The only thing I did remotely athletic was run cross country. And that didn't require equipment except expensive shoes," she said.

"You have nice, firm legs. I could tell you had some sport background. I was going to guess ballet, but cross country makes sense," I said. Her blush was delightful. "I played soccer for a bit. I wasn't very good. And I played volleyball."

She pointed at me. "I can see that. You have the height for it. Did you enjoy it?"

"I enjoyed the competition. As I'm sure you could guess. We did okay overall. I played all four years through high school." I was just about to tell her about my first girlfriend when Emery walked over. "Oh, my God. What are you doing here? It's so good to see you." I stood and hugged her.

Emery held up a large paper bag. "I told Claire I would grab dinner on the way home." She looked at Lucky then back at me. "Hi, I'm Emery."

I shook my head. "I'm so sorry. Emery, this is Lucky. Lucky this is my good friend Emery."

Lucky shook Emery's hand. "I've heard so much about you and your wife. It's nice to finally meet you."

"Likewise." Emery thumbed in my direction. "This one only has good things to say about you," she said. I hadn't seen Emery smile that big ever. I knew to expect a phone call from Claire later. "Okay, well, enjoy your dinner. Let's plan for a get-together soon. Maybe a couples' dinner?" I nodded and gave her another hug.

"So, that's Emery," Lucky said.

"She's the best. And she's perfect for Claire. I've never seen two people so much in love before."

"Tell me about Claire. She used to work for Titan and Spector, right?"

"Yes, but that was before I really knew her. She's a great lawyer. Very smart and knows the law like nobody else. Now she's a judge. A really good judge."

"Have you ever been in front of her in court?" Lucky asked.

"No. If for some reason, she's the judge on the case, she'll recuse herself. But only if I'm lead. Honestly, only about ten percent of our cases make it to the courtroom. Lawyering is all about dealing."

"That's very sexy. What you do." She took a sip of her margarita. When her tongue flicked out to gather salt that stuck to her upper lip, I almost moaned.

"Why are you tempting me right now?" I asked.

She wiped her mouth with her napkin. "For once, I wasn't trying to."

"You don't play fair, do you, Lucky Chance?" Her laugh was delightful.

"What's fair? I know what I want and I go for it. I think we are very similar. You obviously get what you want," she said.

I leaned back in my chair and smiled. She wasn't wrong. "My friends are going to love you. If you think I get what I want, wait until you meet Claire."

"I'd love to meet her. You told me that they were your favorite power couple. And Emery seems super nice," Lucky said.

"Great. I'll reach out to them and we can have dinner one night soon," I said. I didn't introduce my friends to the people I dated because most of them were just casual hook-ups. Lucky was different. Even though we had sex early in our relationship, I was excited for the people in my life to meet her. That never happened before. At least not since college.

After a ninety-minute dinner, I stalled. I didn't want our night to end but I had to get back to the office. Holding her hand on our way back to the car felt natural and nice. Her touch made me happy. Lucky was starting to mean something more than just a flirtation. I pulled her close when we got to the car. "Thank you for suggesting dinner. It was nice to step away from work."

She wrapped her arms around me and kissed me softly. "I knew you were probably working too hard. Besides, you're so close."

"Just a note away."

CHAPTER SIXTEEN

LUCKY CHANCE—CELEBRATING TOO EARLY

They signed the contract but had strict stipulations." Darian was brimming with excitement in our meeting with Miranda.

Miranda drummed her fingertips on the table as she thought about what Titan and Spector wanted—a quick turnaround. I was good with the two-month lead time—I just needed the content. "Lucky, how much time will you need to mock up the website? What date is good for you?"

"Honestly, I'll need two solid weeks. Content and IT cleanup will take the longest so I'm at the mercy of everyone else," I said. Two weeks was pushing it, but I was willing to work overtime to get the project behind me. And since it was Bri's place of employment, I was going to do a bang-up job. I could tell Miranda was skeptical. "It's what I do, boss. Trust me."

She turned to Darian. "Can we do a great job in eight weeks?"

I could almost feel Darian's energy ramping up. "They liked the mock-up. I think the commercials will take the most time."

"And we can slip those in after a soft launch," Elliot added.

"So, everyone's on board with being able to get this done on time? Have you checked with AV on their schedule?" Miranda asked.

Elliot shrugged. "They said they were light and could make something fast. The company agreed to use models, not employees, sadly, and they liked Lucky's mock-ups of thirty-second commercials."

Miranda swiveled. "You are mocking up commercials now?"

She knew damn well I led the entire team back in Boston for the Connecticut Cheetahs account. That was one of the things she pointed out when I interviewed. "Never stopped."

"Hm." Her eyes darted from Darian to Elliot to me. She didn't even look at Noelle who was still sulking from last week's blow-up. I shook my head. Thank God pre-contract work was done and I didn't have to deal with her on this project anymore.

"What happens now?" I asked. Darian opened her iPad and scrolled through her notes.

"We divide up the work and get the departments on the schedule. Obviously, we need the AV department to get started. Lucky, why don't you set up a meeting today or first thing tomorrow?" Darian asked.

Miranda interrupted. "Include me on the invite. I want to make sure everybody's on the same page. Sometimes they need a friendly push."

"Will do," I said. We broke the meeting with a list of things each of us needed to do.

I was bummed that Bri hadn't been at the meeting today, but I knew she was getting ready for trial. She texted me right before it started saying she was too busy with trial prep. Only four Titan and Spector employees met with us. According to them, we were neck and neck with our competition and if we could beat their time frame, they would sign with us. The other agency came in at ten to twelve weeks, and they wanted eight. We agreed. Did I think Web Pioneer could do it that quickly? Yes. Did I think my team could do it? Not at all. I came from a place where teams burned the midnight oil and we clicked. I was still finding my footing with this location. Maybe the AV department would be easier. I emailed Ruth, the manager of the department, copied Miranda, and moved on to the next task.

I'm sorry I wasn't there. I was really hoping they'd want to close this case instead of taking it to trial. Looks like I'll be here for a bit.

I sighed when I read Bri's text. Trials sucked. *Need anything? You're so sweet. No, thank you.* Her text made me smile.

Well, if you get too tired, you can always stay here. Sleeping only. I don't think you've slept more than three hours every night all week. I was the reason she wasn't sleeping, but I was selfish and wanted the time with her.

Sleeping is overrated. Besides I'm wound too tight for sleep.

Hmm. I wonder what we could do to relax you? I smiled knowing that would get her attention. I snapped a quick photo of my neck with the top two buttons of my shirt open and sent it to her. My cleavage was up front and center. Who was I? There was something so decadent about Bri and taking risks like this. Anyone could've seen me.

I held my phone waiting for her response. She didn't disappoint. She sent me a photo of her desk cleared off and my ripped panties crumpled up in her hand. I covered my mouth to stop the squeal of both excitement and embarrassment. She never gave me back my panties. The caption said motivation. Another ding and another photo. This time it was of her looking longingly in the distance. It was the only photo I had of her face and it was beautiful. That meant I probably wouldn't see her tonight. That was fine. I could work on another small project Web Pioneer gave me. Or I could go to Katrina's.

I sighed. I knew better than to rely on only one person to spend time with. Mia taught me that valuable lesson. I decided a quick drink at Katrina's might be fun. I hadn't seen Frankie for over a week and I needed something familiar. By the time I got home and changed, it was six thirty. Super early to go to a bar, but also I wouldn't have to fight the crowd. It was too hot for jeans so I wore a knee-length lilac-colored summer dress with spaghetti straps and slip-on sandals. My hair fell in just the right way and I prayed that the heat wouldn't melt my makeup. The moment I stepped outside, I knew I should've put my hair up. I slipped into my car and drove the short distance to Katrina's.

"Lucky Chance! Where have you been?" Frankie was busy making a fruity cocktail.

"Working hard." I sat on a barstool in front of her and ordered whatever she was making. It looked refreshing and sweet.

"But it's summer. You should be having a blast and coming to our games and going to all the cool concerts around here."

I made a face. "I'm still trying to prove myself at work so I've been putting in extra hours. How's softball?"

"You should come to the game on Sunday. It starts at ten, so it won't be that hot yet," she said. She held her finger up indicating she'd be back and disappeared to deliver a tray of drinks. When she returned to the bar, she yelled at people walking in. "Go ahead and sit anywhere. I'll be with you in a minute."

"Are you the only one working?" I looked around knowing that by nine, this place would be packed.

"There are a few other servers, but they are either in the kitchen or on break. It's still pretty slow right now." She nodded to somebody who approached the bar. "What can I get you?"

I glanced over at the person who stood near my chair. It was Emery! We looked at each other surprised. "Hi!" It was impossible to keep the excitement out of my voice.

"Hi, Lucky. It's great to see you again." She looked around. "Are you here with Brianna?"

It was weird to hear people call her Brianna. "No. She's prepping for a trial that starts next week. I'm just grabbing a quick drink."

Emery pointed behind her. "I'm here with Claire and a few people from the Kansas City Diversity and Inclusion Club. Would you like to join us?"

"Oh, I don't want to intrude. I'm sure you all are busy," My anxiety was high just thinking about sitting with people I didn't know.

"No, seriously. Please join us. It'll give them fresh blood to recruit," she said.

"What can I get you?" Frankie asked.

"Three Boulevard Wheats and an old-fashioned," Emery said. She handed Frankie her credit card. "Keep it open."

"Sure thing. Go ahead and have a seat. I'll bring them out to the table," Frankie said.

"I'd love for you to meet Claire," Emery said to me. I hadn't prepared myself mentally to meet anyone tonight, especially one of Bri's best friends, but it would've been rude to turn Emery down. She was insistent and excited.

"Okay. I'd like that." I grabbed my drink and followed Emery to the table.

"Everyone, this is Lucky. She's my new friend and somebody Brianna is seeing."

Did I feel like there was a spotlight on me? Yes. Did it bother me? Absolutely. Emery pulled a chair over from an empty table.

"Hello." I gave them all my best smile and sat in the chair tucked at the front of the table. Emery was dapper and suave, but Claire? Claire was beautiful. No, that word didn't do her justice. She was drop-dead gorgeous and full of smiles. Even though she maintained eye contact with me, I knew she was sizing me up. Not in a bad way, but in a curious way.

"Hi, Lucky. I'm Claire. It's nice to finally meet you," she said. She shook my hand. Even her voice sounded sexy. And she was a judge?

"Same. What brings you all to Katrina's?" I asked after all the introductions were made. This was not an establishment I expected to see them in. Ever. There were so many upscale bourbon bars and wine bars close by. Katrina's wasn't a dump, but it could use a boost into this decade.

"We were wrapping up a quick meeting about summer fundraising events. More than what's already on the schedule," Lisa said. She was the director and, Karlye, sitting next to Lisa, was in charge of the center's finances.

"And what better place than Katrina's?" Emery asked.

"Yeah, I really like this place. Frankie has always been nice and tried to get me more involved in the queer community," I said. I didn't go into the whole attempted softball recruitment. They didn't seem the type.

"This is definitely the table you want to be at if you're looking to become more involved," Lisa said.

"But you're under no obligation," Claire said. "By the way, where's Brianna tonight?"

"She's getting ready for a case," I said. Even though Claire seemed relaxed and carefree, I could almost feel the power that radiated from her. I took a small sip from the stirring straw in my drink. The last thing I needed was to spill my drink all over me, so small sips only. I was sure I looked extremely nervous. They were kind enough to include me in the conversation, but not push.

"So, you said you're new to the area. How long have you lived here?" Lisa asked.

"Almost eight months. This is the only bar I've found for queer people and it's thankfully close."

"Sadly, our bars are dwindling in numbers. But also it's more acceptable to be queer in regular bars than it was a few years ago," Lisa said.

I had a feeling Lisa was a wealth of queer information. She was loud and proud and I liked her immediately. Maybe if my life settled, I could volunteer and get more involved in the community. It didn't take long for me to loosen up around them and before I knew it, it was nine and the bar was filling up with people looking for a good time on a Friday night. The music was getting louder and I found myself leaning in closer to hear our group. I saw my phone light up with a message. It was Brianna. I couldn't help but smile.

I can't believe they won't settle. We're going to destroy them in court. How are you?

"Is that Brianna?" Emery said. I nodded. "We should send her a selfie." She held her phone up and motioned for me to get between her and Claire. I squatted so that my face was between theirs. They both smelled wonderful. Claire smelled like vanilla and jasmine, and Emery smelled like bergamot and black pepper. "Smile!" She took several photos and showed me and Claire the photo she was going to send to Bri. I approved. She hit send and I was trying hard not to giggle imagining Bri's reaction.

OMG. You're with Emery and Claire! How? Where are you? She punctuated the text with several hearts. *What a beautiful picture.*

"Oh. She responded." Emery laughed and held up her hand for our attention. "*I'm so jealous. It's not fair that my friends are playing and I'm working. You all look beautiful.*"

I quickly sent her a text. *They showed up at Katrina's. I came down here to have a drink with Frankie and they walked in. Emery invited me over and I got to meet Claire. I'm so nervous.*

You don't look nervous. You look beautiful. Truly. I'm sad I'm missing out. A row of sad, crying faces followed that sweet message.

I'm going to finish my drink and head home. Are you leaving any time soon?

I was going to sneak over to Katrina's. Stay long enough? My heart did a funny up and down flip at her text.

"She's going to swing by," I said. I tried to hide my excitement, but they knew. Claire gave me a knowing smile.

"You all stay, but it's getting late and I need to make sure the kids haven't turned into wildings. I need to get home," Lisa said. She opened her wallet to pay but Emery stopped her.

"Like I told Karlye, it was our invitation. Don't worry about it," she said. Karlye left about ten minutes ago and fought the same fight with Emery.

"Thanks, Em. It was nice to meet you, Lucky. I hope to see more of you. Swing by the club any time and I'll give you a tour. Our new location is pretty impressive." She hugged Claire and Emery and waved before leaving.

"She seems really nice." It was just me and them. It was more stressful when the conversation fell on me.

"Lisa's a gem. She really tries hard to keep the community involved so more people can find us. There are at least two events every month and we always get new people," Emery said.

"How long have you been involved with the club?" I asked.

"It's changed names over the years, but about ten years. I recruited Emery because, well, we're married and she has to do what I say," Claire said.

It was cute the way they looked at one another. I could tell their relationship was solid. They seemed perfect together. Successful, smart, and respectful. Their small touches and closeness made me miss Bri. We weren't at their level. We were still learning how to be comfortable around each other even though we'd had sex too many times to count.

I didn't know if I looked up right when Bri walked in because I felt her or because I was waiting for her. Our eyes met and she gave me that look. The heated look that made my stomach quiver and my pussy tense. It was a look for only me. When I turned to Emery and Claire to let them know she was here, Claire was smiling at me secretively. She saw. She knew.

"I hope I'm not too late," Bri said. She pulled out the vacant chair next to me and kissed me after she sat. She touched my chin. "It's nice to see you."

I almost melted. She radiated power, like Claire, only she was mine. "I'm glad you could make it."

"Um, hello? We're here, too," Emery said.

"Thanks for sending me motivation." Bri looked at them briefly, but her eyes were on me. I put my hand on my stomach to keep the imaginary butterflies inside. I liked the fluttering, light feeling, but I was also very aware of Claire and Emery watching our dynamic.

"Can I get you something to drink?" I asked.

"I can get it. I don't mind."

I put my hand on hers. "You've worked a long day. Let me do this," I said.

She smiled thankfully at me. "Okay. I'll take a rum and Coke. Top shelf," she said.

"Does anybody else want anything?" I asked.

Emery and Claire shook their heads. "Tell Frankie to add it to my tab," Emery said.

I felt like I floated to the bar. I didn't remember getting out of my chair, but suddenly I was in front of Frankie.

"Oh, good. Bri showed up. What does she want?"

I gave Frankie her order and turned to watch them. All three of them had their heads close together and I could only imagine they were talking about me. I thought I did a great job of not embarrassing me or her tonight. I was riding high and only had one drink.

"One overpriced rum and Coke. And tell Bri I said hello." Frankie set the drink on the counter and scurried off to fill another order. The line behind me was starting to snake around the bar so I quickly grabbed Bri's drink and headed back to the table.

"Thank you." She accepted the drink and kissed me softly when I sat. I smiled when she scooted closer.

"Tell me what I've missed," Bri said.

"Well, we missed you, but we learned a lot about Lucky," Claire said.

"Your friends are really nice," I said. I was giddy that she was here. I couldn't stop smiling. "And you look incredible. I haven't seen you in this suit before." Bri was wearing a charcoal gray pants suit with a black shell.

"That reminds me. It's hot in here."

I watched her take off her jacket and hang it on the back of the chair. She was graceful and it was stunning to watch. I bet she slayed in a courtroom. "I want to see you in action."

She arched her brow at me and bit her bottom lip. "Okay, wow. I need to do a better job then."

I covered my mouth in horror once I realized what I insinuated. Bri laughed and pulled me close enough to kiss.

"You're adorable," she said.

"Ack. I meant in the courtroom," Lucky said.

Emery tapped her glass of beer against my water glass. "I feel this so hard. Sexy, hot partners who know the law and aren't afraid to fight for the underdog. We're the lucky ones, Lucky." She dropped a sly wink.

"If we go to trial, maybe you can sneak away for a bit and watch me in action," she said. I blushed accordingly.

"I get it," Emery said. She fanned herself with a cocktail napkin. "I've seen Claire in the courthouse, and let me tell you something. Watching her work, or as you like to put it, watching her in action, is incredible. The power, the control. Still gives me the shivers."

It was wonderful being open and public with Bri. Claire and Emery were very nice and very smart. Bri was playful and attentive, kissing me on my cheek or my temple or running her fingers up my arm or across my back. I was having the time of my life. For the first time since I moved here, I felt like I belonged. Listening to Claire's and Emery's stories of their family and Emery's dangerous job, I was on the edge of my seat most of the evening.

"It's eleven. Why are we still in this bar?" Emery had to yell when the music got louder so we could hear her. "Let's get out of here." She signaled for us to meet her outside while she settled the bill.

The temperature was still stifling, but at least we could hear one another. Bri pulled me closer and gave me a soft kiss. The brush of her lips, not the pressure, made my pulse dance. I was happy. When Mia walked by us and gawked, I stood a little closer to Bri. Not knowing what was happening, Bri tilted my head back and kissed me thoroughly and I almost melted at the sheer power of it. Her lips were incredible. Mia's friends pushed her in the bar even though she couldn't stop staring at us. Emery slipped out while they walked in. Nobody knew what happened in that moment except for me and Mia. I didn't feel the same sharpness at seeing her. She was just somebody I knew once. That was a breakthrough I didn't see happening any time soon and the feeling was liberating.

"So, how about dinner after the trial is over?" Claire asked.

"That sounds great. I'll let you know what happens next week and reach out. Thanks for hanging around and letting me crash your party," Bri said.

I hugged Claire and Emery and thanked them for being so kind and inviting me to their table. They walked down the block to their car.

"I really like your friends. And Claire wasn't scary at all," I said.

Bri threw back her head and laughed. She put her arm around my shoulder and pulled me close. "I never said she was."

"You said powerful. And that's scary," I said.

She stopped and made me face her. "Am I scary?" she asked.

I almost leaned forward to kiss her, but I realized she was serious. I chose to be, too. "Only what you're doing to me." Neither one of us moved. Maybe she didn't want to hear it, but I was caught up in the moment and her brown, expressive eyes were like a truth serum.

"What am I doing to you?" she asked.

My heart was frantic. It beat against my chest as though trying to break free and fly away. What was happening? What did she want from me? Could I tell her the truth?

"Are you all leaving? Can we have your spot?"

I snapped out of my trance and stared at the carload of eager lesbians looking for a parking spot so they could party in Katrina's. "Um, sure. Yeah. We're leaving." I faced Bri. "Are you coming over?" Her shoulders dropped and I knew the answer.

"I would love to, but I have too much to do. We're meeting in the morning first thing," she said. My face said everything my mouth didn't. She could tell I was disappointed. "It's not always like this. We rarely go to trial."

"Hey, not to interrupt a private moment, but we have people behind us."

"Sure, I'll move." I wasn't going to let this bother me. I told Bri I would be supportive and I meant that. "Call me tomorrow?" I tried hard to keep the desperation out of my voice.

"I promise," she said.

A shift happened tonight. Even though we never had the opportunity to talk about it, we were turning into a relationship.

CHAPTER SEVENTEEN

BRIANNA JAMESON—ALL WORK AND ALL PLAY

It was nine o'clock on Sunday morning and I was at Lucky's place with breakfast from First Watch. She answered the door wearing boy shorts and a small camisole. My weary body stood at attention.

"They settled. I brought breakfast," I said. I placed a swift kiss on her sleepy mouth and invited myself in. "Tito. I have something for you, too."

"What a nice surprise." Lucky hid a yawn behind her palm and stretched. It was hard to ignore her perky breasts and her tight ass hanging out of her pajamas.

"You barely dressed is the real nice surprise," I said.

She playfully groaned and covered her face. "I'm a mess. Give me two minutes. I'll be back," she said.

I found two plates and split the mushroom and cheese omelet. I gave her the fresh fruit with a dollop of whipped cream and buttered the toast. I smiled when I felt her hands wrap around my waist and her warm cheek press against my shoulder. This was starting to become our thing.

"Congratulations. You must be so relieved."

"Wait. Are you sleeping against me?" I felt her giggle. I turned so we were facing one another. "And thank you. I'm so happy they settled. The client got everything they wanted and I get to spend one day of the weekend with my girlfriend." The look on her face made me rethink labeling us. "I mean, a day with just us." Nervous laughter that I didn't recognize bubbled up in my throat. "Anyway, I hope you're hungry. I bought a lot of food. And I even got a side of scramble eggs for Tito."

Her hand on mine stopped my movements. "Hey. Let's talk."

"Okay. What's on your mind?" I asked even though I knew full well.

Her smile was adorable and her disheveled look made me want to sink into her. She ran her fingertips over my cheek. It was a loving gesture and one I tried not to read into.

"You just called me your girlfriend. Is that what we are?" Lucky asked.

"I'm weighing our options, but I think it would be a good idea if we were exclusive," I said.

She twirled a piece of my hair playfully. "I mean, I guess I could delete my Tinder and HER accounts. I wasn't getting a lot of attention there anyway." She held up a finger as though deep in thought. "Although there's this incredibly sexy gorgeous woman who I see from time to time. Best sex of my life, except she's super busy lawyering and stuff."

I put my hands on her hips and pulled her closer. "Lawyering, huh? That sounds boring."

"Oh, not at all. It's exciting to see her in action," Lucky said. She closed her eyes and made a moaning sound. "The first time I saw her at her job, we had sex in her office." She licked her lips but kept her eyes closed.

"I guess that was exciting to you," I said.

Different emotions swirled in her blue eyes when she finally opened them. "Oh, it most definitely was," Lucky said. She ran her fingertips across my collarbone.

I lifted my chin when she touched my neck and pulled her close. "You're very exciting. It's hard not to want to touch you every time we are together, but I have Tito pawing my pants and your stomach is rumbling, so let's eat first." I kissed her pouting lips and moved around her to put the plates on the small table she had next to the other large window.

"Thank you for breakfast. It smells delicious," she said.

I put the small serving of scrambled eggs in Tito's bowl before I sat across from her. "Is he humming?" I asked.

"He's a happy eater. Those are happy hums, or happy purrs. Whatever." She took a bite and hummed, too.

I rolled with it. I wasn't a cat expert and Tito had already surpassed all my expectations. "Since we're sitting here, why don't we talk about relationship goals."

"Goals?" She shook her head and pointed her fork at me. "You're lawyering right now."

"Honestly, it's been so long since my last relationship, I don't know how people do this." I took a sip of lukewarm coffee regretting that I didn't nuke it before we sat. "Do I send you a note and you check the box if we want to be exclusive or not? I want it to be just us. I know we did this relationship backwards." I paused to stop myself from saying too much. I was sleep deprived and a tad emotional.

"Backwards? What do you mean?" Lucky asked.

Maybe things had changed and having sex first wasn't a big deal. "We didn't have a lot of dates before our four o'clock meeting in my office," I said.

"But we've had several since. And yes, a lot of sex, but that's healthy. We are two women who enjoy sex and each other's company," she said.

That was fairly unemotional and not what I wanted to hear. It sounded like something I would say if I was trying to avoid a relationship. I was vulnerable and I had a moment of regret for racing over here before getting rest. "That's true. I guess we can just leave things the way they are."

"No, wait. I want to talk about it." Lucky covered my hand with hers. "I'm sorry. I'm still sleepy. I got to bed about four hours ago."

"Work?" I asked.

"I want to make sure I do the best job for my girlfriend's law firm," she said.

I almost choked on my swig of coffee. She called me her girlfriend. I played it cool. "Not her firm but the firm she works for. Big difference." My phone dinged. I ignored it.

"Sounds important," Lucky said after it beeped a second time two minutes later.

I waved her off. "I'm with you. That can wait."

"I think you should read it," she said. She tilted her head and took another bite of a strawberry. I made the right call giving her the fresh fruit. Watching her sink her teeth into the sweet flesh was such a turn on. At first, she didn't realize what she was doing. Until she did. I blatantly stared. "Your phone."

"What about it?" I asked.

She rolled her eyes. "It dinged again."

"Oh. Oh!" I pulled my phone out and smiled when I read the message from her. *Will I be your girlfriend? Of course, I will.* What did that mean? "So, exclusive rights to one another's bodies. You can only kiss me in public and private. What else?"

"Seriously? I know it's been a year or so since your last girlfriend," Lucky said.

I put my hand on my heart and winced. "Ouch. Ouch! That hurt." She was right though. I wasn't the best at intimate relationships. "Do you feel like I'm too soon after your last girlfriend?"

"No. I mean, you're not my rebound if that's what you're asking. I mean, most rebounds are just quick and desperate attempts to erase the person you were with, but let me tell you something. You are everything. You're smart, beautiful, sexy as hell, and you have a great heart. Why you're single, I have no idea. Who let you go?" she asked.

"Nobody let me go." I thought about how my career was always first. I frowned wondering if I gave my career my best years. "But also it's what I've wanted. I like what I do. I get the chance to help people." Even though I knew she said it to make me feel better, I felt worse. She must've sensed my mood because she put her strawberry down and scooted so that she was right next to me.

"I only meant it in the best possible way. I'm not even kidding when I say you're perfect," Lucky said. She moved my plate away and straddled my lap. "Why can't you see that? I meant what I said. I want us. The exclusive us. The one where you put your arm around me or hold my hand when we go out. Where you kiss me senseless and I don't even care that the whole world is watching." Her kiss tasted like strawberries and cream. She didn't understand that she was a catch, too. That her girlfriend was stupid to dump her. Lucky was a bit naive, but otherwise perfect. The eight year difference bothered me more than her. I nodded and kissed her back. I was tired of talking.

"You know what I want?" I asked.

"Me?" She sounded helpful.

"Definitely you. But I could also use a nap. I'm so tired, babe," I said, not thinking of the term of endearment. She pulled me over to the bed.

"Let's take off these clothes and snuggle," she said. My clothes were off in a flash. I slipped under the covers feeling instantly safe. Lucky crawled in beside me and put her arm around my waist. It was such a satisfying feeling. Trust.

"Are you sure you can't stay? Maybe you should keep a suit or two over here because you work right there." Lucky pointed across the street. The idea had merit, but I thought it might be too soon.

"I'm not that far away," I said, hoping the lightness in my voice didn't upset her. "Ten-minute drive."

"Back and forth is going to get old. Maybe we should have a weekend at your place," Lucky said.

I touched her chin. "Agreed. Or, hear me out, maybe we can sneak away for a weekend. Just you and me."

Her eyes lit up. "We can go to Boston! I know that city better than my hometown." She looked so cute with her pouting bottom lip and pleading blue eyes.

"I would be up for that. Let's see how work pans out the next few weeks. Maybe the first weekend of August?" I asked. She thought for a moment and nodded. "What's a good hotel? I'll book the room."

Lucky linked her fingers behind my neck. "Absolutely not. My town. My treat."

No way was I going to let her pay for the bulk of it. "Then let me get us there, okay?" She nodded. "Okay, let me out of your clutches, you sexy siren, so I can go home, change, and get to the office early. We have a lot to go over today. I don't even want to think about the paperwork. Sebastian's going to have one hell of a day."

❖

I was right. Even though a lot of people were buzzing about getting paperwork copied, scanned, couriered, and filed, it was a good feeling. Charlie made a big production of knocking on my door even though I saw him coming toward me and we held eye contact the entire time. He made himself comfortable on my couch. I didn't move from behind my desk. It made for an awkward conversation across the room.

"Way to close the deal, Brianna. I didn't think it was going to happen, but you held strong up until the very end. I'm proud of you." He made an uppercut motion with his fist. "This looks good to the partners."

"My billings are amazing this month. I'm sure they see that, too. Any idea on when they are going to make a decision?" My confidence was at an all-time high. How could they not pick me?

He shook his finger at me. "You've had a lot of great cases come through."

I stopped him. "And I worked hard on all those cases. They didn't just land on my desk." Maybe one or two did, but the ones that gave us large payouts were cases referred to me by past clients who were pleased with my services. That was the good thing about personal injury law. Somebody always knew somebody who needed a lawyer.

"Oh, I didn't mean anything by it," he said. He adjusted his tie and fidgeted with a button on his suit jacket. "You've surpassed my expectations. You are in the prime of your career and you're doing a fantastic job."

I sat back and studied him. "What's going on, Charlie? Do you know something I don't?"

"I don't know anything yet." He sounded defensive. "I just wanted to congratulate you on settling a great case," he said.

"I would've loved a jury on this one. They would've given my client the moon. He just wanted it to stop." Very few people wanted to go to trial. Everyone wanted to settle. Trials were expensive and time-consuming. Everyone worked late hours up to and during them. And when appeals were filed, everything got delayed. It was best to settle, but I loved a good trial. I was probably the only one, besides Tyler, who liked to get in front of a judge and jury

"Money helps the pain go away and the sooner it's in their hands, the better they feel," he said. He pointed at me as he stood. "Trust me. I've been doing this a long time."

I didn't stand because he did. "I'm sure you've seen a lot over your career." Did I just call him old? Maybe. He didn't seem offended. "Thanks for stopping by, Charlie."

"Keep it up, kiddo."

The weird thing about all of this was that I closed bigger cases than this one, and he never stopped by to congratulate me. Granted, nobody thought C-M Steel would settle, because they never had before, but here we were, signing paperwork and putting the case behind us.

"Sebastian, was that odd?"

"Big dog showing up out of the blue to congratulate you, which he's never done before? Nah. Not weird at all," he said. He shrugged and grabbed a stack of paperwork off his desk. "Off to make copies. Call if you need anything."

My schedule was clear. Everyone thought we'd be in court. I decided to look at some of the cases that I only had time to skim last week. Most of them would be easy. A slip and fall, a car wreck with questionable injuries but enough that I was interested in it, and somebody who wanted to sue a pharmaceutical company. All the cases on my desks were referrals, but already signed to Titan and Spector. I was too busy to entertain any thoughts of working anywhere else.

CHAPTER EIGHTEEN

LUCKY CHANCE—ALL OR NOTHING

I met Claire and Emery in the best way possible. By accident and in an extremely fun and relaxed setting. Had I not, sitting across from them at Chaz Restaurant tonight would have skyrocketed my anxiety. Instead, I was laughing and having a nice time. Bri had her hands on me the entire night, whether it was holding my hand, her hand resting on my knee, or her arm resting on the back of my chair and her fingers brushing my shoulders. She looked so casual doing it like every touch wasn't a big deal. My body responded every time. I was hyper aware of her the entire night. After dinner, we had tickets to the Kansas City Symphony. I had imposter syndrome bad. I was out with a judge, a lawyer, well, two lawyers, and a fire investigator. People looked at us.

"So, Lucky, how is your job going? I'm afraid we've whined the entire evening about our jobs." Claire made sipping wine an art form. Her energy flowed smoothly. It was hard not to stare just to admire her grace.

As much as I wanted to brag, I couldn't. "Honestly, not great. That's why I'm going to ensure my team does a great job for Titan and Spector. If we do, then I can go back to my own schedule and work from home."

"Do you like being in marketing?" Emery said.

"It's okay. I like coming up with fresh ideas for people. The business world is always changing and the internet grows by leaps and bounds. If you don't stay on top of it, you're going to fall behind," I said. Everyone focusing on me made my palms sweat.

"Being creative sounds like fun," Emery said.

"Meh. Sometimes customers don't like it when you're too creative. They want clever, but nothing over the top. My last two clients wanted exactly what they already had from thirty years ago. Blows my mind that nobody wants to upgrade and update to new things."

"That doesn't even make sense," Emery said.

"Right? I feel like so many companies here in the Midwest want change, but then when you make suggestions, they don't want to take them. It's been an adjustment trying to fit into this demographic."

"The coasts are way ahead of us, but there are a lot of companies who like forward progress. It's just going to take some time to find the right ones," Claire said.

"I'm sure what the team has planned will be great. I've seen her work and I'm impressed." Bri squeezed my hand and smiled sweetly.

"Let's hope you're not the only one," I said.

"When does the website go live?" Claire asked.

"In a couple of weeks. I should get all content by tomorrow. I'm going to hole up and work until it's done." I didn't plan on going into the office for the next two weeks. It was too distracting. Miranda would understand.

"You're going to hole up? Without me?" Bri asked. She moved closer and lowered her voice but not so low that they couldn't hear her. "Am I allowed to visit? I'll bring dinner." I touched her face forgetting that we had an audience.

"Of course. Anytime you want." I kissed her because I couldn't help myself.

We were interrupted as the waiter delivered our plates. Claire and I ordered the pan seared scallops, Bri ordered the garden quinoa, and after much debate, Emery picked the beef Wellington. We spent the first five minutes of the meal arguing about who had ordered the best plate.

"This is healthy and delicious." Bri pointed at her plate with her fork. "You can't beat this flavor. And scallops have no taste," she said.

Such simple banter and I couldn't stop smiling. "Everything is delicious. There. Settled."

"Smart woman," Emery said.

As much as I wanted to stay and drink wine and get to know them better, we had a concert in thirty minutes. I loved music, but I wasn't an aficionado like they were. I was just happy to be out with Bri and her friends. I really was lucky.

"What do you think? Is this your first time at the Kauffman Center?" Bri had laced her fingers with mine and strolled with me along the ginormous wall of glass that overlooked the city.

"It's beautiful. I live like eight blocks away. Why haven't I been here yet?" Because I didn't have any friends and I was embarrassed to go places by myself.

"They have so many amazing events here, not just the symphony. National Geographic has a whole series where photographers come out to show and discuss their work. Those are a lot of fun. I'll have to check the schedule to see who's coming and maybe we can pick a few out. I think you'll really enjoy it," Bri said.

"Are you ready? The concert is going to start in a few minutes." Emery finished her drink and motioned for us to follow them. I leaned my shoulder against Bri's.

"I'm having the best time. Thank you for inviting me," I said. She kissed my temple.

"I know the next two weeks are going to be rough for you so I figured a nice evening out might get your mind off things. Besides, you took care of me when I was prepping for trial," she said.

I almost snorted. It wasn't the same. "Thank you. That's very sweet. I'm having a fantastic time." The only thing better would be a hot and heavy make out session after the concert. I took extra time to make sure I looked my best for Bri. I wanted to look good for her, her friends, and good enough for her to come back home with me.

Not only did the concert go on longer than anticipated, Claire and Emery were chatty after the concert. We stood around a high table and drank wine while everyone else was hustling to the cars. According to them, it was best to either leave early, or have a drink at the bar and wait for the garage to clear out. By ten thirty, I fake yawned until Bri got the hint.

"We should probably get out of here. I'm sure the traffic's died down," Bri said.

"I think so, too. I had a wonderful night tonight. Thank you for inviting us to dinner," I said.

"Thank you for coming even though you have a massive project starting in the morning. Please remember to take breaks, drink water, and sleep," Claire said.

It was such a motherly thing to say, but it melted my heart, too. "I will. Good luck in court this week and, Emery, make them sweat." I hugged them both when we got to Emery's SUV. "Thank you for being so kind to me. I really appreciate it."

Claire put both hands over her heart. "It's been our pleasure. You and Brianna are so cute together. I'm glad she has somebody like you in her life."

I wanted to ask what she meant by that, but also I wanted to get laid. Instead, I just smiled and stepped out of the way when Emery opened the door for Claire.

"Have a great night," Emery said. She gave me a small wink. She knew I wanted alone time with Bri.

"Can we please get home so I can take off this beautiful dress?" I tugged at the silky material gathered at Bri's waist and gave her a promising look.

"I thought you'd never ask." She picked up her pace so fast she made me laugh all the way back to the car.

When Darian pulled up the link that had all the content perfectly placed in the website back at the office and, instead, a lot of gibberish showed up, I nearly fainted. Immediately, I knew something was wrong and it wasn't just a computer glitch. The logo was a preliminary sketch from the beginning, the Meet Our Lawyers section had fake résumés that we pulled from another site just as filler, and the testimonials were quotes from a modeling agency. What the fuck was going on? Either we were hacked or somebody sabotaged the account. I knew I wasn't liked, but I didn't think somebody would actually set out to destroy me.

"What's going on here? I don't understand. Is there a problem?" Charles asked. He was super tense. His face was beet red and he kept running his forefinger along his collar to alleviate the heat or the tightness of the shirt. Or maybe he was legit having a heart attack.

This was totally my problem and I had to step up. I pulled out my laptop and searched the three places I saved it to the cloud. All gibberish. Names were misspelled. Head shots were under the wrong names. Panic set in. Another reason I hated working in teams. Too many people had access to projects.

"Well, I'm not sure what's going on. The link should take us right to your newly designed website. It worked all day yesterday and this morning." My heart was pounding in my ears. The glass of water on the table seemed too far away. I needed Bri, but she had a last-minute meeting and told me she would still come, but she would be late. Nothing was going right.

"Lucky, can you fix this?" Miranda asked.

"I'm really trying. If we could reconvene in fifteen minutes, I can have the correct website up." I had a copy at my loft that didn't have the final tweaks, but it was a lot better than this. The stress of having everyone staring at me was almost too much. I had to concentrate hard even though I could feel my career spiraling downward. I could hear Miranda and Darian try to smooth things out in the background which only flustered me more. "I'm not IT, but this file is corrupt." I knew damn well that it was perfect in the office this morning. My team knew it was ready and loved it. Miranda's face was pinched with anger. "Everything was fine an hour ago."

"Well, if this is an indication of how great your security system is, we are seriously going to have to reconsider the contract. You haven't provided what we'd asked for and we're all sitting around wasting valuable time." Charles looked at his watch and stood. "This meeting is over. If you think you can get it fixed before the weekend, call me. If not, just know the contract we signed is null and void."

"Of course, Mr. Spector. We'll get back to you immediately," Miranda said.

I was still digging around looking for the root of the problem when Miranda spat out my name. I looked up. It was just our team in their conference room. Everyone else had left.

"What did you do?" she hissed. I'd never seen her look so angry before.

I slid the chair away from the laptop and looked at her incredulously. "What do you mean, what did I do? There were no issues when we left. Plus, I have a copy at my loft. I just needed somebody to settle them down for ten minutes while I ran across the street to get it." I hoped somebody on my team would stand up for me, but there was no getting through to Miranda. They looked just as frightened as I felt.

"Darian. Elliot. Head back to the office. I'll meet you there." Miranda's voice was low and brimming with anger. I was about to be on the receiving end of her wrath. They both avoided eye contact and bolted.

"This has never happened before, Miranda. I seriously don't know what's going on," I said.

"Where are your notes?" she asked.

"My iPad is in the top drawer in my desk at the office. Why?" I asked. When the realization hit, I stood and faced her. "Why, Miranda?" I could hear myself breathing hard and felt my chest tighten as though clutching my heart in place.

"Lucky, we gave you a big responsibility and you failed. And you did it in front of the customer which makes all of us look bad. I've given you job after job and every single one was a failure."

"That's not true. You're only choosing to remember the ones who didn't sign with us. How many did Jared lose or even superstar Darian?" That wasn't fair to Darian, but I'd reached the desperate phase of my job.

"Moonlight Crackers was supposed to be a slam dunk. And you should have knocked Bethany's Boutique out of the park. They were simple, cut and paste projects and you couldn't even do that right." Miranda's voice was getting louder and it suddenly occurred to me that we weren't in the privacy of our offices, but we were still at Titan and Spector.

"We need to take this back to the office," I said.

When Miranda leaned back in the chair and crossed her arms, I knew. The sinking feeling in the pit of my stomach grew and I waited for her to utter the career-ending words.

"You're fired."

Chapter Nineteen

Brianna Jameson—Everyone Remembers Their First Client

I was furious, but I couldn't react until I knew for sure. Sebastian heard from someone in the mailroom that Tyler made partner over me. An interoffice memo addressed from Charlie and Robert to Tyler with confidential stamped on the outside was making its way up to our floor.

"I was really tempted to grab it and run," Sebastian said. He was more nervous than I was. I was angry.

"Like how? How did they pick him over me?" I was stunned. Sebastian pushed me into my office and shut the door.

"I shouldn't have said anything. Maybe it was nothing," he said.

I crossed my arms and stared at him. It's not his fault, I told myself. He's your true ally here. Don't push him away. "How can we find out for sure?"

"Hang around Tyler's office and listen?" he suggested.

"Well, I can't, but you can," I said.

"I tried, but he's not there. He's in a meeting." Sebastian looked at the office calendar. "He's in Conference Room B. Oh, shit. How did I miss this? He's in the Web Pioneer website drop meeting. The same one you should be in."

"Shit." I didn't want to miss Lucky's presentation, but I lost track of time and spent fifteen minutes trying to locate any of the partners to find out if the rumor was true. "Where's Charlie? Is he in that meeting, too?" I looked over his shoulder. "Fuck. I can't believe I lost track of time."

Sebastian twirled in his chair. "You go to the meeting and I'm going to snoop around. Somebody's going to cave." He stopped me. "I need you to relax. You look like you're out for blood."

I took several deep breaths. I was itching to get my hands on somebody and the person I had in my crosshairs was Charlie. "You're right. I need to calm down." But also, I needed to support Lucky. "I'm going to go to the meeting, but keep me posted." I waved my phone at him and worked my way to the elevators. The meeting was on the fifth floor. When I got there, I marched into an empty conference room. "What happened to the meeting in Conference Room B? Did it get changed?" I asked the receptionist. My body language must've screamed out of my way because he shrunk back in fear.

"Uh, no. They're done. It didn't last long."

I looked at my watch. I was twenty-two minutes late and it was already over? How was that even possible?" I texted Lucky. *Where are you? Is the meeting over? I'm down in B and nobody's here.*

I got fired.

I immediately called Lucky. She didn't pick up. I called Sebastian. "I'm going to be out of the office for half an hour. What do I have on my schedule?" He didn't ask where I was going. He knew better.

"You're good until one."

"I'll be back by then." I pushed the down button repeatedly on the elevator. Come on. Come on. I had to get to Lucky and find out what happened. I raced across the street and punched in the code to her building. I only slowed down when I got to her door. I knocked softly. "Lucky? Please open the door." I paused and put my ear to the door. I heard her rustling around. "Please?" When she opened the door, she fell into my arms sobbing. I walked us into the loft and closed the door. I held her until she was ready to talk.

She pulled away and sniffled. "Miranda just fired me. She did it in your conference room. There wasn't a meeting with human resources or anything. Just 'you're fired' and she left. It was humiliating. I don't know if anyone heard but I kept it together long enough to get here."

It was hard to understand her while the tears fell. "Did she give a reason?"

Lucky sat on the couch and reached for a tissue. "The meeting was awful. Nothing worked. The link we were supposed to use that had the entire website up, was broken. It pulled up garbage. It worked fine up until we left but someone messed with it and Miranda blamed me."

"Did everyone see it when it was working?" I asked.

"Just my team. Miranda didn't see it. She was too busy doing whatever. She's the kind of boss that only likes to be there when things are really good or really bad."

"Was it human error or was it malicious—like did somebody maybe mess with it on purpose?"

Lucky looked at me like I was bonkers. "Now who would—?" She paused and dropped her head in her hands. "Shit. I bet you it was Noelle. She 'accidentally' messed with Darian's initial presentation. She had access to the account since she was precontract. I bet you it was her! She's such an asshole."

"Do you know anybody on the team who could check it out?" I asked.

"I'm sure they've been told to not have any communication with me. I'm sure I'm locked out of everything by now," Lucky said.

"Can't hurt to try," I said.

She picked up her phone and sent a message to Elliot. She read a few other texts that had come through when she was avoiding her phone. "Darian wants to know where I am. So does Elliot. I'm sure they know by now."

I had no advice to give her. Missouri was an at-will state and employers could fire any employee for any reason unless discrimination was involved. Everyone at her job knew she was queer, but the only person who said anything remotely negative was Noelle. But if Lucky had evidence that Noelle tampered with her project, I could go to Web Pioneer with guns blazing. But getting it would mean a lot of people would be sticking their necks out and that rarely happened. People valued their jobs more than doing the right thing and helping out others.

"I told Elliot I got fired. He and Darian are in shock."

She told me everything Charles said to her and my rage continued to grow. I kept it hidden from her because right now, I just needed to support her. "I'm so sorry I wasn't there. I could've jumped in and diffused the situation and calmed him down." Fuck. Why did I miss such an important meeting?

"I think Miranda would've fired me anyway. She's been looking for a way," Lucky said.

"I don't like her," I said.

"I don't either."

I pulled her close and she rested her head on my shoulder. Twelve hours ago, our lives were peaceful. Now we were both spiraling. My phone dinged. I ignored it.

"You should get that." She sat up. "You should probably go back to work. I'll be fine."

She didn't look like she would be fine, but she was right. Today was a bad day to skip work. Too much was happening and I needed to be in the thick of it. I reluctantly pulled out my phone and saw a message from Sebastian that made my arms and legs suddenly heavy and my blood turn cold.

Not confirmed but the rumor mill is loud about Tyler making partner. Charlie is looking for you.

My phone chimed again. this time with a message from Charlie. *Since you're out of the office, let's go to lunch. Sebastian said your next appointment is at one. Can you meet me at Grinders?*

Fuck, really? Grinders? To hand me the worst news of my career you want to take me to a hole in the wall? *I'm across the street. I'll meet you in your office in ten minutes.*

"What's wrong?" Lucky asked.

I smiled at her and kissed her softly. "Nothing's wrong, but I need to get back to the office to take care of one thing and then I'll be back. Can I get you anything?"

"No, thank you," she said. I held her and kissed her hair and her cheek until I felt her arms relax and let me go. "I'll let you know if I hear anything."

One last kiss and I was out the door. Fuck Charlie and all the hard work I'd put in over the last eight years. I made him and the partners millionaires several times over. My phone dinged again and again. I ignored Charlie's message and focused on the three Lucky just sent me.

Holy shit! Elliot sent me two screen shots and both show that Noelle logged into the file right after we left.

I stopped to read the screenshots. One showed Noelle's login and the other screen shot was the time Noelle accessed the file. The meeting with Titan and Spector was at ten. She accessed the file at nine fifty-two. That was a smoking gun. *I'm so glad Elliot came through for you. Now don't contact anyone. Don't say a word. After this meeting, I'll be over and we can figure out a course of action.*

Okay. I won't answer any texts from anybody at Web Pioneer. I'll wait for you. That way I won't be tempted.

Atta, girl. I sent her a kissing emoji and put my phone away. I was out for blood. I called Sebastian. He answered the phone quietly. "Brianna Jameson's office." Someone was there.

I lowered my voice. "Is it Charlie?"

"Yes, ma'am. I can get that copied and sent to you right away."

"I'll be there in two," I said.

"That will work."

"Sebastian? Get the letter ready," I said.

The gasp of surprise wasn't a surprise to me. "Are you sure?" He lowered his voice. "We're talking about the letter?" He emphasized the word *the*.

"That's the one. Almost there. You good?" I asked him.

"Yes, ma'am."

I knew it was a lot for him to process. The letter was one I had drafted the moment I heard that Tyler might make partner over me.

When I wrote it, I didn't intend to actually send it out. I was just angry and it made me feel better. Now I was glad I'd kept it ready to go. Sebastian was to eblast my resignation letter to all my clients, past and present, and tell them Charles Spector would be taking over their cases and, as partner, he would do an excellent job representing them. I ignored all looks as I swiftly walked to my office.

"Charlie, good to see you. Come in." I nodded to Sebastian and shut the door.

This time he sat in one of my guest chairs. I folded my hands in front of me and waited for him to drop the news.

"I'm sure you've heard the rumors already," he said.

"Rumors? Or truth? Don't sugarcoat it, Charlie. Just give it to me straight." I always hated when people tried to lessen the blow by dropping compliment after compliment, then wham! They deliver bad news. His shoulders sagged and he ran his palms up and down his face a few times. He looked haggard and stressed. I realized how much he'd aged since I started working for him.

"Bri, they made Tyler partner." He held up his hand before I had a chance to tear into him. "They want to make it up to you by changing your salary to more of a base plus commission. You've brought in so much business that, technically, you'll be making more than Tyler."

I snorted. "Until they cut the partners' end of year checks." I stood because my anger wouldn't allow me to stay seated. I started pacing. "Why him?"

"They feel Tyler is a better fit right now."

I held up my hand to stop him. "Oh, please." I held up a finger with each emphasis. "I've closed more cases, I've signed more clients, and I've even been to court more times. Every single person knows I'm the right fit for the job."

"And that's why we want to rework your payment structure. To make it fair."

I snorted again. "Bullshit. There's no such thing as fairness here. The patriarchy is alive and well at Titan and Spector. You will continue to give all advantages to entitled white men because you're threatened by successful women. Well, guess what, Charlie?

I'm done. I'm out. I quit." I sat as the realization set in. I just quit my job.

"You can't quit," he said and waved me off.

"What do you mean I can't quit? I sure as hell can. Do you know how many law firms try to poach me from here? All of them. Sebastian fields recruitment calls daily." It was more like weekly, but I was in high demand.

"I won't accept your resignation," he said.

"You don't have a choice. I know exactly what my contract says, Charlie. I know because I drafted it. I can leave any time I want without notice." I knew the interrupting knock on the door was Sebastian. "Come in," I said.

He handed me a letter and quickly scurried out. I took a deep breath and signed it. I slid it across the desk. "Here's my resignation letter effective immediately. All my clients have been notified that you are my successor, and that you will do a bang up job for them. Or you can always push them off on Tyler since he's a better fit."

His hand shook as he read the letter. "You can't do this!"

"Of course I can. You should read my contract, Charlie." I leaned forward to ensure my point was made. "I'm a really good lawyer." I gave him a wink and grabbed three framed photos off my credenza and put them in my briefcase. I removed my two framed diplomas from the wall and secured them under my arm. I paused for a few moments to look around the room and think about the people I helped over the years in this office. It was a lot of hard work and shaped me into who I was today, but it was time to move on. "You know what, Charlie? I'm not even mad. Deep down, I expect this from Titan and Spector. Making Tyler partner over me was exactly the swift kick I needed." I grabbed the door handle and paused. "And another thing. You got my girlfriend fired today and I won't ever forget that."

Sebastian stood when I opened the door. "Sebastian, it's been a pleasure working with you." I hugged him as though this was it, but we had a plan. He'd agreed to work for me if I decided to start my own business. He would get a substantial raise, but I had to figure everything else out like insurance, a physical office, and how to get started, but I had a few ideas. Now was not the best time for him to Jerry Maguire.

Again, I ignored stares as I walked through the office. I was sure that everyone knew by now. A lightness filled my chest with every step I took. Even though Lucky was right across the street, I had to get my car out of the garage while my keycard still worked. I knew how fast things changed when you quit or were fired. None of my key cards would work by the end of the day. I didn't care. I didn't need a single thing from that office. I found street parking a half a block up from Lucky's.

I sent her a text. *Are you okay?*

I am. Are you already done with your meeting?

Yes. I'm downstairs. I'll be up in a minute.

She was waiting for me in the doorway. "Is everything okay?" she asked.

I smiled at her before planting a swift kiss on her soft lips. "How would you, Lucky Chance, like to be my first client?"

CHAPTER TWENTY

LUCKY CHANCE—LUCKED OUT!

I didn't understand. She already had plenty of clients. "What do you mean?"

"They made Tyler partner over me so I quit."

"Really?" I was stunned. "You did it. You really did it?"

Bri nodded. "Yep. It was as amazing as I thought it would be. I feel liberated."

I hugged her and whooped with delight. "I'm so proud of you. Good for you. I think you'll be a lot happier on your own," I said.

"Honestly, I'm pretty pumped myself. But right now, we need to talk about your situation. As your lawyer, we have a case of wrongful termination. It's not my specialty, but I have enough knowledge to be dangerous. You have proof that somebody went into your file and changed it without permission. What messages do you have from your co-workers?" she asked.

I handed her my phone. A few people I'd only talked to in passing reached out. Elliot was more vocal than Darian, but both apologized for not sticking up for me when everything went down in Titan and Spector's conference room. Their excuse was that they were too shocked to speak. That was probably true. The whole experience was jaw-dropping.

"Is there anything here worth noting other than the screen shots from Elliot?" she asked. She scrolled through the message thread I had with the team. "Tell me about Noelle."

I scowled. "She's hateful. If it wasn't for Elliot, who's queer, I wouldn't have lasted."

"What makes her homophobic? Did she say anything, write anything? Explain her to me," Bri said. I told her about seeing the rainbow on Titan and Spector's website and how she said it wasn't important and had a negative attitude about me in general. "That could just be jealousy. You are extremely attractive and smart so maybe she didn't like competition," she said.

I blushed. "That's sweet. She's attractive but her personality makes her ugly, you know?" When I first started, I worked one week in the office to get a feel for it and meet some co-workers. I sat with Noelle for about an hour to learn about her role at Web Pioneer. She immediately bristled when I told her I moved here to be with my girlfriend and promptly passed me off to the next employee. I didn't think much about it until I was forced to work with her. "So, what happens now?"

"Do you want your job back or no?" Bri asked.

I shook my head. "No. Absolutely not. Miranda is just mean. And apparently, she's been going through anger management classes. There've been several incidents." Bri raised her eyebrow but didn't interrupt so I continued. "She never gave me a chance. I'm starting to think she gave me jobs she knew I'd suck at just so I would transfer back or quit."

"Would you transfer back?" she asked.

"To Boston?" My voice got a little higher. "No. I don't want to work for a company that treats its employees so poorly regardless of where the office is." I didn't want to think about leaving Kansas City because even though my career was tanking, I was in a healthy relationship for the first time in my life. I didn't want to leave Bri. I would find something here in town. "Do you have a plan?"

"I guess let's teach them a lesson," Bri said.

"What does that mean?" I asked.

"Nobody likes bad press. And technically you've only been fired for two hours now so we can't sue for lost wages, but we can still make them sweat."

"Can you charge them legal fees?" I asked. I knew nothing about the law.

"I'm not worried about getting paid, although you need to give me a dollar for retention. This is the perfect case for me to start off my new business. I have a lot of anger, and putting my energy into Lucky Chance versus Web Pioneer will be therapeutic," she said.

"Do you have to have your own business in order to help me?" I was concerned that she was rushing and would somehow get into trouble. Just because I didn't know, didn't mean she didn't.

"I have a license to practice in the state of Missouri. No worries. I'm going to have Claire sign off on a spoliation letter and we'll see what happens." At my puzzled look, she elaborated. "It's a letter that tells them not to destroy any evidence relating to the case." She pulled out her laptop. "May I use your desk?"

"Of course. Wherever you want. Can I do anything? Get you anything? Why am I so nervous?" I was a mess.

She pulled me in her arms and held me. "You've had three life changes in less than a year. Moving here, the breakup, and then losing your job. I'm surprised you're not curled up on the bed asleep. Maybe that's not a bad idea," Bri said. Her smile was encouraging but I saw the stress in her eyes.

"Can we both just stretch out for a minute?" I could feel a wave of panic rise in my chest, ready to crash and wash over me and I wasn't sure I wanted Bri to witness my breakdown. I needed her strength, not to have her tuck me in and leave me. Tears stung my eyes. I looked away suddenly very interested in Tito on the couch.

She embraced me from behind. "Today was a lot. You're right. Let's go lie down," she said.

The tears fell before we got to my bed. She was so kind and gentle and held me as I cried. "I'm so sorry. I'm normally not this emotional."

"Babe, just relax. We have no worries right now. Free of any obligations," she said. That made me cry harder. "I mean that in the best way possible."

"But it's the middle of the week and we're jobless." The last thing I wanted to do was whine about money. I had some money saved, but it wasn't enough to last the year. My lease was up in December and for sure I didn't have enough to cover expenses until then.

"You're going to be fine. You're very good at what you do. I know. I've seen your work. Barkley or Crossroads Design would love to have you. Or maybe you can be a consultant and freelance," she said.

I wiped my eyes and leaned up. "Do you think so? I mean, could I drum up enough business on my own? I'm so new to the area."

She stroked my hair. "I think you're brilliant and you can do anything you set your mind to. I'm not worried at all. You've got this. I mean, both of us are ready to set this town on fire if we want to."

"I love how positive you are," I said. I didn't have her confidence level. Plus, this was her hometown, and she knew a lot of people. I knew like ten. I kissed her. "Thank you for believing in me and jumping to my rescue after everything that happened today."

Whatever letter Bri sent to Web Pioneer had everyone over there stressed. My phone was blowing up with phone calls and messages, none of which I answered. I couldn't answer Bri when she asked me what I wanted out of it. I wanted Noelle to be reprimanded for her behavior. I wanted them to know what she did and why she did it. I wanted her fired. At the very least, I wanted her sent to sensitivity training and be put on probation. I wasn't going to get what I wanted though. Nobody could force an employee to do anything they didn't want to. She could just quit and move on to another firm. Plus, there was no proof that I was the actual target. I knew, but proving it would be next to impossible. Her social media accounts switched to private but not before I did a deep dive and found several random tweets and liked posts against the queer community. I had screenshots, but they only showed that she was a homophobe.

When Mom's name appeared on my phone, I cringed. I forgot to tell her what happened. "Hi, Mom."

"What's wrong, honey?" She always knew when things were off. Today was no exception.

"I don't want you to worry, but I got fired." I held the phone away from my ear as my mother's voice rose several octaves.

"Oh, my God. What happened?" She sounded scared and upset.

"Just some shitty politics at work, but Bri is helping me fight it."

"It's that crappy boss of yours, isn't it? I always knew she was such a bitch." The fire in my mother's voice was unmistakable.

"You're right, Mom. Bri already sent them a letter. I don't know if anything will come of it, but she's pissed," I said.

"I'm glad she's doing something. Let me know if you need anything at all. Do you?" she asked.

"No, thanks. I promise I'm fine. This was the best thing that could've happened to me. Now I can focus on a positive work environment instead."

"What about getting your old job back in Boston? It's worth a shot, right?" My mother had no idea how hard I struggled here fitting in.

"I don't want to work for a company that won't support me. Besides, Kansas City is starting to grow on me. If I can't find a job by the end of the year, I'll think about going back. Right now I just need to breathe and not panic." I tried to keep my voice calm so that my mother didn't panic either. We fed off each other's energy all the time. Today wasn't the day for that kind of exchange. "I promise to keep you posted, but right now I have to focus. I'm talking with Bri about a course of action."

I disconnected the call with Mom and returned my attention to a book I wasn't reading but held onto it like it was the only thing keeping my anxiety at bay. I didn't think much would happen after Bri sent the letter, but according to a text message from Elliot, the entire company knew about it in a flash. I was nervous about poking the bear, but Bri assured me we were in the right.

"I know lawyers who would jump in and help pro bono if this goes in a direction we don't anticipate," Bri said.

"What do you think is going to happen?" I asked.

"If we don't hear from them by the end of the week, on Monday I'm going to file with the court," Bri said.

Everything was happening so fast. I started pacing. "Hey, can we go to a park or something for lunch? Or can we run any errands you might have? I just need to get out."

Bri understood. "Let's grab something from the food trucks near Barney Allis Plaza. I could use some fresh air and sunshine, too."

"Before we go, can I just tell you how cute you look today? Don't get me wrong, I love the sexy, power suit look, but this?" I pointed up and down at her. She was wearing shorts, a tank top, sandals, and a baseball cap. Bri had nice, defined arms and the tank really showed them off. "This is adorable. Still sexy, but more of a relaxed sexy. Want me to put sunscreen on you?"

"Let's have lunch first and then you can rub me down with lotion." She winked at me and pulled me onto her lap. "Once I feel your fingers on my body, we'll never leave your loft. And then we'll wither away because we cannot live off sex alone," she said. She put her fingertips against my pouting lips. I kissed them but nodded.

"You're not wrong, but let me put some on before we head out." Bri had darker skin than I did. I would blister and she would tan. I grabbed a Boston Red Sox hat and sunglasses after slathering SPF 50 all over my arms and legs.

I felt guilty because Bri was working hard on my case and also trying to button up everything with Titan and Spector. She had taken several calls from the other partners and explained her position and wished them well. Sebastian was working on transitioning her clients to other lawyers. It would keep him busy and employed until she found a place for them to land and launch.

We grabbed hot dogs and sodas from a food truck on the street and found shade under a tree. "Where would you like your office to be? Down here or on the plaza? Or Crossroads?"

"I want to find a place where people can get to me easily enough. Downtown is great, but it doesn't have great parking. I want everything to be convenient for my clients. Since I'm a personal injury lawyer, a lot of my clients are disabled," she said. She finished the last bite of her hot dog and wiped her hands clean.

"You're just so nice. You have the best heart," I said.

She leaned against me and put her head on my shoulder. It was very sweet and I didn't move on purpose.

"Brianna? Is that you?" The douchey guy from the Titan and Spector meeting whipped off his sunglasses and sneered down at us. A small mustard stain dotted his tie so he must've grabbed a hot dog off the same truck we did. I felt Bri tense, but she remained calm. He squatted so he was eye level with us.

"Tyler." That was all she said.

"You won't take my calls, but you're hanging at my favorite lunch spot? Are you looking for me? Well, you found me. I'm here." He gave a smarmy smile "Look, I'm sorry I got partner over you, but come on. You didn't have to quit about that. We both know Charlie's only in it for a few more years, then another partner spot will open up." He was smiling when he said it.

I didn't believe him and I knew she didn't either. I wanted to mouth off to him, but I stayed quiet. It wasn't my place and Bri didn't need me defending her.

"That's not how it works," she said.

"Come back. We'll make it worth your while," he said.

Bri pulled off her glasses to look him in the eye. "Oh, I'm good right where I am. Good luck, Tyler. I'm sure we'll run into each other."

He got the hint and stood. "I'm sure we will," he said.

I waited until he was out of earshot. "What a fucking tool."

"I loathe him," she said. She scooped up her trash and helped me to my feet. "Do you want to go look at office spaces with me this afternoon?"

I didn't hesitate. "Yes. Definitely." It was the least I could do. She was putting off starting her business by helping me. "Do you have appointments?"

"I have a commercial real estate friend who can send me a list of available office spaces and meet us at three if that works for us," she said.

"Oh? A friend?" I hadn't heard of this friend yet.

"Old client. I settled a case for her about three years ago. She still sends me Christmas cards," she said.

At least it wasn't an ex. I learned to be a jealous person because of Mia, but Bri never gave me a reason to doubt her or our budding relationship. "That's great. I like that you still have a relationship with your clients. Lawyers get a bad rap."

"Most lawyers deserve a bad rap. I strongly believe in maintaining relationships because everyone needs a lawyer at some point. Or knows somebody who needs one. And I know somebody who needs one so I need to make a quick call before massages," she said.

I perked up. "We're getting massages?" I completely forgot about the conversation earlier. She leaned closer.

"Instead of sunscreen, I'm going to use sweet almond oil and rub it over every inch of your skin," she said.

I shuddered at her promise. I didn't know how we were going to fit everything in this afternoon, but I didn't question her. "Sounds amazing and I'm going to need you to walk faster." If she wanted to meet with her real estate client at three, that only gave us two hours to do stress relief exercises.

CHAPTER TWENTY-ONE

BRIANNA JAMESON—MANAGING PARTNER, JAMESON LAW

How do you feel about ten thousand dollars?" I asked.

Lucky looked up from her laptop and blinked at me as her eyes adjusted from bright computer screen to me in the semi-dark room. "Like in general or what do you mean?" She had sent her résumé to every web designer and marketing company within a thirty-mile radius.

I pointed to my screen. "Looks like Web Pioneer is offering a settlement."

Lucky jumped up from her desk and raced over. "Wait, what? Why do they want to give me money?" She twisted her hair around her forefinger, a nervous habit I recently discovered since spending several days with her and Tito. "Should we accept? What should I do?"

My phone rang and I had to put her on pause. "I have to take this." Lucky nodded and I swiped the call. "Gabriel. Thank you for calling me. How are you?"

"I'm doing okay. Just taking it day by day," he said.

"I wanted to find out if you ever signed with a lawyer." Selfishly, I hoped that he hadn't. I wanted to plug my energy into this case because I felt so strongly about it.

"I signed with some guy, but he hasn't done anything. I can't even get him to talk to my insurance company."

I heard the stress in his voice. "Did you sign any documents with your insurance company?"

"No. I only signed a letter with the lawyer. I'm too busy with doctor appointments. Did you know we moved in with my aunt?"

"I'm sorry this has been difficult, but listen, I want to help. Fire your lawyer. I started my own company, Jameson Law, and I want to sign you as one of my first clients." Lucky was technically my first, but Gabriel was going to be my breakout case.

"You left Titan and Spector?" He sounded like every other person—total disbelief at first and then thrilled for me. "I think that's great. And yes, please, I would love to be one of your first clients."

I did a silent fist pump and Lucky did a small, quiet dance. She knew how much I wanted to sign him. "Great. I'm still looking for office space, but I can meet you anywhere."

"This is wonderful news, Brianna. I don't know how to thank you. I'm just…"

I could tell he was either crying or close to it. "Listen, I believe your story and now I get to work on it full time. We're going to clear your name." We made a plan to have breakfast in the morning. I disconnected the call and added our appointment to my calendar. I needed Sebastian. I was bad at scheduling and organizing. I motioned for Lucky. "Now, let's get back to you. They are offering the money because they either know it looks bad and want to make this go away or they know they did something wrong and want to make this go away. What would you like me to do?"

"I have no idea. What should I do?"

Understandably, Lucky was on edge since she got fired. It had been a couple of weeks and, like I promised, I filed the suit against Pioneer Web last Monday. Notices were sent out. I also filed the paperwork for Jameson Law. "If I were you, I'd counter for twenty and the written apology that they ignored in their offer. Now that the suit is out there for the public to see, they are going to want to bury this quickly."

"I really don't want to seem greedy though," Lucky said.

"You've already lost two weeks' worth of employment. You no longer have free health insurance, stock options, and all that adds up quickly. Ten isn't enough. Twenty is acceptable and a number they would agree to, but if they want to take this to court, I'll pour my heart and soul into the case and get Avery involved. You remember Avery, right? We went to law school together. She's the best employment discrimination attorney in the area and would totally jump at the chance to help." I could tell Lucky was struggling with the decision. I remained quiet and patient while she paced.

"Okay. I trust you. Let's counter with twenty and the apology and then I can move on," she said.

I gave her a thumbs up and responded to their offer listing out everything I said—loss of salary, expensive COBRA insurance, and mental anguish for being wrongfully and publicly fired at a client's site.

"I'm glad you're my lawyer. If not, I would've packed up and moved back to Enfield or Boston with my tail between my legs." She kissed me with meaning. "Thank you for helping me."

"You're my girlfriend. I'd do anything for you." I meant that. We agreed to be exclusive, but we never talked about our feelings. I knew I was falling for Lucky, but we had so much going on that it was hard to focus on just us.

"Counselor." She paused. "Am I saying that right?" At my nod, she continued. "I'd do anything for you, too." She looked at her watch. "Like going to see the office space in the River Market area."

I jumped up, startling Tito who was asleep in the chair next to me. "Oh, shit. I forgot."

"I'm trying hard to be a stand-in for Sebastian."

I grabbed my keys and her hand. "You're doing great, babe."

We were only five minutes late for our meeting. I was looking at the ground floor of a two-story building that was two blocks east of the heart of the River Market. There was ample, gated parking and it was only a few minutes off the highway. I asked Sebastian to meet us if he had time and he promised to make it.

"What do you think?" the Realtor asked.

I looked at Lucky. "I like it, but I want Sebastian's opinion."

"I like it, too. It's close, it's spacious, and there's room to grow," she said. The space seemed cold and clinical, but paint and the right furniture was going to make it feel comfortable and safe. There were four decent-sized offices, a small kitchenette, two unisex bathrooms, and a large reception area. It needed work, but it was affordable and I felt good about it.

Sebastian walked in and nodded. "Great location, boss," he said. I hugged him. It felt like a lifetime when I sat down with him earlier in the week.

"It's nice to see you again, Sebastian," Lucky said.

He smirked at me before turning back to her. "You, too. How are you holding up?"

She shrugged. "I can't remember the last time things felt normal, but I'm doing okay. Bri is doing a great job of keeping me positive and focused," she said.

"She's the best. I can't wait to get out of there and get in here," he said. He studied the space. "You know what? You should reach out to Norman Busby. Do you remember him? He and his wife have that interior decorating business. I bet they would give you a good quote."

"Who's Norman Busby?" Lucky asked.

"His wife was in a car wreck last year. Their case was one that went to trial. We got them a huge payout." It was a lot of hard work and I can honestly say we earned every penny of our fee. It was Sebastian's first case with me.

"Can you get me his number?" I asked Sebastian. He scrolled on his phone for about ten seconds and sent me a message.

"There you go," he said.

I added Norman's info to my phone and looked at Sebastian. "I can't wait for us to get started. I've missed you."

❖

"Can we just turn off the outside world and pretend things are normal for one night?" Lucky leaned against me as we walked down the hall to her loft. We'd spent most nights at her place because neither one of us wanted to leave Tito and we didn't want to be apart. I made a big production of turning off my phone and slipping my phone into my bag. She did the same.

"Done," I said. I put the takeout on plates and sat on the couch beside Lucky.

"Why do I feel so drained but also why am I so hungry?" she asked.

"Adrenaline. This has been a lot. At some point we're going to crash. You're right in powering down. Let's just eat, curl up, watch a mindless movie," I said. It didn't take long for us to eat and get comfortable on her couch. I was asleep before we picked a movie.

"Wake up." I heard Lucky's voice and felt soft lips on the back of my neck, but I was too groggy to respond. I moaned when Lucky's fingertips slipped under my clothes and softly touched my skin. Chill bumps popped up and I felt my nipples harden as her palm skimmed my breast.

I groaned when she moved her hand. "No," I said.

"You want me to stop?" she asked.

"What? No. Put your hand back." I was still groggy. My voice sounded gravelly and low. Damn, I was tired but Lucky was doing a wonderful job of waking me up. I sighed when her fingers pressed into my breast. Her warmth made me shiver.

"Now are you awake?" she asked.

"Not yet."

Lucky's hand slid down my stomach and slipped under the waistband of my shorts. She rubbed my pussy softly at first and harder when I rolled my hips. "Now?" she asked.

I rolled over and looked at her. "I think I'm still dreaming."

"Oh, yeah?" Lucky pulled my bottom lip with her teeth, gently biting into the sensitive flesh. It made me moan. I nodded. She slipped her tongue into my mouth, slowly moving it against my tongue. I put my hand on the back of her head and deepened the kiss. I grasped her hips to settle between my legs and pulled at her T-shirt.

"Let's take this off," I said. She leaned up and pulled it over her head. I loved her creamy and smooth skin. It felt like silk under my touch.

Lucky quickly kicked off her shorts. "What is it about my couch?" she asked.

"I think the real question is what is it about you?" I thought I was being flirty and fun, but realized I was serious. I'd never been as comfortable or happy as I was with Lucky. My pulse spiked when she was near. I was always aware of where she was as though I could sense her. And when she touched me, I forgot about everything.

"Let's agree that it's our chemistry." She reached behind her back and unhooked her bra.

I wanted more from her, but I wasn't going to complain. Lucky gave me everything during sex, but after everything we'd been through—the stress, the physical highs, the emotional lows, and trying to rise above everything going on, I wanted more. I wanted her heart.

"I'm going to say it's more than that," I said right before she returned to her position between my legs with her mouth on mine. I felt her hesitation in our kiss, but she didn't say anything. Usually we were somewhat talkative, but it felt different.

Lucky softened against me. "Can we go to the bed?" she asked.

I nodded and followed her behind the partitions that separated her bed from the rest of the loft. I removed my clothes and joined her under the sheets. I was still tired, but something was happening between us and I was laser-focused on her. I gave her a soft smile expecting her to return one, but her lips pressed in a line. Her eyes searched mine for something.

"What's going on? Is everything okay?" I asked. I brushed her hair away from her face and tucked it behind her ear. She leaned into my touch and closed her eyes. She nodded but didn't say anything. When she opened her eyes, I saw tears. Immediately, I sat up. "Please, Lucky, what's going on?"

"I'm sorry. I've just been so emotional lately with everything. I'm fine," she said.

"Not if you're crying." I pulled her down to rest in my arms. Her body felt tense, and I rubbed her back until I felt her relax into me. "Do you want to talk about it?"

"I don't know," Lucky said.

I checked my libido and pulled the sheet up over us. "Okay. Let's just snuggle." I gave her a squeeze. "What a week, huh?"

"I'm stressed but I can't even fathom what you're going through," Lucky said.

"I eat stress for breakfast. I'm going to be okay, so if you're worried about me, don't. I wanted to start my own firm. It was time." I amped up my excitement for her benefit. "You saw the place. It's perfect. It still has the downtown vibe, but everyone can get to me a lot easier than they could before. I'm not even worried." My words didn't seem to help. "Lucky? What's really going on?"

She sighed and pulled out of my embrace. "I know you don't need added stress…" she started.

Oh, hell. This time my body tensed. "It's okay. Whatever it is, it's okay."

"I'm just going to say it." Lucky took a deep breath. "Bri, I love you. I knew it weeks ago, but then our lives got flipped upside down and then I didn't want you to think that I was saying it just because you were helping me."

I sat up and cupped her face. "What? What?" I couldn't believe it. Here I was thinking the worst and struggling with my own emotions, and it turned out, so was she. "Listen to me. I can't begin to tell you how happy hearing those words makes me. I love you, too, Lucky. I don't know when I fell, but I did."

She clutched me. "Really?" she asked.

I fell back on the bed and laughed. "Oh, my God. Yes."

She pounced on me and kissed me until we were both breathless. I was floating. My heart felt both full and light. I wrapped my arms around her and flipped her.

"I love it when you take charge," Lucky said.

"Me?" I pointed to myself. "You're a bossy bottom."

She laughed. "Not even. Just bossy."

I held her hands above her head. "Don't move." I stripped off the rest of my clothes and pulled her underwear off. "I don't know why you even bother to wear these."

"Especially since you like to rip them." Lucky made an "o" with her mouth as though that was a secret she was bringing to light.

"Sure, one time. I ripped them one time."

"Stop arguing and kiss me," she said. It was a playful demand but one I was willing to give in to. I rested between her legs and kissed her softly while pressing my hips against her core.

"Fuck," she hissed out between clenched teeth.

I loved how quickly her body responded to me. I leaned up on my palms and thrust against her core several times. She lifted her hips for more friction and cupped her breasts. I watched her pinch her nipples and moan until I couldn't stand it. I sucked her nipple into my mouth and ran my tongue around its hardness. She slid her hands into my hair and pressed me harder against her. I opened my mouth wider and sucked as much of her breast into my mouth as I could. She writhed beneath me as her head moved side to side. I pulled away to give her other breast the same attention and got the same response. I slipped my hand between her legs to find her pussy wet and swollen. "Mm. You're ready for me," I said.

"Always, but how about we try something different?" she asked.

I was intrigued. "Oh, what do you mean?"

She moved so that she was beside me instead of underneath me and rested her chin on her hand. Her blue eyes sparkled in the light of the day. "How do you feel about dildos?"

I smiled. "Oh. That kind of different. I think they are sexy and fun and I have a few of my own."

Lucky smiled devilishly at me. "How come I don't know about them?"

"Yet? How come you don't know about them yet? We spend most of our time over here," I said.

"Would you be okay if I grabbed mine? It's a recent purchase that I've only ever used on myself."

I nodded and watched as she reached into the drawer of her nightstand and pulled out a medium-sized dildo and a small bottle of lube.

"Is this okay?" Lucky asked.

"For me or for you or both?" I was down for all of it.

"I was thinking we could start by you using it on me first." She handed it to me and bit her bottom lip.

I leaned back and applied just enough lube. I ran the tip along her slit and watched as a blush crept from her thighs, up her body, and feathered out across her neck and cheeks. Lucky was beautiful and responsive and all mine. "I think I'm going to like this a lot," I said.

She couldn't stand the soft teasing and started rubbing her clit while I softly pushed the tip of the dildo against her pussy. Watching her touch herself wasn't something I thought I'd be into, but I couldn't look away. I was trying to be gentle, but she moved her hips and reached down to push the dildo inside her. It was hot watching her pleasure herself, but I wanted to be the one to do it.

"Grab the headboard, love," I said. She tightened her fists around the slats and closed her eyes as I pushed through the tightness of her opening. I stopped moving until I knew she was completely stretched around it. She sucked in a breath when I moved it a little bit. I stopped. "Is this okay?"

Lucky nodded. "Yes. That feels good." That encouraged me to continue to slowly push and pull. When she started lifting her hips into my thrusts, I pushed in more.

Watching it move in and out of her slowly almost made me come. "Do you want more?" When she nodded, I gave her more. She clutched the covers as I started to move again. Her eyes fluttered shut and she pulled her knees up to her chest. I leaned over her with one palm on the bed beside her head. "Look at me, Lucky." When she opened her eyes and focused on me, I lifted my eyebrow. "Do you want me to go faster?" Oh, God, please say yes. I couldn't wait to make her come this way. Lucky was able to come just by penetration alone. I couldn't remember the last lover I had who could do that. "Because I want to go faster. I want to see your body shake and watch your body explode with an orgasm. Do you know how sexy you are? Do you know what watching you does to me?"

Lucky mumbled something incoherently. I pushed deeper. Her moans were louder. I gripped the dildo and started moving. When she took all of it, I moaned louder than she did. When I pulled all the way out, she groaned her disappointment. I pushed it gently back in and pulled it all the way out until she was sufficiently stretched enough to be able to do what I wanted. Her hips rocked against my hand, wanting more. I held the base and moved my hand as fast as I could. Her eyes flew open and she stared at me while I fucked her hard and fast.

She grabbed my arms and dug her nails into my flesh while moaning, "yes, yes, yes," over and over. When she finally came, I pulled out and watched her body vibrate with pleasure.

I knew she was spent. I pushed her legs straight and massaged them until she stopped jerking. Meanwhile, I practically dripped with wetness after watching her dildo move in and out of her. She was going to be sore for a day or two. I dropped on the bed beside her equal parts exhausted and exhilarated. The side of me that needed to come won out so I licked my finger and started playing with my clit. I wasn't going to last long. Lucky leaned up to watch me. She put her hand on the inside of my thigh and squeezed. The pressure of her holding me down was enough to push me over the edge. I cried out and rode every wave of my orgasm. When I was done, I opened my eyes and stared at her. Beads of sweat lined her forehead and soaked the hair at her temples. Her cheeks were pink and her lips bright red. She was perfect.

"You're so beautiful," I said. I touched her face. "And all mine." I was too tired to hold my arm up, so I turned on my side to face her and draped my arms across her stomach.

"Wouldn't it be great if we never had to work and just had sex every day?" Lucky asked.

"Or, hear me out, we can work and still have sex every day," I said. I giggled when she playfully pinched me.

"Are you going to be the kind of girlfriend who works on our vacations? Because I won't stand for that," she said.

I kissed her lips. "I'm going to be the kind of girlfriend who spends the entire time wooing you to the bedroom on our vacations."

"I'm a sure thing," she said. She raised her eyebrow at me and smirked.

"I don't know what I did to get so lucky," I said. I was sure previous girlfriends used her name in fun little statements. Besides, I was feeling mushy inside at her confession and the great sex we just had.

"No, I'm Lucky," she said.

"But so am I," I said.

I rolled my eyes playfully and groaned. This was one argument this lawyer was never going to win.

CHAPTER TWENTY-TWO

LUCKY CHANCE—HOW DID I GET SO LUCKY?

Web Pioneer's legal team sat across from us. Their lead, Johnston Stone, had slicked back hair and halitosis. He played with his watch so much that I wanted to reach across the table to still his movements. "We're very sorry about the circumstances and hope that this helps as you transition to another job. Web Pioneer is sad to see you go, but we understand. Noelle has been put on suspension and has agreed to attend sensitivity training," he said.

Smarmy jerk, I thought. I was done with Web Pioneer. I didn't want to give them any more of my time.

"My client believes this is fair compensation for having to start all over with a different company," Bri said. She looked directly at Miranda. "I hope you realize what a valuable employee you lost. She did an amazing job on Titan and Spector's website."

Miranda's lips were a white line. She was trying hard to keep her cool. I knew the signs. She moved around in her chair a lot. She fidgeted with the buttons on her jacket. My favorite? She couldn't look me in the eye. I was waiting for her apology. I wasn't leaving until I got it from her, not "Ponyboy" Johnston. The lawyers shuffled papers around and one of them cleared his throat. Finally, she folded her hands in front of her and spoke.

"Lucky, I wanted great things for you. I'm sorry it didn't work out for you here," she said.

"That's not really an apology. You fired me in a client's place without any regard for the truth. You didn't give me the benefit of a doubt. You assumed I sabotaged it to get back at you. Newsflash, Miranda. I value my name a lot more than trying to make you look bad." I was starting to get worked up. When Bri lightly touched my arm, I backed down.

"You're right. I'm sorry I did that. I hope you find success in your future endeavors," she said. This time she looked at me. She looked nervous. It was the first time I felt any power over her.

"Apology accepted," I said. There was a collective sigh of relief. Johnston slid the paperwork over to Bri. We all sat in silence while she reviewed it. I couldn't help but watch her. Her hair was down and tucked behind her ear. I watched her eyes flicker over the paperwork, nodding with what she read. Today she wore her black suit on purpose, because she knew it was my favorite. Watching her calmly shred this company was a massive turn-on and I couldn't wait to get out of there and celebrate. The settlement wasn't a lot of money, but it was enough of a cushion to cover me until I found a job I liked. I felt like I needed more Kansas City customers under my belt before I ventured out to do my own thing. Next week I had an in-person interview with Crossroads Design. The salary was the same, but the benefits were better. The only thing I didn't like was that I was expected to be in the office every Monday for weekly meetings. But it was a good company and they liked my more edgy work.

"Sign here and here, but please review." Bri pointed at the two places pre-marked with red arrow stickers. She gave me a quick wink letting me know everything was fine. I read the agreement which, in a nutshell, said neither parties were going to talk about it and they had satisfied my demands. I signed and slid the paperwork back to Bri who reviewed it a second time before handing it over to Johnston. He handed Bri a check that she added to the folder.

Johnston and his team stood and shook our hands. "Thank you for working with us."

I followed Bri out but stopped in the doorway and turned back to Miranda. "Just so you know, Moonlight Crackers did everything

I suggested. Check out their website. Maybe the issue wasn't me." Miranda looked shocked but her lips remained firmly pressed together. This entire meeting must've been hard for her. Good riddance, I thought as I walked out the door.

"You did great back there, babe," Bri said. She squeezed my hand. "How do you feel?"

I thought about it. "I did everything they ever asked me to do, but it was never going to work. I feel liberated." This was a new start for me. "And by the way, you were amazing. Sexy and powerful." I growled with pleasure. "Remind me to show you how much later," I said once we left the building.

"I'm sorry we had to have the meeting there," Bri said. Meeting them at their place wasn't ideal, but Jameson Law didn't have a physical place yet.

"It didn't bother me. My anxiety was going to be high regardless of where we had the meeting," I said. I slipped into her car and leaned over the armrest. "I really want to kiss you right now, but with everyone watching, that's probably not the best idea." She held up her finger and started the car.

"Hold that delicious thought," she said. She merged into traffic only to pull over two blocks away. She put the car in park and unclicked her seat belt. "Now then, what were you saying?"

I leaned over and kissed her hard. Her lips were hot and demanding and I felt that kiss with every part of my body. I had one of two options—pull back or have sex with her on Main Street where we'd probably have an audience and get arrested. "Counselor. What are you doing to me?" My lips tingled and my body throbbed. She threw me a sexy smile and slipped on her sunglasses.

"Loving you, that's what."

I leaned back in the seat full of warm fuzzies and heat. How could anyone make me feel this complete? I thought I was in love with Mia, but that was only a fraction of what I felt for Bri. I put my hand on her thigh because I wanted the connection. Her strength gave me strength. "Where are we going?"

"To the bank so they don't cancel the check," she said.

I sat up straight. "Are you serious? People do that?" My voice boomed in the small space.

"Ow. I was kidding. They don't, but since we're going to meet with Norman in half an hour, we might as well just go to the bank. I'd hate to go home, say hi to Tito, then say bye to Tito. You know how my heart hurts when we have to leave him."

I smiled my cheesy grin and touched Bri's face. "You said home." She bit her bottom lip and looked away.

"Well, you know what I mean."

"I think it's sweet. You're worried about the boy. And I agree. We have a lot going on. Let's go to the bank." I didn't want us to be stereotypical lesbians and move in after two months of dating. I made that mistake once. Bri and Mia were completely different people and I trusted Bri on a whole different level than I did Mia.

"Pull out the file, please." Bri pointed to her briefcase on the floor of the passenger seat. I grabbed it and set it on my lap.

"Done, boss."

"Get the check. It should be right on top," she said.

I looked at it and waved it at her. "Bri, this is twenty-five thousand dollars. I thought you countered with twenty?"

She shrugged. "This could have been a big, messy case and they knew it. They wanted to get rid of you. I think you made the right call by settling, but I would have gone to trial for you."

I kissed her softly this time. "I love you. I'm so glad you're on my team."

"Anything for you," she said.

I believed her. "A lot has happened in the last three months, huh?" I asked.

"A lot, but all good. Well, except for the part where they fired you, but hopefully you get a good job where people respect you and your creativity and you don't have to deal with unprofessionalism like you did at Web Pioneer," Bri said.

I was a little melancholy about Web Pioneer. I had a massive account that I created and it catapulted me to the top. Had I stayed in Boston, who knows where I would be in my career. One bad decision brought me here, but had I not made the leap, I would've never met Bri.

I deposited the check while Bri waited in the car. "Okay. I've never had that much money in my account before."

"It's a nice feeling, isn't it?" she asked.

"Speaking of money and banks, were you able to get Commerce Bank to change the meeting tomorrow to ten?" I asked.

"I did. I can't imagine they would turn me down," she said.

I hoped at one point in my life I could be as confident as she was. She feared nothing and no one. Bri loved fiercely and fought loyally. "You're going to kill it. If not, I have twenty-five thousand dollars to invest in Jameson Law. I can be a silent partner."

She squeezed my hand. "That's a very generous offer, but you keep your money. I'm going to be fine," she said.

I worried. I didn't know everything that went into starting a business, but Bri was constantly fielding calls about all different insurances, licenses, fees, and things I didn't even know about. Secretly, listening to her scared me about opening my own web design business. I would need my hand held through it and Bri had enough going on. "Well, I'm hoping to be employed by next week so just know it's there."

Bri pulled into the back of the parking lot so she could look at the building she was considering leasing. "I like how the second-floor office has a separate entrance." She pointed to a door near the back of the building. "And it even has a small elevator. Who would've thought?"

"It has charm. Just ignore the bars on the windows. I feel better that they are there. Now I won't worry about you working late down here." Crime was everywhere. You just had to be aware of your surroundings. "It looks like the outside has a fresh coat of paint and I love the black shutters. A lot of East Coast businesses are in grand, old houses. This reminds me of back home."

"It's too bad it's not move-in ready," Bri said.

"And that's why we're meeting your friend. Come on. Let's go pick out colors and furniture." I waited until we were both out of the car. "But I get to pick out your desk." She shot me her sexy look that made me melt.

"Deal. We'll make sure it's big enough."

Norman pulled up the same time the Realtor did. She had to let us in so that Norman could bid the project. Bri hadn't signed the lease yet, but there wasn't a rush. The Realtor said nobody had looked at the property in months. Bri wanted to wait until she got the loan from the bank before committing.

"Norman, this is my girlfriend, Lucky. Lucky, this is Norman. A near and dear client who sends me flowers on my birthday," she said.

"Should I be jealous?" I asked jokingly.

He threw his head back and roared out a laugh. It was startling. "She's perfect for you, Bri," he said. He shook my hand enthusiastically. "It's nice to meet you, Lucky."

The Realtor held the door open and ushered us in. Norman wanted to get the full experience so he entered first. He had great ideas about the space including knocking down a wall and making Bri's office larger with a small conference room table nestled in the corner instead of two separate offices. Sebastian would get the office closest to Bri, and if business boomed, there was an empty office for another lawyer. I was excited for Bri. I believed Norman's vision.

I wanted to ignore my mother's call when my phone buzzed, but I owed her an update. "Hi, Mom." I pointed to my phone as though Bri didn't hear me. She tossed me the fob to her car so I had privacy. I blew her a kiss and walked out to her car. "Sorry about that. Bri and I were talking to her contractor slash interior decorator."

"She hit the ground running, didn't she? I can't wait to meet her."

Even though I signed a nondisclosure about the settlement, I was pretty sure mothers were excluded. "She got me twenty-five thousand dollars that went straight into the bank."

"Honey, that's great. I'm glad you're out of there. I didn't like the way they treated you. I don't understand why people have to be so hateful. Your life isn't any of their business."

"I know. Miranda had to apologize to me. It was so poetic," I said.

"I told you she was a bad egg. I could just tell. And with a name like Miranda, of course she's going to be an evil boss." Huh. I hadn't thought about *The Devil Wears Prada*. My mom nailed it.

"Well, I don't have to worry about her anymore. And I have at least one interview next week," I said.

"We'd love to have you move back, but I understand about you wanting to stay in Kansas City. We loved it and it sounds like you're starting to like the place," she said.

I knew my mother would bring up moving home, but this was the first time she didn't prod and poke me. I think she was starting to understand I was a grown-up capable of making the right decisions for myself. It helped that my girlfriend was a lawyer. My mother equated Bri's job with success, and she wasn't wrong. Only Bri wasn't rolling in the dough. Yet. I predicted she would have to hire another lawyer before the end of the year.

"Listen, Mom. I'm going to have to call you later. We're at Bri's new place chatting with the designer. I'll call you tonight." I disconnected the call and hoped I would remember to call her.

I walked back inside the building. "What do you think, Norman?"

"It has potential. The location is great. Look at these color schemes." He waved me over and showed me a handful of earth tones. I liked the colors, but I was afraid they would be out of style in a few years.

"Ooh, I like this amber. How do we feel about the longevity of it?" I asked.

"Well, the lease would be for two years. We can always repaint. I wanted warm, inviting colors. Seeing a lawyer is a very stressful situation. I want clients to feel welcome," Bri said.

"I think it's the right choice. I like the dark blue accent color," I said.

"I've noted everything and will get back to you with a bid." He shook our hands again. "I'm happy for you, Brianna. I think you're making a bold move and it will pay off. I have a friend who might need your services. I'll give him your number."

"Thanks, Norman. That's very sweet of you. I appreciate it," Bri said.

We sat in the car for another ten minutes discussing the layout, the location, and if this was going to work for her. I already had an idea for what to do for her website. There was no question that I would be in charge of her marketing rollout, and it would be brilliant. She gave me full creative license, but I wanted her input every step of the way.

"How long will construction take?" I asked.

"Norman's crew will knock that wall down in a day. I bet he will get everything done in three to four weeks. Which is perfect, because that'll be the time I get back all my paperwork for Jameson Law from the state," she said.

Her excitement was infectious. I couldn't wait to get started. Norman had given us a website to look at for office furniture. I pulled out my iPad and we looked at furniture while sitting in her car. I found the perfect office set for her which included a large, spacious desk. She picked out guest and lobby chairs. Based on the prices, I was going to suggest a cheaper furniture place, but I wasn't sure what kind of deal Norman was going to offer.

"Let's go home to celebrate. While I love the leather interior and how I can barely feel the sun through the windows, nothing beats time at home, in our lounge wear, loving on Tito."

Bri put the car in gear and pointed it home. It took less than five minutes to get to my loft. It was about seven minutes from her place. The location was ideal. I didn't want to push her to sign because she knew what she was doing. I was there to support and encourage her every step of the way.

"I'm proud of you," I said.

She looked at me in surprise. "What do you mean?"

I held her hand as we walked to the apartment elevator. "You're an amazing woman, Brianna Jameson. You're using your superpowers for the greater good."

She playfully swung my arm with hers. "Nah. I don't have any superpowers. I live off justice and love and use those two things to save humanity."

I laughed. "Justice and love? Well, I can't argue with you there. You are an amazing woman."

"I'm the lucky one." She smacked her forehead. "I'm going to have to come up with something else, aren't I?"

"I could always go by Lucinda," I said.

She pulled me close. "I love your name. It's perfect."

"Okay, so you love my name, but what about me?" I asked. I would never get tired of her telling me she loved me. I wanted to hear it every time I saw her.

"You?" She kissed my lips softly. "I love you so much. Besides, you're my lucky chance."

CHAPTER TWENTY-THREE

BRIANNA JAMESON—NEW LAW FIRM IN TOWN

I tried not to shout with joy when I left Thomas Miller's house. In my hand, I had a signed statement saying he saw Gabriel Andrews veer off the road into oncoming traffic to avoid hitting two small children who chased after a soccer ball. Even better, I also had a video of the crash obtained from his doorbell camera. He put it on an old flash drive that I carefully zipped up in my briefcase. It verified what the street camera showed. Not only did Gabriel quickly swerve to avoid them, but it showed the Lickety Split driver not paying attention to traffic. He was looking down and, judging by a blurry but bright rectangle in his hand, he was on his phone.

Thomas saved his Ring video of the crash. He had emailed it to the police, but the file was too big and the email never got to them. He said he figured since nobody reached out, he assumed the case was closed. I discovered the undeliverable mail when he downloaded the file to the thumb drive. I wasn't even going to tell him about the cloud and how he could've sent it that way. I didn't have hours to explain how the internet worked.

Could I really be this lucky? Claire had pulled some strings with the Kansas City police department and was able to get me footage from the street cam in no time flat. It went against the police report. They didn't care enough to look around for other witnesses other than the cluster of people who only saw the aftermath of the crash, not the cause of it. Everyone thought it was Gabriel's fault.

Trying to capitalize on my good luck, I went next door to see if the mother of the two children was home. I very casually rang the bell.

"Can I help you?" a voice asked from the doorbell camera.

I leaned forward so she could get a good look at me. "Hi, yes. My name is Brianna Jameson and I'm looking for Renee Jones."

"What do you want?" she asked.

"I'm a lawyer for Gabriel Andrews. He was in an accident several months ago on this street and I believe you might be able shed some light about what happened." There was a long pause. "Hello? Are you still there?"

"I didn't see anything." Her clipped answer sounded angry, but I knew she was just scared.

"Ms. Jones? I know that your children were playing outside and chased after a ball. That's okay. Kids will be kids. Your children did nothing wrong. Nobody is getting in trouble. I just need to clear my client's name. He avoided hitting your children. He lost his job, his friends, and is permanently injured. I need your help to clear his name." Another long pause. "Are your children okay?" I knew they were since I'd seen them run off in the video, but asking was a good way to get a mother to respond.

"They're fine. Look, I'm thankful he didn't hit my children, but I don't want any trouble," she said. Obviously, she had been reading too many John Grisham books or watching too many crime movies.

"Ms. Jones, I don't want anything other than a statement from you. Can I come in and talk to you for a few minutes?"

My knees felt weak when I heard the click of the door unlocking. A woman in her mid-twenties with long bleach-blonde hair tied back in a ponytail opened the door. She was wearing a long T-shirt and shorts that were barely visible. She looked tired.

"All right. Come in," she said. She stepped aside.

I walked into a house that smelled like chili. The dated flower wallpaper was taped to the wall in several places. Family photos showed a polished version of the family in front of me. Two children with juice-stained faces were playing on a gaming system and didn't hear me or acknowledge me. Ms. Jones stacked the dishes from the table to make room for me. She pointed at the only empty chair. I gingerly sat on the edge of it afraid to get pancake syrup on my suit.

"Here, let me wipe that up." She came back with a washcloth. "Sorry about the mess. We don't get a lot of company."

I waved her off like it wasn't a big deal. "Thank you for talking to me."

She moved a stack of papers from the chair opposite me and started puffing on a vape. I very slowly sat back in the chair and tried not to inhale the sweet-smelling vapor.

"So, nothing's going to happen to me or my kids if I tell you what happened?"

I shook my head. "No, ma'am. It was an accident, but I need you to tell me what you remember. Mr. Miller gave me a statement so I know what he saw. What can you tell me about that day?"

She sighed and sucked in a long drag of her vape before blowing it out five seconds later. "I just remember seeing the kids run out in the street. I yelled at them from the kitchen window, but they didn't listen. Just look at them now. They aren't listening. They probably don't even know you're here." Another drag and a cloud of vapor that she blew out away from me, but the window air conditioning unit that grumbled and whined three feet behind her blew it right back.

I tried not to blink or cough. Her statement would mean everything and I didn't want to spook her. I had to make her feel comfortable with me. "I'm sure I didn't listen to my mother either. Sometimes when you're playing hard, you just don't want to stop. Kids are great at magically tuning things out."

"You got kids?" she asked.

"Not yet. But maybe someday," I said. I was indifferent about children, but I was never going to be an absent parent. If my partner wanted kids, then we were going to have them. It was too soon to have the talk with Lucky. Both of us were obsessed with our careers.

"Well, you're smart for waiting. I didn't." She was struggling.

I lowered my voice. "Are you doing this alone?"

"Yep. Sometimes their worthless father sends money, but mostly it's just me."

I briefly touched her hand. "I'm sorry. It must be hard."

She leaned back in the chair and shrugged. "Oh well. What's done is done. So, what do you need from me?"

"Just your account of what happened that day. What you saw. Right now, I'm trying to get the facts straight so I can clear Mr. Andrews's name."

She stared at me for a long time before asking the question I knew she wanted to ask. "Will I get paid for this information?"

"If this goes to trial, then yes. You will get paid for your time, travel expenses, daycare expenses, and any other expenses we can think of. Right now, I need a statement. I'm asking you to be a Good Samaritan and help out a guy who is on the brink of losing everything. He has two children as well, and he can't work."

I sent a spoliation letter to Lickety Split the day I signed Gabriel. I believed him, and after getting concrete evidence that he wasn't entirely at fault, I knew I had a massive case. After a lengthy conversation, she gave me a signed statement. I stuck around for two hours just talking to her. I needed her to trust me because Lickety Split would contact her asking the same questions.

"If you need anything at all or have any questions, call me. Here's my card. And thank you, Renee. I know Gabriel really appreciates the help."

I had a long journey ahead. Jameson Law was up and running and I even had a handful of clients. Gabriel was my largest and I knew I was going to drop a lot of money getting ready for the case. Watching the video over and over was hard, especially seeing it from different angles. The Lickety Split driver had the opportunity to slow down, but since he was busy with his phone, he hit Gabriel head-on and going well over the speed limit. I was anxious to get my hands on all the information and have an expert reconstruct the crash scene. They would be able to tell me exactly how fast both drivers were going. As long as Gabriel was less than fifty percent at fault, he stood to gain a lot of money. I checked my phone when I got to my car. Sebastian had called and texted about two other possible clients. Plus, he wanted to ensure that somebody hadn't kidnapped me while I canvassed the area for more witnesses. I called him back as I walked to my car.

"I'm fine. Everything's fine. No, actually, everything is great," I said. I brought him up to speed and told him I'd be in the office in ten minutes. I was going to work with him on the paperwork and get this case filed today.

"We're going to need a new person sooner rather than later. You can barely keep up with the cases we have." Sebastian handed me a stack of folders.

"Have I told you how much I appreciate you being here?" I asked.

"Every day. Never stop," he said.

"Never will." I was a bit stressed about money because we only closed a few cases and the fees weren't enough to cover payroll and the loan payments. In my head, I had everything paid off in six months, but it would take a case like Gabriel's to bump us to where we needed to be.

❖

"Long day, babe?" Lucky asked when I dragged my weary body through the door. Funny how I spent most nights here when my townhouse was five times the size of her loft. My place felt empty. Tito didn't like traveling back and forth so we spent the week at the loft and the weekends at my place.

"Long but worth it. Major breakthrough on Gabriel's case." I dropped my briefcase by the door and walked directly into her arms. This was my favorite part of my day. Even Tito rubbed against my leg to greet me.

"Oh, that's great. I'm so happy," she said. She knew I couldn't talk about specifics since I signed him.

"How's the Bateman account?" I asked.

"I love it. He's the best client and I'm working with him every step of the way. It's nice working with a company who really values me," she said. Lucky had taken the job at Crossroads Design. The benefits were great and she really liked her co-workers. "Listen, I've been thinking about something." She wrapped her arms around my waist.

"Uh-oh. Do I need to sit?" I asked. I kissed her lips. "You look very serious."

"Yes, because I know you're tired," Lucky said. She pulled me down on the couch after I kicked off my shoes. "Our relationship is wonderful. I love you and I love spending every day with you."

I was hesitant. "Okay." The flutter in my chest was alarming, but I remained calm.

"I think you should move in with us. Me and Tito. Sell your townhouse. You have a lot going on with the new business so it'll be one less thing for you to worry about."

I chewed on my bottom lip as I thought about her idea. I wasn't opposed and it was a seller's market. I could make a lot of money. "But your lease is up in like two months, right?"

"So that's the second part. The guy across the hall is moving out at the end of December. It's a two-bedroom loft that faces west so we won't have to see any part of Titan and Spector. We both like the neighborhood and by the end of next year you'll be well established, and we can take our time looking for something permanent. There's plenty of room in the loft for your nice living room set. I can get rid of my couch. And your bed is nicer. What we can't fit, we can throw in storage," she said.

"Lucky Chance, are you asking me to move in with you?"

She cocked her head and smiled. "I guess I am."

"But I insist on paying at least half the rent."

Lucky shook her head. "You cover utilities and food. I get paid well and things are going great at my job. I'll take care of us now, and when you're rolling in dough, you can take care of us. Deal?"

I was a strong and determined woman, but I also knew when to accept help. I loved Lucky. I loved how well we fit. All my friends loved her. Her mother loved me. She gave me hope. I took a deep breath and let it out slowly. "Okay, Lucky. I'll take a chance on you." I leaned forward to kiss her, but she pushed my face away and groaned.

"I can't believe you said that." She threw her hands up.

I pulled her hips down on the couch so she was underneath me. "I love that I can have fun with you. Let's take it even one step further. Instead of a chance, let's make it official." I could stare into her blue eyes forever.

"I thought we decided months ago we're girlfriends?" She quirked her eyebrows at me.

It came from my heart. After hard days and good ones, I loved coming home to her. Lucky grounded me. We fed off one another's energy. I knew when to leave her alone and when she needed extra attention. She knew when I needed a hug or needed to bounce ideas around. She never put herself first. I would be crazy to let her go.

"Lucky Chance." She rolled her eyes. I put my finger on her lips and shushed her. "Let me find the right words. Lucky Chance, you took a chance on me and I got lucky!" This time she put her finger on my lips. I moved my head back. "Wait. I'm not doing this right." I sat and pulled her up so we were face-to-face. "I really did get lucky with you." I touched her face and ran my thumb across her bottom lip. Her mouth could give me pleasure beyond anything I'd ever experienced before. She filled my heart so much that at times it hurt. She was everything to me. Everything. "I'll just make it simple. Lucky Chance, will you marry me?"

EPILOGUE

LUCKY CHANCE—LUCKY IN LOVE

Can you swing by the office? Bri's text didn't feel like anything out of the ordinary.

I checked my watch. I was ahead on my projects and could use a break. I put on my snow boots and heavy coat and headed out. *On my way.* The cold air stung my face and took my breath away so I quickened my pace in the garage. I didn't mind the cold, but I didn't love it either.

"Why aren't you wearing gloves?" Bri asked when I showed up at Jameson Law. She blew warm breath over my cold fingers and rubbed them with her hands.

"I don't want to snag my ring," I said. We'd been engaged for almost fourteen months. Our destination wedding was in June. I held my hand up so the light caught the diamond just right so that it sparkled. It was lovely.

"But I don't want you to lose your fingers. We need them," Bri said. She wiggled her eyebrows at me. "Anyway, come into my office. I want to show you something."

Something was happening. The energy in the office was amped. Sebastian was on two different phone calls, the administrative assistant was on the phone, and even the new lawyer, Kasey Stevens, was talking to somebody and furiously scribbling notes as I walked by. "What's happening? Why is everybody on the phone?"

Bri waved them off. "Come on. I'll tell you all about it."

I wrapped my arm around her waist and leaned close. "Oh, are we having a desk date?" I asked. Bri locked the door behind us. She took my coat and hung it on the coat rack near the door. I noticed her hand was slightly shaking. I looked at her in alarm. "You're scaring me. What's going on?" She pulled me next to her on her couch.

"Gabriel's case settled." She waited patiently for my reaction. Her eyes widened when mine did.

"Oh, my God. You settled his case. This is the best news!" I hugged her. This was a monumental case for Jameson Law. Bri worked endlessly for Gabriel and plugged a lot of money into the case believing it was going to pay off. She had the smoking gun and kept pushing for it to go to trial. She shut down all talks of settlements for several months until they started upping the numbers. The case was going to trial in less than a month and she wasn't budging.

"They called today. I just got off the phone with Gabriel. Because of his health issues and a bunch of other things, they offered him four million and he accepted." She squeezed my hands as I processed the information. She nodded at me when I finally did the math.

"Are you serious?" Tears sprang to my eyes, which, in turn, made her tear up. "Bri! That means you get over a million dollars." I stood. "Holy shit!"

"The company does, but that gives us so much breathing room." She leaned against the back of the couch and pulled me into her embrace.

I was stunned. Jameson Law was starting to gain momentum. Bri was already looking to expand. The leasing company was transplanting the business upstairs so Bri could have both floors. That meant more offices, a large conference room, and more breathing room overall.

"Is that why the phones are ringing off the hook?" I asked.

"We're getting a lot of referrals right now and reporters are calling. I even heard from Titan and Spector. Charlie had the nerve to email me."

"Please tell me you told him off," I said.

"Oh, it was poetic justice telling him that he should've listened to me. I was right all along."

I knew she wasn't being egotistical. Ever since day one, she had a hunch about Gabriel and it paid off big time. I was so proud of her.

"So, Claire called. They want to have drinks tonight to celebrate. How does that sound?" she asked.

"I love it. Yes. But we need to leave early so we can celebrate properly." I kissed her hungrily. Our passion and chemistry were still as strong as when we first started dating. "You locked the door, right?" I asked. She nodded. I pulled her over to her desk and slid her jacket off. Neither of us cared that it pooled on the floor. She pulled me flush against her and lifted me so that I was sitting on her desk. It was one of my favorite places to be.

"I should've told you to wear a skirt," she said.

I frowned and looked down at my very unsexy leggings and sweater. "I miss dressing up," I said.

"You look so beautiful in whatever you wear. Besides, it's like I'm unwrapping a gift. It's not about the paper, it's about what's in it." I leaned back on my elbows and lifted my hips so she could pull my leggings off. She pulled them down past my knees but kept them on. I looked at her in surprise. "I don't want you to get cold."

My body felt like it was on fire. She knew everywhere I liked to be touched, licked, and kissed. I moaned when her fingers slipped inside.

"You're so wet for me," she said against my mouth.

"Always." I meant it. She felt so good inside, but I wanted more. As if reading my mind, she slipped out and pulled me to my feet. "What's wrong?" I asked.

She made a circular motion with her finger. "Turn around."

A shiver of delight worked itself over my body. She didn't even have to tell me to bend over. I moaned when I felt her fingers press inside and fill me up. I grabbed the front of her desk and held on waiting anxiously for her to draw out at least one orgasm. I closed my eyes when she dropped to her knees and used her tongue to heighten my pleasure.

"You're the best thing to ever happen to me, Brianna Jameson." Without a doubt, I was a lucky girl.

About the Author

Multi-award-winning author Kris Bryant was born in Tacoma, WA, but has lived all over the world and now considers Kansas City her home. She received her BA in English from the University of Missouri and spends a lot of her time buried in books. She enjoys binge-watching television shows, photography, and co-hosting the Queerly Recommended podcast.

Her first novel, *Jolt*, was a Lambda Literary Award Finalist. *Forget-Me-Not* was selected by the American Library Association's 2018 Over the Rainbow book list and was a Golden Crown Finalist for Contemporary Romance. *Breakthrough* won a 2019 Goldie for Contemporary Romance, *Listen* won a 2020 Goldie for Contemporary Romance, and *Temptation* won a 2021 Goldie for Contemporary Romance. *Not Guilty* won a 2022 Goldie for Erotica and *Cherish* won a 2023 Goldie for Contemporary Romance. Her novel *Catch* was a 2023 Lambda Literary Award Finalist.

Books Available from Bold Strokes Books

All For Her: Forbidden Romance Novellas by Gun Brooke, J.J. Hale, Aurora Rey. Explore the angst and excitement of forbidden love few would dare in this heart-stopping novella collection. (978-1-63679-713-7)

Finding Harmony by CF Frizzell. Rock star Harper Cushing has to rearrange her grandmother's future and sell the family store out from under her, but she reassesses everything because Gram's helper, Frankie, could be offering the harmony her heart has been missing. (978-1-63679-741-0)

Gaze by Kris Bryant. Love at first sight is for dreamers, but the more time Lucky and Brianna spend together, the more they realize the chemistry of a gaze can make anything possible. (978-1-63679-711-3)

Laying of Hands by Patricia Evans. The mysterious new writing instructor at camp makes Grace Waters brave enough to wonder what would happen if she dared to write her own story. (978-1-63679-782-3)

Seducing the Widow by Jane Walsh. Former rival debutantes have a second chance at love after fifteen years apart when a spinster persuades her ex-lover to help save her family business. (978-1-63679-747-2)

The Naked Truth by Sandy Lowe. How far are Rowan and Genevieve willing to go and how much will they risk to make their most captivating and forbidden fantasies a reality? (978-1-63679-426-6)

The Roommate by Claire Forsythe. Jess Black's boyfriend is handsome and successful. That's why it comes as a shock when she meets a woman on the train who makes her pulse race. (978-1-63679-757-1)

Close to Home by Allisa Bahney. Eli Thomas has to decide if avoiding her hometown forever is worth losing the people who used to mean the most to her, especially Aracely Hernandez, the girl who got away. (978-1-63679-661-1)

Golden Girl by Julie Tizard. In 1993, "Don't ask, don't tell" forces everyone to lie, but Air Force nurse Lt. Sofia Sanchez and injured instructor pilot Lt. Gillian Guthman have to risk telling each other the truth in order to fly and survive. (978-1-63679-751-9)

Innis Harbor by Patricia Evans. When Amir Farzaneh meets and falls in love with Loch, a dark secret lurking in her past reappears, threatening the happiness she'd just started to believe could be hers. (978-1-63679-781-6)

The Blessed by Anne Shade. Layla and Suri are brought together by fate to defeat the darkness threatening to tear their world apart. What they don't expect to discover is a love that might set them free. (978-1-63679-715-1)

The Guardians by Sheri Lewis Wohl. Dogs, devotion, and determination are all that stand between darkness and light. (978-1-63679-681-9)

The Mogul Meets Her Match by Julia Underwood. When CEO Claire Beauchamp goes undercover as a customer of Abby Pita's café to help seal a deal that will solidify her career, she doesn't expect to be so drawn to her. When the truth is revealed, will she break Abby's heart? (978-1-63679-784-7)

Trial Run by Carsen Taite. When Reggie Knoll and Brooke Dawson wind up serving on a jury together, their one task—reaching a unanimous verdict—is derailed by the fiery clash of their personalities, the intensity of their attraction, and a secret that could threaten Brooke's life. (978-1-63555-865-4)

Waterlogged by Nance Sparks. When conservation warden Jordan Pearce discovers a body floating in the flowage, the serenity of the Northwoods is rocked. (978-1-63679-699-4)

Accidentally in Love by Kimberly Cooper Griffin. Nic and Lee have good reasons for keeping their distance. So why does their growing attraction seem more like a love-hate relationship? (978-1-63679-759-5)

Fatal Foul Play by David S. Pederson. After eight friends are stranded in an old lodge by a blinding snowstorm, a brutal murder leaves Mark Maddox to solve the crime as he discovers deadly secrets about people he thought he knew. (978-1-63679-794-6)

Frosted by the Girl Next Door by Aurora Rey and Jaime Clevenger. When heartbroken Casey Stevens opens a sex shop next door to uptight cupcake baker Tara McCoy, things get a little frosty. (978-1-63679-723-6)

Ghost of the Heart by Catherine Friend. Being possessed by a ghost was not on Gwen's bucket list, but she must admit that ghosts might be real, and one is obviously trying to send her a message. (978-1-63555-112-9)

Hot Honey Love by Nan Campbell. When chef Stef Lombardozzi puts her cooking career into the hands of filmmaker Mallory Radowski—the pickiest eater alive—she doesn't anticipate how hard she falls for her. (978-1-63679-743-4)

London by Patricia Evans. Jaq's and Bronwyn's lives become entwined as dangerous secrets emerge and Bronwyn's seemingly perfect life starts to unravel. (978-1-63679-778-6)

This Christmas by Georgia Beers. When Sam's grandmother rigs the Christmas parade to make Sam and Keegan queen and queen, sparks fly, but they can't forget the Big Embarrassing Thing that makes romance a total nope. (978-1-63679-729-8)

Unwrapped by D. Jackson Leigh. Asia du Muir is not going to let some party girl actress ruin her best chance to get noticed by a Broadway critic. Everyone knows you should never mix business and pleasure. (978-1-63679-667-3)

Language Lessons by Sage Donnell. Grace and Lenka never expected to fall in love. Is home really where the heart is if it means giving up your dreams? (978-1-63679-725-0)

New Horizons by Shia Woods. When Quinn Collins meets Alex Anders, Horizon Theater's enigmatic managing director, a passionate connection ignites, but amidst the complex backdrop of theater politics, their budding romance faces a formidable challenge. (978-1-63679-683-3)

Scrambled: A Tuesday Night Book Club Mystery by Jaime Maddox. Avery Hutchins makes a discovery about her father's death that will force her to face an impossible choice between doing what is right and finally finding a way to regain a part of herself she had lost. (978-1-63679-703-8)

Stolen Hearts by Michele Castleman. Finding the thief who stole a precious heirloom will become Ella's first move in a dangerous game of wits that exposes family secrets and could lead to her family's financial ruin. (978-1-63679-733-5)

Synchronicity by J.J. Hale. Dance, destiny, and undeniable passion collide at a summer camp as Haley and Cal navigate a love story that intertwines past scars with present desires. (978-1-63679-677-2)

The First Kiss by Patricia Evans. As the intrigue surrounding her latest case spins dangerously out of control, military police detective Parker Haven must choose between her career and the woman she's falling in love with. (978-1-63679-775-5)

Wild Fire by Radclyffe & Julie Cannon. When Olivia returns to the Red Sky Ranch, Riley's carefully crafted safe world goes up in flames. Can they take a risk and cross the fire line to find love? (978-1-63679-727-4)

Writ of Love by Cassidy Crane. Kelly and Jillian struggle to navigate the ruthless battleground of Big Law, grappling with desire, ambition, and the thin line between success and surrender. (978-1-63679-738-0)